THE STREETS OF FLORIA

J. B. ARNOLD

TWISTED TALES

For my daughter Aubrey, thanks for the motivation kiddo. I would have never accomplished this without your inspiration.

PRAISE FOR THE STREETS OF FLORIA

"**Immersive and haunting, with twists around every corner.** Fans of spooky period mysteries will delight in their adventure through the Streets of Floria!" — A.G. Mock, Amazon charts #1 bestselling author of The Little Woods.

"**A marvelous and dark tale!**" – Steven Cortinas, author and producer/director of the award-winning "Legacy Universe" audiobook series.

"**The Streets of Floria is an easy 5 stars for me.** Really enjoyed the book" – Author John Watson, Bestselling horror author of Karaoke Night, Off The Grid, Cradle Robber, and more.

"**Debut novel! Amazing!**" - Chad Miller, author of The Prisoner of Fear and The Paroxysm of Fear.

CONTENTS

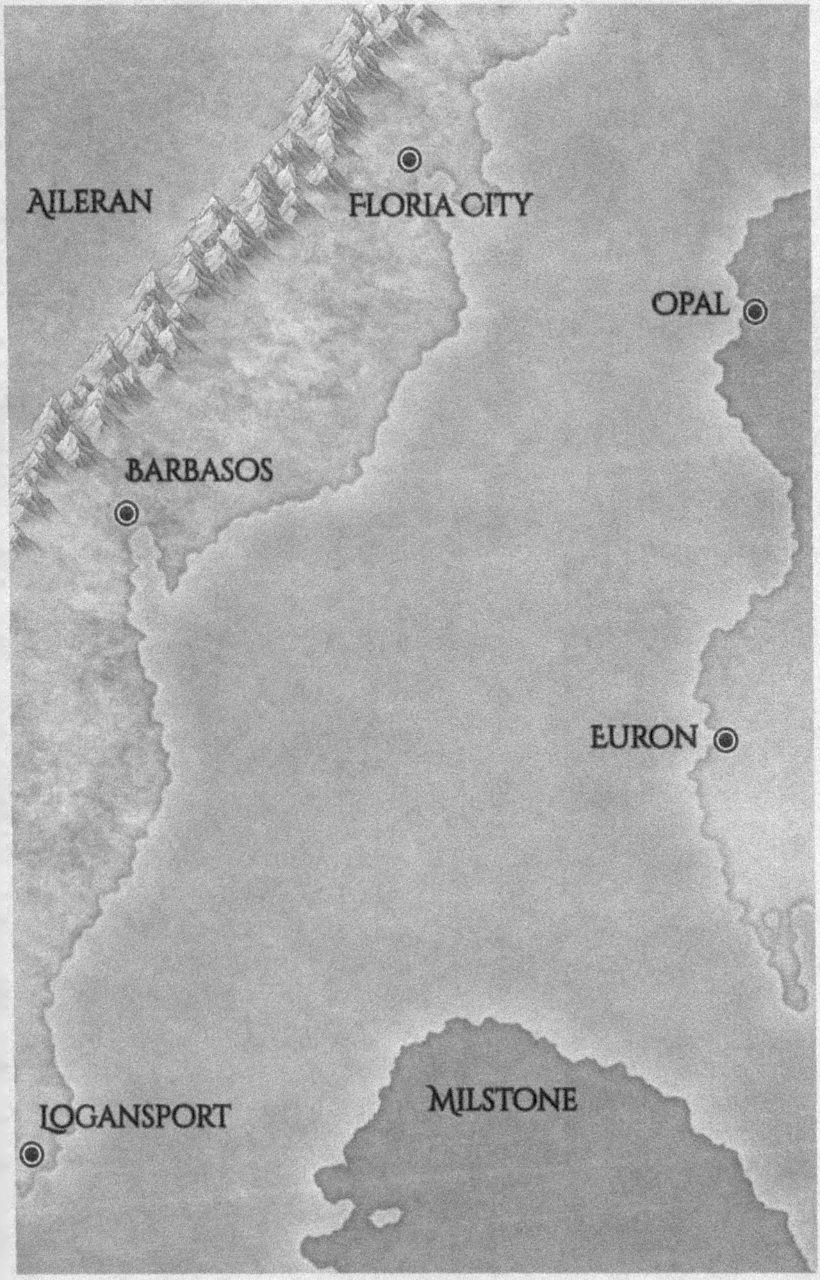
AILERAN
FLORIA CITY
OPAL
BARBASOS
EURON
MILSTONE
LOGANSPORT

FLORIA

FLORIA IS JUST LIKE most port cities along the coast of Aileran and the Green Sea. It's a bustling metropolis overflowing with thousands of peasants scraping by any way that they can. Those that have meager jobs get by, unless what they earn is stolen from them. Others beg, barter, or sell merchandise to make it through another longing day in the city. Life is not grand here, or happy for that matter. It's hard. The peasants that call this life are not citizens, they are slaves to the city and its internal functions.

From the docks, the city stretches out over a square league from Kobalt Harbor to the foothills below the Lemurian Mountains. The docks extend for leagues in each direction, and hundreds of ships can be viewed waiting in the calm green waters at any given time. Taverns, brothels, and markets line the streets, mirroring the docks,' calling those that step foot off of the vessels that brought them here. This is not a charming part of the city by any means, but if you are looking for a good time, you will find it here, unless you are looking for something else of course. You will probably find that too.

The docks are always busiest in the morning. This is when the fresh catch is hauled in from the Green Sea. Sailors, rousters, and dock hands scurry around like ants obeying their queen, tying off the vessels returning from the long night. At first glance, it looks quite chaotic;

however, there is a beautiful dance to be witnessed if you observe long enough.

The older dock hands, have a simple routine hidden amongst the shouts and mayhem of the morning. They effortlessly leap aboard the vessels and open the hull. This is where the treasure lays to be brought ashore and sold. Creatures of the sea are tossed to waiting arms lining the docks. The rousters catch and group the incoming harvest, then sort them based on value, size, and demand.

Waiting and already bullying their way forward, the shop owners and merchants begin their bidding war for the newly arrived catch. As the freshly acquired goods are presented, aging entrepreneurs flex their power using coins and intimidation. The rousters start this spectacle by opening up a rare species and presenting the pink, succulent meat to those strong enough to make their way towards the front of the docks. This is where the battle begins.

Usually, an arrogant well-aged merchant will start the bidding at such a low price it is laughable. Next comes a more sensible individual who is also attempting to lowball the price but offers something worth considering. Then, without notice, strategies change and greed sets in. The next bidder will demand that the catch be sold below the previous price. Sometimes this works, but the captains of the vessels know there will be at least two more bids if they are patient. Eventually, without fail, the catch is sold for equal or more each time a fresh treasure is delivered to the docks of Floria. Supply and demand at its finest.

After the catch is sold, the docks quiet down and become almost somber. The ships slowly rock back and forth in the steady tide of the bay patiently waiting for their next voyage. Most of the sailors, dock hands, and rousters, on the other hand, make their way to the brothels and taverns to spend their coppers as quickly as they earned them. There are the few who venture farther inland to their waiting wives and children outside the walls of the manors, but this is an exception. The business of the docks moves onto the nightlife for a time. Sometimes days go by without much action, but the song and dance always continues and the docks will once again be alive when the next catch returns.

Past the docks, brothels, and taverns of Floria is the market district. If you are looking for anything of interest or pleasure, you will find it in this part of the city. Five leagues wide and another long, this district has a little bit of everything. Merchants of all races erect tents from crude poles and dyed fabrics. A mixture of ivory, teals, greens, and oranges dominate and enclose the sides of the streets. This forms a minute walkway down the center of the streets which forces visitors to see and smell all that is available. Walking down the narrow corridors of the district will open your senses to a myriad of new possibilities and desires. Even if you do not buy anything, you will remember this market district.

Merchants line the streets selling exotic garments and decor from lands beyond the Lemurians and across the Green Sea. Rare, and even mysterious creatures can be bought for the right price if you know the right merchant. Wines and spirits from across the Green Sea are accessible without much bother too. If ale is your choice, there are numerous taps available to sample for a copper or two. But of all the oddities you will find in the district, the food is what makes the district so unique.

Baked goods from Opal and seasoned meats from Euron can be found throughout the market. You will also find the common deli-cacies of the region too; stews, porridges, and salted fish, fresh off the docks of course. The scents from a thousand dishes linger in the air from corner to corner, luring the intrigued and hungry. Many visit

Floria just to whet their pallet with the strange and exotic flavors of the city.

As the city ascends the slopes of the foothills, two- and three-story manors and keeps built of stone and mortar reach for the heavens. Towering pillars accompanied with arrow slits and tremendous turrets line the horizon leading towards the Lemurians. The legendary sigils from the most powerful families in the city are on display for all to see from the tops of these turrets. Golden krakens, emerald eagles, navy rays, and white gulls dominate this display.

This is where the Lords of Floria rest their weary bones at night while counting their coppers, silvers, and golds - often sipping on imported spirits or enjoying the company of paid for guests. This area of the city is off limits to many, unless you have the proper ranking or purpose of being there. Undesirables are removed immediately.

A wall reaching twenty feet tall separates this part of Floria from the lower slums and markets of the city. There are two gates to the Manors of Floria, as it is known. The North gate has two iron gates that swing out towards the city when opened. The West gate is a portcullis made of iron like its counterpart to the North. Patrols are always on watch with orders to protect the lords at all costs. They man the gates, watch towers, and the wall from dusk until dawn.

Few trespassers live to tell their tale amongst the common folk of the city. Those that have been mentioned to breach the walls, are never seen or heard from again with the exception of a few old, salty sailors who like to boast of their triumphs beyond the wall. Most simply vanish without a trace. The few that claim they have been over the wall and back are unreliable. Untrustworthy peasants or sailors with a habitual tendency to fabricate the truth. The Manors of Floria are not impenetrable, but close, so there may be some truth to their tales after all.

The hierarchy of Floria is that of any city: the poor scavenge for their next fix or to feed their kin. They beg or do what is necessary to survive. In the slums near the docks, you can find countless peasants missing fingers or hands due to their petty crimes committed in the city.

The Lords are swift with their justice, guilty or not. The ones not begging, stealing, or scraping by have found other ways to survive. The brothels are always needing new, talented volunteers, both male and female, to keep those with a few coppers in their purse happy for an hour or two.

The poor of the city build crude structures out of driftwood and bland tapestries bought or stolen from the markets. They scavenge for usable material after storms and are quite resourceful in their building. Some of the erected structures are old enough the wood and tapestries have been replaced with brick and mortar. These structures populate numerous families at a time. Other non-permanent structures are visible throughout the slums. Many merely find a suitable flat location to pitch a tent.

The middle class is, for the most part, honorable families leading exemplary lives, following laws, and holding themselves in high regard. With the right Lord watching over them, they can become significant in the city. Most of them are shop owners and merchants. Some use their savings to extend their reach within the market district. Some have even monopolized their niche, aggressively oppressing others from dabbling in their market. Others fall into the pit of the city and blow their earnings without a breadcrumb to show for it.

Then, there are the rich Lords. Those who can claim this title have been privileged with opportunities others can only dream of, while watching their treasures swell from the labors of others. Their beautiful gardens and sun rooms overlook the wall segregating them from the slums and market district. Stained glass, marble statues, and hand-scraped wooden floors are just a few of the luxuries the rich dismiss as a birthright.

They govern Floria, controlling all aspects of city life. The Lords of the realm make the laws, convict the guilty, and pass sentence willingly. Every peasant, merchant, and shop owner within Floria's domain must answer to a Lord. Their vast wealth can hold great influence for those around them.

But there is something else in the city that has even more influence than the rich. It works in the shadows and behind closed doors. It is sometimes referenced but never cited by those brave enough to mention its presence. The mystery behind its existence has never been made public. Few even believe that it is real; however, the few that believe know it has something to do with all of disappearances. It is the gatekeeper, key holder, and the watcher of the city. Without it, there would be no mystery to Floria. The locals in the city have many names for it; darkness, beast, or even creature, but it is referred to most commonly as The Eyes.

PART 1

A CITY'S SECRETS

1

"KOBALT HARBOR," THE BARRELMAN bellowed from the top of his crow's nest, spyglass in hand. "The docks of Floria, in three leagues!"

With the silence of the dawn broken, the crack of the shout shuddered to the cabin below, snapping out Odin from his slumber. He jumped from his warm bed, startled, reaching out for his dirk before really taking in his surroundings: he was alone. Once he caught his breath and his heart settled, he fell back into the straw mattress with a sigh.

"Already here with time to spare," Odin muttered while looking up at the cabin's roof. "I guess Captain Balfour was right. What an old coot, but a man of his word."

He laid still for a few moments, relishing the comforts a few coins could buy on a ship like the Blue Gypsy. He laid there, finally free of the burdens of his past, given the opportunity for change. With a deep exhale, he rolled out of bed and walked towards his garment trunk kept in the cabin's corner, mentally preparing for his first day in this new city.

The old trunk carried everything he still had to his name. Two pairs of tan breeches, one black and three white poet shirts, a navy waistcoat, a pair of soldier boots and a pair of square-toed shoes, both black as soot. Hidden under his cower of a closet was a decorative boot knife, a gift from his father. It rested on the trunk's bottom, safely sheathed in brown leather. Then there was the matching leather coin purse, worn and loved to the bone, almost empty. A few wrinkled pieces of parchment were stuffed in as well, even though he seldom wrote.

Odin chose simplicity today. Not that he had a choice, but he felt content in his tan breeches and white shirt. He also tailored himself with the black boots and his knife. Before leaving the cabin, he caught his own eyes in the cracked mirror beside the door. He couldn't see much of himself, with the spider web of shards and dingy musk, but he felt content. He brushed a strand of wavy hair from his eyes thinking, *not bad, not bad at all*.

After a moment, he turned to the door, forcing it open with a grunt. The hall was vacant, just the rays of morning sun to greet him. He trudged down the hall, feeling the planks under his boots groan in protest.

A spiral staircase led to the lower decks, where the mess hall waited. Odin descended the stairs smelling the comforts awaiting. Fresh eggs and sausage lingered in the air, making his mouth water and stomach grumble. He paused as he stepped off the last stair, taking in the sounds and action around him. The ship's crew frantically worked, preparing to land. He shook his head while releasing a chuckle, not envying the life of a sailor, before walking towards the mess hall's doors and entering.

Few were inside where the rich scents originated, but Captain Balfour was there, gazing out over the green bay they were entering. His mind worked steady, thinking about journeys of the past-remembering the good and the bad and everything-in between. The captain's gaze broke as the sound of footsteps fell behind him. He pivoted, turning and taking in his newest passenger.

"Ah, Odin. I trust you slept well last night." He slapped a hand across Odin's shoulder. "Your new quarters are far superior to where you laid your head before boarding my ship, I would presume."

"That... is an understatement, Captain." Odin countered, never breaking eye contact. "It was quite comfortable. Much better than sharing quarters with three cabin boys on the Moonlight Dawn. A week of my life I wish to forget, to be honest with you." His eyes closed as he shook his head, feeling disgusted by the memory. "I never want to return to Barbasos. Captain, I am amazed that we have arrived in Floria, though. I didn't think you could get us here in such a short time, with the bloody storms looming." A twinkle danced in his eyes, mutely thanking him

"Ah, this old ship has been through many storms, lad," Captain Balfour insisted, his voice filled with pride, standing a little taller. "She's tough as nails and stronger than an ox. She might not be the prettiest bird on the sea, but she makes up for it with speed, boy. Have I ever told you about the time..."

The pride in the captain's voice filled his ears with fond memories. Memories of the past... of his father. He listened to each word as the captain continued rambling on about how long he had owned the Blue Gypsy, of battles with plundering pirates, and the countless times he thought he was going down with his ship.

His gaze slowly wandered towards the nook in the hall with the freshly cooked breakfast. "Thank you again for letting me board," Odin interrupted, "but... if you'll excuse me, I'm famished and need to eat."

Captain Balfour stopped mid-sentence, apologizing for the situation. "Of course, of course! Excuse an old man and his unfortunate habits and babblings." He stepped to the side and waved his arm towards the nook that Odin was eyeing. "Breakfast is served. Have as many helpings as you like."

After three plates of runny fried eggs and burnt sausage, Odin left the mess hall. With a full stomach and the sun shining high above, he felt like today was the start of his new life. The memories of his past were fresh, but suppressing them and starting over was his only choice. There was no turning back now.

As he strolled back up the spiral, rusty staircase to the second deck, he could see they were in the bay. The docks were within a league, and the caws of gulls echoed in the distance. From the railing outside his cabin, he watched sea lions and otters basking in the warm morning sunlight. Over a hundred ships, swaying back and forth to the rhythm of the bay and its gentle glide, were visible. He had arrived.

The Blue Gypsy slowed almost to a halt as she approached the docks. Odin was in his cabin collecting his few belongings and placing them in his old trunk when the sudden descent of speed rocked him forward. He steadied himself, closing one of the trunk's two hasps. The other no longer worked. There was no draw bolt for the lock any longer. He glared down at the trunk, thinking to himself, *What a piece of junk*. The trunk had seen better days, but it was functional for this journey, which he prayed was his last.

Carrying the beaten-up trunk by both handles, he made his way out of the cramped cabin he called home for the last three nights. The trunk's top obstructed his sight, and he smashed his right hand against the railing. The trunk fell to the wooden deck with a thud. "Damn it," he swore, grimacing as he cradled his injured hand.

His attention left the throbs pulsing in his fingers and landed on the calamity in front of him. The single hasp had sprung and his belongings spilled out over the deck. Cursing under his breath, he crouched down, gathering his garments.

"Need some help there, mate?" called a short, stout deckhand that he had played cards with his first night aboard the ship. Odin couldn't quite make out the man's accent. Maybe from beyond the Lemurians, maybe south of his native Milstone? He wasn't sure.

The deckhand seemed a few years older than Odin, deep lines running along his forehead. His arms were muscular and heavily tattooed. He had a clean-shaven head with a long, full beard graying around his square chin. But his rigid exterior didn't quite match the friendliness baked in his gestures and mannerisms.

"No, no, I'm fine," startled and still a little upset, Odin raised his arm to ward off the oncoming deckhand. "Just pissed at myself for rushing things. Thank you, though."

The deckhand ignored his request and continued forward, kneeling and picking up the clothes, throwing them back into the even more beaten-up trunk. "No worries, all's good." A toothy grin emerged as he locked eyes with Odin. "Can't tell ya how many times I've been there. This all ya got with ya?"

Odin placed the last of his belongings back into the trunk and closed the lid. "Thanks friend, what was your name again?" He latched the one functional hasp and stared at the deckhand for a few heartbeats before continuing. "We... played cards the other night, right? Simon, is it?"

The deckhand stood, smiling that toothy grin. "Ya remember. Aye, that's what my mum called me. Ya name's Odie, right?" He paused for a moment, leaning over the railing at the captain's quarters on the main deck. "Balfour's been talkin' 'bout you a bit. What's ya surname, Odie? Headin' to Floria, eh?"

Odin paused, looking at the man with confusion in his eyes. "The name's Odin, just Odin."

"That's what I said, mate - Odie." Simon cocked his head to the side.

With a slight shake of his head, Odin's sight drifted to the view of the docks and the colossal city stretching towards the mountains in the distance. It was larger than he thought it would be. Busier too. The docks were alive this morning with fishing vessels returning with their catch from the night. The previous night's storm had not deterred them from the treasures awaiting from the deep emerald waters. He could also see a large crowd gathering near the front of the docks. From the distance, it sounded like they were shouting at one another, not necessarily in anger though.

Turning his attention back to the deckhand, and ignoring the question about his surname, Odin responded, "Yes, yes, Floria. I've traveled for two long weeks to get here. Traveled all the way from Logansport. Spent a few dreadful nights in Barbasos, too." A slight cringe appeared on his face.

"Barbasos?" Simon said, disgust seeping out of every pore. "Dreadful place from what I've heard. Never been there, though."

Odin mirrored the look. "I know, I know. It really lives up to its reputation. Do you know Floria well? I could use some advice while I am here, friend."

"Advice? Well, that depends, mate. What's ya business in the city? Trade, booze, women?" The deckhand asked, while pulling down on his long beard in smooth strokes. "If it's women, there's a place across from the docks called The Blind Beggar. Dark and damp, but lots of choices. Most of the ladies are clean, too."

Odin waited a moment before responding to his new friend. He hadn't told a soul of his business in Floria and would not do it now. These questions raised some suspicion in his mind. He had traveled five-hundred leagues in the last two weeks, with no one questioning his destination or motives. Why was this deckhand probing him now? Was there a reason, or was he just being cordial and friendly?

"Just looking for something new," Odin sighed, thinking about his homeland. Thinking about those he had departed. The guilt. "Thanks for your help, friend. I've got it from here."

Simon stepped aside and smiled his toothy grin again. "No worries, mate. Happy to help. That's what Balfour pays for me for on this rusty can." The deckhand dropped his eyes from Odin and looked to the side as though he was deep in thought for a moment, stroking his long beard once again. "He doesn't pay me that well though, a few coppers a week? Think I should ask for a raise?" His eyes drifted back to Odin.

Odin looked at the man, but didn't think to answer his question. *Is this guy serious?* He thought. "Farewell Simon. Perhaps I'll see you in the city sometime." He raised his hand to his brow in a friendly gesture.

The deckhand nodded and mirrored the action. Then he swiveled and fell in line with the rest of the ship's crew, moving crates and trunks around the stern of the ship.

Odin gripped both handles of his old trunk once again and navigated towards the spiral staircase, being very cautious of the railing that had hampered his right-hand minutes before. As he descended the stairs, a few other passengers aboard the ship that he had seen but never talked to were already waiting with their luggage near the gangway, ready to deboard the ship.

An older man and who Odin assumed were his two daughters were chatting about the manors they could see below the mountains as they gazed at the sprawling city. The man was pointing and saying something about the Golden Kraken sigil dominantly displayed on the north side. Based on their garments, he knew they weren't peasants. The young girls, probably fifteen and ten, wore skirts and gowns of neutral coloring. The cleanliness and colors of the fabrics suggested the girls were cared for, but not a member of a Lordship. The father wore tan breeches and a dark navy doublet.

Besides the father and daughters, there was a tall, very thin man, much older than Odin, carrying a small bag hanging over his sagging shoulder. He had thinning, white hair with dark sun spots on his scalp. A crooked nose and gnarled, yellowed teeth draped his face. When he shouted towards the deckhands to hurry, spat flung out of his mouth and ran down his chin, glistening in the morning sunlight. He wiped it away with the back of his hand and scowled, impatience driving his actions.

Odin knew men like this: angry, resentful, self-righteous. He glanced down at his left boot for a split second, observing the knife's hilt hidden there. He approached the other passengers and waited a suitable distance behind the man that was alone. Something deep within told him that this was not a man he wanted to get too close to.

As the gangway touched down, the father and his daughters crossed over first, followed by the thin man that was alone. Trying to be as cautious as possible, and worrying about falling into the green waters below, Odin grasped the handles of his trunk and gripped it against his chest, making sure he could see over it. He hesitated a few moments, waiting for the gangway to clear.

After a deep sigh, he stepped off the ship and continued down the ten-foot path towards his future. Once across and finally back on dry land, he lowered his old trunk to the ground. He took a seat on top of it to take in the city's view. After a few moments of admiring the city with his senses, he picked his old trunk back up and started walking towards the many buildings lining the docks. Shabby taverns, lit brothels, and run-down inns were right in front of him. As he made his stroll forward, a slight smirk came to his lips.

2

ODIN LOWERED HIS TRUNK to the ground in front of a bleak, old tavern. A weathered wooden sign, painted with the name The Whisky Dip, was nailed into the siding near the entrance. The establishment was dark and motionless as he approached, probably because of the time of day. It was a two-story structure with a tavern on the first floor and six small boarding rooms above facing Kobalt Bay, numbered one through six in weathered white paint. A switchback staircase led the occupants up to the rooms on each side of the tavern. It wasn't the most appealing establishment, but it would do. He wanted to see what this place was all about.

He left the old, tattered trunk on the walkway as he sauntered forward towards the tavern. As he approached, the scent of stale ale and fried fish filled the walkway. An old woman and older man, clad in ripped and soiled attire, sat on the faded old deck with their backs against the wall, nibbling on scraps. Pity filled his veins seeing people live like this, but he had more important matters to deal with. Before stepping inside, he called out towards the man, "Watch my trunk for me," as he flipped a copper in the man's direction. An initial curse came from the man's lips, but vanished, replaced by a toothy grin instead once he realized what he was holding in his hands.

Once he stepped inside, laughter quickly came from his right where a group of sweaty, disheveled men crowded around a round table, nursing their morning ales. The group ignored his entrance as he continued forward, finding an empty stool in front of the bar. His eyes drifted around, appreciating the full stock of spirits, wines, and ales. But that's not all he admired.

The barkeep tending to patrons this morning was younger than him. Very attractive too. He immediately felt a little uncomfortable being near her. He hadn't thought about a woman in a long time, but he couldn't help himself. There was just something different about her.

Another burst of laughter came from the table of men, momentarily grabbing his attention. He watched as they laughed and clinked their glass mugs together. *Celebrating this early*? he wondered. *Or was this a daily way of life down here near the docks?* His eyes shifted back, focused on this mystery in front of him.

She was tending to an older man as he watched her, taking in her features. She had long hair in a tight braid that hung over her left shoulder. Her light brown eyes were noticeable even in the dim light as she finished serving the old man that appeared to have already had his limit for the day. Her low-cut blue dress flaunted her voluptuous figure. As she finished with the man, she walked towards the center of the bar, swaying her thick hips back and forth in a flirtatious manner, knowing he was watching and waiting for her. She rinsed her hands in a bowl, toweled them off, and strode in his direction with a contemptuous smile on her face.

"What can I getcha, sir?" The barkeep asked with a tone that said something more like, I don't care what you want.

"Just an ale will be fine, miss. Don't want to bother you," Odin stated while not making eye contact. He swiveled in his stool, turning his attention towards the windows leading out towards the bay, even though he could barely see out of them because of the grime. Her presence made him uneasy, nervous.

The barkeep sneered in his direction, acknowledging the uncomfortable manners with a slight smirk on her face. She had seen his type before. New to town, looking for a friend for the night. She gripped the bottom of the bar with both hands and leaned forward, revealing her cleavage even more. "It's a magnificent view, huh?" She paused, averting her stare to the windows, too. "My daddy tries to clean the windows at least weekly, but he's been missing for a while." She wrinkled her nose. "He does this from time to time."

Feeling a little nervous, Odin glanced from the windows back to the barkeep for a split second before staring down at his hands in his lap. "The... the bay is great. Busy this time of day, but really beautiful." He paused, not knowing what else to say. "Can I get that ale, miss?"

"Ale, oh yeah? Ya got it, stranger." The barkeep smiled, turned around, and made her way towards the center of the bar, swaying her hips with each step. She lifted an empty glass from a rack below the bar and placed it under the tap labeled Iron Bros. and poured a fresh pint. She walked back towards Odin carrying the ale in her right hand, trying not to spill the perfect foam head. "Here ya go mister, the finest we got."

Odin looked at the ale with appreciation. "Thank you, miss." He took a long drink from the glass while holding eye contact with her. This mysterious woman was very attractive and interesting. He mustered some courage, suppressing the nerves. "I... I just landed off the Blue Gypsy, Captain Balfour's ship. Looking for work and board. Not sure if you can help me with either of those, though?"

"Balfour?" The barkeep squeaked. "I haven't seen that old man in months. I used to see him at least once a week, staying a night or two or just coming in for a drop." She paused and shook her head.

"He's a good man, rambles on about the past though. Sometimes I just smile when he does." The barkeep changed her conversation towards business while wiping down the top of the bar with a cloth. "Anyway, I have two rooms available upstairs if ya want to rent one, numbers two and six. Can't say much about them other than that they have four walls and a roof. I think six has a leak in the roof in the privy, though." She shrugged her shoulders. "Interested?"

Odin nodded, mind working while his intrigue was escalating. He hadn't spoken with a woman casually in a long time, but it felt good. "When I'm done with my ale, I'd like to see number two. Is that something we can do, miss?"

The barkeep smiled, "That... can be arranged stranger, and please call me Lilly. I'll be ya contact here if ya stay with us." She strolled away from him to tend to the old man at the other end of the bar, again swaying her hips back and forth with each step. She glanced over her shoulder before reaching her destination with a smirk.

He watched her for some time, admiring the kindness that she showed towards the old man as she served him a fresh ale. The way she moved and laughed at the man's gestures and jokes made him smile with curiosity and amusement. She was great at her job and seemed to love doing it, too. He had met female barkeeps before, but they never had the energy and beauty of this one. He knew she was special.

Odin sat on his stool, appreciating the moment, slowly sipping on his frothy ale. Only an hour in the city and he had possibly landed a room. Maybe a new friend, too. He stared thoughtfully out of the dirty, silt covered windows and felt more comfortable than he had in weeks.

3

ODIN FOLLOWED LILLY UP the staircase on the left side of the tavern leading to the boarding rooms. The morning sun highlighted her dark-brown hair and olive skin tone. Seeing her in the bright daylight justified his thoughts of how beautiful she really was. He stayed a few paces behind her as he climbed, eyes drifting to her backside with each step, cautious of her noticing. *Why hasn't a Lord made you his wife yet?* He thought.

Once they reached the deck of the second floor, Lilly led him towards room number two. She reached into her pocket and pulled out a ring of keys, glistening in the sunlight. She fumbled through a few before finding the right one. "Number two's been empty for a few weeks. Might be a little musty, so just keep the door open for a while. It'll be fine." She opened the door and stepped aside, letting Odin enter first.

The room was small by most standards, but he had grown used to cramped spaces spending the last month boarding cabins on ships. One small window, surprisingly clean, showcased a magnificent view of the bay and all its activity. The privy was in the back left corner, no running water or door, of course. A dingy straw mattress that had seen many years of use laid in the back right corner of the room.

He didn't seem disappointed by the room, though. He felt that this would be the perfect start to his new life in Floria. The smell that Lilly warned him about seemed faint while standing in the room's center. He turned his attention towards her and asked, "What's the rate per week?"

"Five coppers a night or twenty-five per week." Lilly stated with precision. "I can charge ya by the month as well if that works? The going rate per month is seventy-five. If that's outside of what ya pockets can handle, I'm sure ya can help me around the tavern to cover the rest. Mugs always need washing and this old place needs a fresh coat of paint."

Odin thought about the proposal for a few moments before responding. She had stepped away, wiping down the windowsill with a cloth from the apron she wore around her waist. "A week sounds great to start with, miss. I appreciate your help and the offer for work. I need to check on a few things in the market before I commit to anything, though." He reached into the small bag tied around his waist and pulled out a handful of coins. He carefully counted out twenty-five coppers and placed them in her hand. His fingers gently touched her soft palm before he pulled back. "First week, thanks again, miss."

"Call me Lilly, and no worries. Let me know if ya need anything. As I said, there's always something to be done in this old place. Since my daddy's disappeared, there has been little upkeep going on and I'm so busy with the bar. I could use another set of hands around here, and I promise, I won't bite - very hard, that is." Lilly gave Odin a flirtatious smile and walked out of the room, leaving him to settle in.

Once she was out of sight, he flung himself on the mattress and sprawled out. He kicked off his boots and listened to the many sounds that the bay brought with the door open. The caws of the gulls and the crash of the waves in the bay were music to his ears. He stared at the ceiling, fingers interlocked behind his head. He was at peace and not thinking about his past. *This might work.*

A few moments later, Lilly popped her head back into the quaint room and said with a slight grin, "Sorry to interrupt. I know ya need a few moments to settle in, but I didn't catch ya name, stranger."

He gazed at her with a thoughtful grin. *Why is this gorgeous woman alone in this city? What in the bloody hell can be wrong with her?* After a few seconds, he finally responded, "My name's Odin. Thank you again, Lilly."

4

AFTER LUGGING THE OLD trunk up the stairs and into his new room, Odin set off towards the markets. He wanted to see what kind of work was available in the city before agreeing to help Lilly around the tavern. He locked the door to number two with the brass key she had handed him, put it safely in the small bag hanging from his waist, and strode down the stairs back to the street facing the docks and harbor.

Once back on the street, he turned left, passing many other establishments very similar to his new home. Taverns, brothels, and markets selling the spoils of life as far as the eye could see. He finally came to an intersection where a wide street crossed the walkway. Looking up the street, he could see that it meandered for at least a league through the foothills below the Lumerians.

He turned, following it up the incline, guessing that this must be the way into the markets. After clearing the initial incline, the street opened up to flat land and had quite an extraordinary view. This was the legendary market district Captain Balfour had raved about during the last days of the voyage.

Merchants of many cultures and dialects erected their tents and stalls. The variety of colors and shapes were an impressive sight as he walked forward. Teal, green, and orange were the most common as he gazed at this strange yet inviting place. Many of the merchants were still setting up for the day as he approached. He could hear the echoes and chants from them offering items for sale.

As he sauntered forward, trying to ignore those enticing calls, he noticed the district continued out on parallel streets as well. There was no telling exactly how large the district was, but he knew it was colossal.

He continued to explore the markets, stopping occasionally to sample curious foods offered for free - fried squid on a stick, eel eggs slathered in honey, and something very spicy called sardinja. The myriad of tastes and smells were intoxicating, overloading his senses.

After an hour or so, he eventually came across a tent predominantly selling clothing and accessories. The structures in this part of the district were a dull teal fabric with gray accents. One in particular caught his attention, bringing with it a hint of nostalgia. There was a massive ram's skull hanging proudly above the two open flaps marking the entrance. The spiraling horns were easily three feet long and in very good shape. He looked up at them appreciatively as he entered.

The scent of burning incense hit him quickly, causing an involuntary cough. Two men were looking at some knives displayed on a table, but briefly glanced towards him at the noise.

"Excuse me," he politely stated in a hushed voice while striding forward. The men went back to admiring the blades in front of them and continued their whispered conversation.

The tent had six oak tables spread out in an array. Each table had plenty of room around it to give visitors the ability to browse the merchandise freely. Two tables near the front of the tent displayed jewelry for both men and women. Rings filled with gemstones, gold earrings, and colorful beaded necklaces hung from decorative tree branches painted teal. Bangles and cuffs overflowed wicker baskets. Chains of all lengths and metals also hung proudly.

The two tables in the center of the tent showcased bags, coin purses and pouches. These handcrafted items were stitched from leather, suede, and cotton in many hues and colors.

The two tables in the back of the tent, where the two strangers stood, housed many knives, dirks, and sabers. Besides the tables full of merchandise, he observed tunics, jerkins, and breeches lining the dull teal walls. The sigil of the Golden Kraken was painted on the back wall - proudly on display, possibly as a warning. Odin also noticed man sitting on a stool in the back right of the tent. The man was older, with gray hair and a thin mustache that matched.

As Odin walked slowly forward, the man stood and called to him. "Anything of interest, kind sir?"

Odin acknowledged the merchant with a smile. "Just looking. Thank you, though."

"Whatever ya are looking for, I probably got it, or know a bloke who does," the merchant replied while eyeing the two men looking at his blades.

Odin approached the tables with the coin purses and pouches. He picked up a dark navy pouch made of suede, smelling the newness of the material as he examined it close to his face. There was a single strap with notches cut in it for latching. He turned toward the merchant again. "I've been looking for one like this for quite some time. What's the price, friend?"

The merchant's eyes widened, preparing to lure his new catch in. "Ah, a wonderful choice. That one's from Celonia across the Green Sea. Hand stitched, sturdy, and dependable. The Celonians know how to stitch as well as they know how to steal, if ya know what I mean." He paused momentarily, rolling his eyes. "Five coppers," the merchant said in an inattentive tone.

Odin held the merchant's green eyes and placed the pouch back on the table. "Five? Not sure if I can afford that right now. I just landed and most of my coin is already spoken for with boarding. Perhaps when I earn again after finding some work."

The man nodded in agreement, understanding the situation. "New to the city, eh? Well, words of wisdom, be careful. Wouldn't want to vanish on ya first day here, would ya?" He smiled, but something hid behind the words.

"I know a bloke up the street that needs some help with his bakery. Bloody peasants keep stealing from him." He paused, shaking his head in annoyance. "He had a lad watching over the baked goods, but the boy ran off. Baker, nor his parents, know where he went." The merchant crossed his arms over his broad chest, puzzlement swimming in his eyes.

Well, I've done worse. Odin thought about the idea of chasing off peasants trying to steal a loaf of bread for their hungry children. He was familiar with the task from years of working for his father. "What's the baker's name, if you don't mind?"

The merchant started rearranging the pouches on the table, not looking up. "His name's Derby. Got a bakery two streets up and he might help ya. Just look for the big green tent with the brick ovens sticking out of the back. The smell will probably lead ya right to him." The man finished with his merchandise and looked at Odin. "If there's anything else I can help ya with, let me know. I'm James, by the way." He held out his hand in a gesture of friendship.

Odin gripped the man's hand tightly with a sense of appreciation. "I was wondering as I came in, James - where did you get the ram's skull outside? I haven't seen one since I left my homeland."

James looked at him with amusement, releasing the crushing grip. "I've had that old thing for decades. Killed it in the south when I was much younger. Paid a hefty price to hunt it, too. Only reason I went to Milstone was because of the giant rams. Were ya born there, son?"

Odin smiled at the man, thinking about his homeland. "Yes, born and raised. Left there recently to start over, though. The name's Odin. Thanks for your time, James. I'll be back for the pouch once I've landed a proper job and can spare the *four* coppers."

The merchant's smile widened as he watched Odin turn and make his way towards the tent's opening. "Five! Five coppers, Odin! Nice try lad. Be careful out there. Don't go disappearing on me." He nodded. "See ya around."

Odin returned the smile, left the tent, and started in the baker's direction. The scent of freshly baked bread was already heavy in the air, and he walked towards it in a hurry.

5

THE GREEN TENT WAS twice the size of the one with the enormous ram's skull hanging from it. Taller too. Odin had no problem seeing the large brick oven hanging out of the back. It was made of red bricks and mortar, including a ten-foot-tall chimney bellowing with brown smoke. Odin approached reluctantly, not wanting to be seen as too forward by the baker.

As he approached the tent's flaps, he noticed one table lined with muffins and another lined with assorted flatbreads. Both were very exotic looking, based on the simplicity of the bakeries from Milstone. Fruits, nuts, and cheeses were baked within the goods or generously sprinkled on top. They all looked delicious and curious at the same time. Odin took in the smell of all the oddities, and then walked into the tent.

Once inside, Odin observed wicker baskets lining the walls, filled with loaves of bread of different kinds. Wheats and white bread were on the left side of the tent, barleys and ryes on the right side. It reminded him of home. There was a woman filling an empty basket with fresh loaves near the left side.

Probably the baker's wife, Odin thought. She was middle aged, a few grey streaks in her long, braided hair. Odin could see the wrinkles on the sides of her eyes as she smiled at him.

"Can I help ya?" the woman asked in a thick Celonian accent. She stopped placing the loaves in the basket and stared at Odin as he walked further into the bakery. She wore a checkered apron that had seen much use during the day, covered in smudges of flour and yeast.

Odin returned the smile and nodded. "Is your husband Derby the baker? I was told to come and see him about some possible work."

The woman placed her hands on her hips and eyed Odin with suspicion. She looked over her right shoulder to the back of the tent towards the oven, then back to Odin. "Who sent ya? What else did they tell ya?"

"I met a man down the street. He said you used to have a boy watching the baked goods, keeping them safe, but he ran off or something. James, the merchant with the ram's skull, told me." Odin kept a hold of the woman's gaze but didn't want to seem aggressive or imposing. A slight smile crossed his lips as he nodded at the woman hoping for approval.

The woman dropped her gaze for a slight moment, considering something. She squished up her face and then redirected her gaze back to Odin. "James is a good man, I hope ya not tryin' to pull somethin' stranger." She paused for a few moments and then looked over her shoulder again and yelled. "Derby, got a man here, says James from down the road sent him!"

Odin could hear someone cursing from behind the brick oven, sounding frustrated. Moments later, a very short, bald-headed man came waddling around from behind the oven. With each step, Odin could see his monstrous belly jiggle under his filthy apron and overalls. This man was an artist and Odin could tell he enjoyed eating his masterpieces.

As the man approached, the sound of his wheezing breath could be heard throughout the tent. With a stream of sweat trickling down his clammy brow, he eyed Odin much the way the woman had. "Ya don't look like ya from 'round here. What James sent ya for?"

Wanting to be as polite as possible, Odin started his rebuttal to the man's question by complimenting his work first. "These baked goods look amazing, sir. I've never seen anything quite like them." He paused for a few seconds nodding at the man and then the woman. "I'm new to the city, just landed this morning. I was asking around if there was any work to be found and James told me that you've had some issues keeping your goods safe. He said peasants come and steal them. I was wondering if I could help with that?" Odin looked at the man with pleading eyes. He knew he would find better work elsewhere, but needed to get to work quickly if he was going to earn some coppers for the next week's boarding.

The baker sized Odin up, judging his brawn and strength. He then pulled a white cloth from his pocket and wiped away the trickle of perspiration that had made its way down his cheek.

"Had a boy watchin' over 'em for a while. He done went and disappeared, though. Seems to happen a lot here in this city. His momma can't find him either. Probably ran off with some girl. Damn shame too, he worked for cheap." The baker nodded in Odin's direction. "The poor come aroun' beggin' for scraps - when I ain't got any to give, they steal. Ya got a good eye?"

"I can handle myself sir, especially if we are talking about some poor peasants. I'll make sure no one takes anything without paying for it. I won't get in your way, either."

The baker's nods became more exaggerated while Odin was talking. Before he could finish, the baker cut him off, "Okay, tomorrow. Sunrise. I can pay ya a copper a day, no more. Ya'll be doin' more than just running off beggars, boy."

The man approached Odin with a smile only a mother could love. He was missing a few teeth, and what was left in his mouth were stained a light brown color. Even with this, the man had a bit of charm to him.

Odin thanked the man and acknowledged his wife as well. "Thank you, sir, the name's Odin. I'll see you at sunrise. I'll do whatever you need from me. Again, I won't get in your way." Odin waved towards the man and stepped out of the tent.

Midday had already passed as he exited the green bakery, Odin started backtracking through the maze of alleys and streets lining this part of the city, making his way back down the incline and to the street facing the docks. He turned towards The Whisky Dip, enjoying the view of the bay and the sounds of the gulls in the distance. He felt a brief moment of optimism about how the day had gone.

6

AFTER RESTING IN HIS room for a few hours, Odin made his way down stairs to the tavern. The place was much busier now than it had been when he entered earlier. Most of the tables and benches were filled with rowdy individuals who seemed to be having a very good time. Their voices were loud with laughter and the sounds of glass mugs clinking together was constant. There was even a musician in the corner playing a flute and singing a crude song about a merchant's wife. The atmosphere was pleasant as Odin made his way back to the bar to get a drink

Finding a stool in the middle of the bar, Odin attempted to get Lilly's attention, but his calls were muffled by the rest of the occupants. He stared at her for a few moments, appreciating the beauty that she brought to this forsaken pub. As she poured the sailors and peasants drinks, that flirtatious smile he saw in the morning never left her lips. She was a natural at this, and her nightly tips proved it from what Odin could see in the large jar on top of the bar. She finished with a group of four sailors at the end of the bar and turned back towards Odin in the middle. With a slight wave, Odin finally got her attention.

"Number two, back so soon huh? Couldn't get me out of ya head, eh?" She smiled at him with her hands on her hips. Her hair was not as tightly braided now, it had a few wisps sticking out and a small curl fell across her left eye. The long shift didn't seem to tire her though.

Odin leaned forward in an attempt to allow his voice to be heard. "Just an ale please."

"Coming right up. Did ya get settled in, by chance?" Lilly asked while pouring a fresh pint of Iron Bros and walking towards Odin.

Odin leaned forward again and started to speak when an obnoxiously loud voice cut him off.

"I'm empty wench! What did I tell ya about that? More wine!"

Odin glanced to his left to see who was speaking and found it to be a thick, middle-aged sailor. His calloused hands were balled up and he was pounding one on the bar while leering at Lilly. He was easily four or five inches taller than Odin with broad shoulders and arms. A massive man in bad spirits. A vertical scar ran down the right side of his gnarled, weathered face. His scowl showed the displeasure he was feeling. Anxiety quickly poured through Odin as he watched the man make his demands.

"Don't just stand there with ya stupid mouth open woman! Get me more wine, NOW!" the sailor shouted. The two associates with him were snickering at the altercation, enjoying the show.

Caught off guard by the cruel demands and insults, Lilly staggered backwards dropping Odin's ale to the floor below.

The sound of glass shattering on the hard stone floor silenced the laughter and shouts, drawing the attention of the rest of the occupants. Odin turned his glare back at Lilly, who's eyes were fixed on the massive sailor.

There was a slight tremble in her voice as she spoke. "O'Doyle, my daddy's already warned ya about acting a fool in his bar. I don't think ya need any more wine, anyways. Take ya goons and get out!" Lilly held her spiteful glare, shaking lightly.

"Ahh, the little bar wench has grown a pair, huh? Where is your daddy, huh? I haven't seen him for a while - in fact no one has. He probably ran off with a brothel girl so he wouldn't have to be reminded of this piss pot ya call home." The sailor looked around the room as dozens of eyes stared at him in disbelief and fear. "What are ya all looking at? Anyone want to make me leave?"

The occupants of the bar dropped their eyes and quietly went back to their drinks and conversations. Odin, still glaring at Lilly, didn't realize that the sailor had noticed his glare towards the barkeep. "Whatcha lookin' at boy?" he asked aggressively, eyeing Odin.

Odin turned his gaze from Lilly and stared at the man contemptuously. "Leave her alone and get out like the lady asked." It had been years since he was involved in a fight but he had a feeling there was no way out of this situation as the hulking sailor stood up from his stool. The rest of the bar silenced once again. A few near the entrance stood up and walked out of the double swinging doors, knowing trouble was brewing.

"Gonna stand up for the wench, eh? New boyfriend huh, Lilly? This should be fun." The sailor walked towards Odin with fists clenched. Odin could see the hilt of a blade sheathed on the man's right hip. Panic and adrenaline shot through Odin's body as the man towered over him leaning down to get face to face. "Ya gonna make me leave, boyfriend?"

Odin could smell the wine on the sailor's breath, being inches away now. As the man spoke, drops of spittle left his lips, landing on Odin's face. He felt petrified as this monster of a man leered at him with dark, violent eyes. Slowly and deliberately, Odin reached behind him and placed his hand on the hilt of his dirk strapped behind his back.

"Ya've made a big mistake, boyfriend! Why don't we take a little stroll outside to take care of this misunderstanding?" The sailor waved his arm towards the double swinging doors exposing a second blade tucked under his left arm.

Not a sound could be heard in the bar as the two held each other's stare. Lilly was still shaking slightly behind the bar, whispering something under her breath, which looked like she was saying "No."

Without notice, the sound of the two double swinging doors being roughly flung open broke the tension and silence in the room. The occupants quickly turned to see what had happened, including the sailor and Odin. It was another sailor though, laughing and stumbling as he came bursting into the bar without a care in the world, singing a song about a fisherman's daughter.

The new occupant stopped singing as he eyed the hulking sailor. "O'Doyle, there ya are, mate!" The man strolled right up to the sailor and slapped him on the back. "This is the third pub I've been in, probably shouldn't have stayed so long in the other two, though." The man's words were high pitched and slurred as he spoke.

The massive sailor known as O'Doyle looked at the man with puzzlement, as did the rest of the bar. Odin took his hand away from the dirk behind his back and stared as the loud, inebriated sailor continued to speak. He quickly glanced over to Lilly to make sure she was safe before standing up and shifting over in front of her. With his back to her now, he faced the two men, listening attentively.

"Ya're piss drunk Simon, what in the bloody hell do ya want?" The sailor snapped as his agitation increased.

Simon steadied himself by reaching out and grabbing O'Doyle's thick arm. "Balfour's sent for ya. Said somethin' 'bout needin' ya in his cabin. Secret stuff I guess. Sent me personally. Did I mention this was the third pub I looked in?"

The shock of the news made O'Doyle's mouth hang with disbelief. "Now? Tonight? What can the old bugger want at this hour?" He leered at Simon with detest and insolence. The scowl on his face as he spoke showed his true age. He stared at the ground for a few moments before calling for his two associates still sitting in their stools at the bar, "Pete, Diggs, back to the ship. Balfour sent for us." The three of them walked past Simon. As he opened the doors, O'Doyle glared back towards the bar where Odin was still standing as he shielded Lilly. "See ya 'round, boyfriend."

As Odin watched him walk out, he turned to Lilly who was now picking up the shattered glass from the stone floor. "Are you alright, Lilly? Who was that guy?"

Lilly was still shaken by the incident, but hesitantly looked up at Odin while sweeping a pile of glass into a tray. "I'm fine. He's been around for a while. Everyone hates him, but they are all too scared to tell him to his face." She stood up at the last moment of her sentence to make sure everyone in the bar heard the that part of her statement. As she was standing there, glaring at the patrons, expecting more out of them, like a disappointed parent, Simon approached the bar.

With a slight stagger to his final steps, Simon had a seat in the stool that O'Doyle previously occupied. With a drunken smile on his face, he acknowledged Lilly. "Hey there darlin', been a while, hasn't it?"

Lilly was still staring daggers through those in her bar but dropped those feelings for a moment and turned her attention towards the drunken sailor. With a long sigh she said, "What can I get ya, Simon?"

"Ya know me, Lilly. A fresh pint of Iron Bros will suffice, my love. Thanks for being so concerned about my well-being, sis." Simon blew a sloppy kiss in her direction while nearly falling off his stool.

Lilly rolled her eyes in frustration, watching Simon try to steady himself on his stool. She sat back and watched as he extended one leg and then the other trying to balance on the stool to prove his sobriety. He looked at her with the most serious of faces and nodded to show her he was well enough for another drink. Eventually, going against her better judgement, she poured him the ale.

"This is it Simon - one drink and ya need to leave, do ya understand?" Her gaze at the man was serious with a hint of sincerity too.

Simon halted his failed attempt at balancing on the stool with his legs in the air and smiled at the barkeep. "Much appreciated, Lilly. Do any of my mates need a new drop?" He turned to the left and then to the right. As he did, he noticed Odin standing at the bar staring at him with a bewildered expression on his face. "Hey Odie, whatcha doin' in this run-down piece?"

Odin sat down with Simon at the bar for the next hour discussing many topics: O'Doyle, Lilly, the docks, and the market district. He discovered that O'Doyle was new to Balfour's ship and was not aboard while Odin was making his way to Floria City. Apparently, he had stayed behind the last time the Blue Gypsy sailed to clear up a misunderstanding with another captain. This other captain claimed that O'Doyle stabbed one of his deck hands in the eye over a card game.

According to Simon, the situation was still unresolved. Odin also learned that O'Doyle had worked on four ships in the past year, stating that he continues to get fired due to insubordination and violence. Based on this evidence, Odin felt relieved that their altercation hadn't become physical.

Simon also provided a vast amount of information about the barkeep Lilly. In his early teens, Simon worked for her father at the tavern and had known Lilly since she was very young. Apparently, she is an only child and had lived solely with her father since she was three, after her mother's death. Simon did not have a clear answer as to how her mother had died though. Odin also learned that Lilly was engaged once to a merchant's son here in the city but the engagement was called off due to a disagreement between the fathers of the betrothed.

In addition, Simon also discussed the disappearance of Lilly's father with Odin. Lilly had confided in Simon that late one night her father mentioned taking the garbage out to the alley behind the tavern. After thirty minutes or so, Lilly became worried because her father did not return. She stepped out into the alley to see if she could find him, but it was eerily empty. She told him there was a strange feeling about the dimness of the alley on that night and not a sound could be heard. She felt like something was watching her every move. Simon stated that she hasn't gone back into the alley since. Odin didn't know if he believed the man.

As the hour passed, Simon continued to enjoy a few tall pints of Iron Bros. They were on the house of course, being such a close family friend. Eventually, Odin decided to cut him off.

"I think you have had enough friend, but thank you for the warm talk." Odin stood and helped Simon to his feet.

Simon nearly fell face down in the bar, but Odin grabbed a hold of the back of his loose poet shirt and steadied him. Simon thanked him and wrapped a strong, tattooed arm around his neck as they made their way to the doors. Before exiting completely, Simon turned to acknowledge Lilly one final time in a slurred drunken voice. "Lilly, my love, thanks for ya hospitality, but I must bid thee adieu." Lilly rolled her eyes with contempt as the two went out into the darkness.

As the two shuffled away from the Whisky Dip, Odin inquired about where Simon was boarding while his ship was docked in the bay. He also made it very clear that he was going nowhere near the Blue Gypsy as long as O'Doyle was around. "Where are we heading Simon? I need to make sure that you get there in one piece."

Simon started to slowly nod off as they made their way down the dimly lit street. "I've got a room over there." Simon pointed up the road near where Odin had turned left earlier in the day to visit the market district.

The two continued their slow shuffle down the road until they finally reached the corner. As they turned the corner, a large group of sailors came walking past them laughing and singing a familiar tune. Simon attempted to sing along but sounded like he was just smashing odd sounds together as he sang. As the song trailed off, Simon pointed to an establishment on the right side of the street. They passed a dark alley on their way across the street. Odin glanced at it suspiciously.

It was a three-story inn with several boarding rooms lining the perimeter. A large enclosed courtyard led towards the front entrance. Odin could see the inn's bright yellow color due to the torches atop poles outside each room as well as hanging on the walls of the upper floors. The rooms were numbered based on their level, from what Odin could observe. All of the rooms on the first level started with one, the rooms on the second floor started with two, and so on. "Simon, which room is yours?" Odin whispered to the drunken man he was nearly carrying.

Simon lifted his head and pointed towards the second floor. "Two, somethin' somethin."

As they approached the inn, Simon's consciousness was starting to become more of a problem. His dead weight was a problem as Odin attempted to drag him along. Odin paused for a moment, and then swiftly threw Simon over his shoulder for the final leg of their journey. "Let's go buddy, second floor it is."

There was a switchback staircase leading to the additional floors on the left side of the inn. Odin began the challenging climb with Simon still hanging over his shoulder, gripping the railing tightly. He could feel his calves straining with each ascent. As he approached the final stair leading to floor number two, he asked Simon about a key with a winded voice. The sailor, barely awake, fumbled in his pocket for a few moments before revealing a dull, brass key with a piece of white parchment attached to it. It read the digits 213.

On the landing to the second floor, Odin finally dropped Simon back to the floor and flung his beefy arm around his neck again. They shuffled past the first room numbered 201.

The second floor decking passed the first eight rooms and then turned left around to the side of the building. This is where rooms 209 through 214 were. The two made their slow stroll around the decking and finally approached room 213. Odin grabbed the key from Simon's sweaty palm and opened the door leading the two of them inside.

The room was smaller than Odin's back at The Whisky Dip, with a straw mattress in the center against the back wall. In the back right corner, Odin observed a privy with a large clay bowl and used hand towels laying on the floor in a pile. There was a single window above the privy facing the alley, covered by a piece of tan fabric which allowed a streak of torch light into the room. Odin led Simon towards the bed and flung him down. As he hit the mattress, a cloud of dust sprung up which Odin could see in the dimness.

"Simon, stay here. I'll check on you in the morning, okay?" Simon mumbled something in return that Odin could not make out. He made his way towards the door and shut it without a sound.

Odin rounded the second floor decking and made his way back to the switchback stairs leading to the ground. He descended them two at a time and was back on the ground in moments. Before he started back to the tavern, he looked up towards the second floor where he had left Simon. *That guy's going to get me in a lot of trouble. He's going to be a lot of fun too.* He gazed up at the crescent moon hanging overhead as he started off towards home.

7

ODIN APPROACHED THE STREET lining the docks but stopped abruptly to stare down the dark alley he and Simon had passed minutes before. He couldn't make it out, but there was something not right about what he was looking at. A feeling from deep within told him to stay out of there. He could vaguely see that the alley was lined with the backside of buildings, cluttered with empty crates, barrels, and debris. The scent of spoiled fish and stale ale lingered in the air as a light breeze made its way towards him from the south.

He knew he could take the alley back to The Whisky Dip but was hesitant due to the lack of lighting - and his gut feeling. In the back of his mind, he was also worried of encountering O'Doyle again on the main street across from the docks, given the Blue Gypsy was docked there for the next few days. He unsheathed the dirk strapped behind his back and stepped wearily into the alley.

As he slowly made his way down the dark corridor, he could hear the scurrying of small animals scavenging through the debris and trash, searching for a free meal. The empty crates lying around created obstructions that he had to go around. He even had to climb over a crate where there was no way around. He stepped forward with his dirk firmly pointed out in front him.

His unease increased with each building that he passed, listening to the sounds of the alley, making his way further into the labyrinth of darkness. The moon above gave off a sliver of light but he was not comforted by it at all. Being alone in this alley made him understand what Simon had revealed to him earlier in the night about Lilly. He recalled Simon stating that when she went to look for her father in the alley, there was an eeriness to it. The darkness and void of sound frightened her, as if there was something there, unseen. He felt it too, now that he was there, utterly alone.

He continued forward, passing the backside of several markets, taverns, and a brothel where a young woman winked at him from an upstairs window. She had long curly red hair and a crooked smile. That red hair brought back fond memories. He didn't respond to her gesture and just continued down the alley attempting to be as stealthy and swift as possible. Deep within his consciousness, he knew if something bad was going to happen, this would be the place.

As he ducked under a broken crate lying upright, he suddenly heard a loud crash and the breaking of glass in front of him. With a startled jump, he halted his steps and pointed his dirk in the direction of the piercing noise. Through the moonlight, he could vaguely see something moving. It was moving slowly in his direction. The appearance of the object began to grow as it inched further. It was a few feet tall from what he could guess and seemed to glide, as if floating off of the ground. He took three steps backwards, never taking his eyes off of the dark mass coming forward, before he bumped into a crate, stopping his retreat. With fear pulsating through him, and a shaky voice, he shouted, "Stop, whoever you are!"

The mass of darkness continued to advance straight towards him, causing sweat to trickle down his brow as he began to panic. He held the dirk firmly towards the thing nearing him, petrified, his back against the crate. It wasn't until it was within twenty feet that Odin realized what it was. An empty bourbon barrel was rolling down the alley in his direction. He could see its oak patterns spiraling around and around now that it inched closer and finally stopped mere feet from the crate he was leaning against.

What the hell is wrong with me? It's just an alley, he thought to himself.

After collecting himself, he pushed off of the crate, wiped his brow, and forced himself to move forward. As he did, the sounds of a group of scurrying animals could be heard ahead. He could see the faint glow of their eyes in the moonlight up the alley. It was just a family of raccoons. Odin reached down to the ground and picked up a stone, rounded and smooth from the sea. He threw it in the raccoons' direction, causing them to dart off into the darkness. "Get out of here!"

The trek down the alley was much swifter now, as he felt more comfortable with his surroundings. He wasn't thinking about what happened to Lilly's father, or that something was wrong with this dark alley. Confidence slowly took over and he decided to sheath his dirk. Walking proudly, he neared the back of The Whisky Dip with a spring to his step.

There was a pathway to the front of the building on each side connecting the front to the back. The path was as dark as the alley but had far fewer crates and barrels in it. Except for an old mattress and a broken piece of furniture, it was clear. The ground was lined with paved stones in the shape of a hexagon. They interlocked to form a strong, steady foundation that made for stable footing. He walked down the path happily, peering up towards the second floor where his room was waiting for him. While rounding the corner to where the stairs were, a sudden shriek was heard close by.

"What the hell was that!" he whispered. He quickly reached for his dirk once more and held the weapon in front of him, knuckles whitening due to the tightness of the grip.

The anxiety and fear from the alley returned in a split second. The feeling of dread pulsed through his body as he wondered who that shriek had come from. Another shriek followed moments later and Odin knew they were very close, possibly coming from the pathway on the other side of the building. He inched around to the front of the tavern towards the other side, dirk pointed out in front of him. Something deep inside told him to bolt up the stairs and lock himself in his room, but he forced himself to move towards the direction of the sound. He leaned forward, peering around the corner, unable to comprehend the sight before him.

Odin could see the back of a person, lifeless and hanging in mid-air, as if suspended by ropes. It was a very tall man. His shoulders were pushed back and his arms were swaying at his sides. His legs were buckled, as if sitting on the edge of a bridge. He could see the top of the man's head, balding with a few sunspots on his scalp, as the man leaned back leering to the heavens. The shock of what he was viewing caused him to freeze, but he couldn't avert his eyes.

What is this? What is happening?

Looking past the man, he could see the view into the alley was obstructed by something. There was a presence there, dark and cloudy, nearly translucent. It filled the entire pathway behind the man, towering high and wide. The darkness of black within the thing terrified Odin as he watched what it was doing to the poor, lifeless man hanging in front of it.

Without warning, there was a sudden rippling effect throughout the dark mass followed by a constant hum. He watched as the entity continued to pulsate. The dim moonlight showed waves of ripples flowing through it, like a stone thrown into a still pond. As this occurred, the man hanging in the air let out another shriek, followed by a series of violent convulsions. Whatever was happening to this poor man was extremely painful.

Suddenly, the man began to move forward through the air towards the thing. As he floated forward, Odin watched in disbelief as the man seemed to slowly dissolve. His arms and legs, already quite thin, seemed to wither away in mere seconds, leaving a torso and head gliding towards the dark mass. This too slowly dissolved into nothingness as it met this evil thing hovering in the pathway. Odin involuntarily released his grip on the blade in shock. The dirk fell to the paved stones below with a loud clank.

The sound caused the rippling and hum of the dark mass to abruptly stop. Odin, now shaking with fear, watched as the thing seemed to notice him and began to slowly move in his direction. It inched effortlessly closer, taking up the space within the path. The fear of death struck Odin without notice and he tried to scream, but no sound exited his mouth. He couldn't scream, move, or take his eyes off of this creature that was now a few feet from him. The terror within became too much for Odin and he felt his body give in. Clutching his chest, he collapsed to the paved stones below.

Before completely blacking out, he looked towards the entity one last time and noticed something - It had eyes. Two crimson red eyes were watching him. As the darkness of unconsciousness took hold, he finally escaped the horror and blacked out, while a last thought flitting through his mind. *How could any of this be real?*

PART 2

SEARCHING FOR ANSWERS

8

A BRIGHT BEAM OF light made its way through the window as the sun rose in the east, its horizontal tendrils reaching out into the unknown. It slowly crawled across the dusty floor of the room towards the bed near the back of the room. As if alive, it made its way up the mattress and across the face being obscured by a flock of wavy, dark hair. The light crossed the man's eyelid causing a shutter and moan of displeasure. He slowly opened one bloodshot eye in annoyance as the light continued to brighten room number two at The Whisky Dip.

Odin was in his boarding room, and he was alive.

With a sudden jolt, he jumped out of bed realizing where he was. Panic set in as his mind started to recall the last moments before blacking out.

"It was a dream, only a dream! What the hell was that?" He was pacing back and forth in front of his bed with his hands on top of his head, fingers locked, mind working erratically.

Suddenly, his frantic activity stopped. He dropped to his knees looking out the window. The sun had risen over the Green Sea and gulls could be seen flying in front of it. Tears were welling in his eyes as the horror slowly started to return. "It wasn't a dream. I know what I saw."

Odin's mind was spinning but he focused on what he could remember. There was a man in the pathway. The man he saw hanging in the air, with the balding white hair and the sunspots on his scalp. He knew that man. He had been on the Blue Gypsy. He had cursed at the sailors while deboarding.

The reality sunk in deeply as Odin stared out of the window. "But why didn't it take me?"

Minutes passed before Odin had the strength to stand. Feeling anxious about his memories from the alley, he opened his old trunk and grasped his boot knife before backing his way into the corner of the room. He slid down to the floor watching the rest of the room, expecting something to happen, something to reveal itself. With frantic eyes, he scoured the room from left to right, never blinking. The knife was held firmly in front of him, as he waited for the horror to return. That dark mass, that nothingness, that *evil*. The paranoia was real and it was sickening. *If it was real, how did I get back to my room?* he thought.

Odin sat in the corner of the room for the next hour, manically waving his knife in the direction of any particle of dust that caught his eye. The disbelief of what he witnessed last night was the only thing on his mind. His fear of the unknown and what he thought he had seen was haunting his every thought. With tears in his eyes, his only other thought was, *Why am I still alive? Why?*

Once the sun was clearly over the horizon of the Green Sea, Odin saw a shadow cross against the bright light entering his quaint little boarding room. He found himself unable to move, paralyzed against the corner of the room. The shadow of light moved from the window towards the door within moments. The seconds seemed like hours as Odin, waiting for the terror to seize him, fixated on the door and the evil that waited beyond it.

The door handle slowly turned, causing him to gasp as he braced to once again see the dark mass that was now haunting his every thought. The door edged open mere inches, allowing more of the radiant morning light to enter. The brightness momentarily blinded him, and he had to shield his eyes with his hand, obscuring his view from what was on the other side. Sheer panic set in as he prepared to face this entity once more.

Beyond the door came a voice though. A voice that saved Odin from blacking out once again. A voice that made him momentarily forget about the alley, the black mass, and how he got back to his room. This voice saved him from the terror of what he lived through and cemented the fact that he was still alive. It was the voice of someone that he recently met, a kind voice.

"Odin. Odin. Are ya decent? I've brought fresh tea."

Lilly pushed the door open and peered in to see Odin sitting in the corner, trembling with fear.

He still had the dirk pointed in her direction and there was an expression of both terror and relief on his face. The sunlight poured in surrounding her as Odin shielded his eyes to see her face. The face of an angel. He momentarily realized that there was good in this world after all. He released his grip, allowing the blade to drop to the floor.

After seeing him cowering in the corner, Lilly rushed into the room, setting a bronze tray down on the floor near his feet. Two mugs of hot tea were sitting on the tray, steam rising into the air. She knelt next to him frantically, taking both of his hands into hers.

"Odin, what's wrong? What happened?" The expression of worry was heavy on her face.

Staring at her with teary eyes, Odin began to break down. He didn't know how to clearly explain what had happened last night or the thing that was haunting all of his thoughts. Without notice, his arms flung around her neck and he held her tightly. The only thing he knew for sure was that he needed another person's embrace in that moment.

Lilly was confused - she had never been near a man so emotionally vulnerable. The men in her life were often tough guys, verbally abusive merchants, drunken sailors, or her father.

Her father was the toughest guy around - you would need to be if you owned an establishment called The Whisky Dip. This man, alone raising a baby girl, was forced to move on with his life after his wife died. The chance to raise an elegant daughter, well educated, and courted by lords or their sires, flew out the window when her mother took her last breath. Instead, she was raised as a barkeep herself - tough, gritty, and stern. She wasn't allowed to be a delicate flower in this city swarming with sharks.

As an only child raised by a bar keep, she had learned to be strong-willed. From an early age, she was told that her emotions needed to remain within, locked up tight. A business owner, especially one that owned a tavern, never showed their emotions, or expressed doubt or fear. It just wasn't the way.

Being in this moment, holding a grown man trembling and in tears - and one that she found relatively attractive - wasn't easy. She put on her best business face and embraced him back, cradling the back of his head and whispering to him, "Odin what happened? I'm here, ya're safe, nothing is wrong. Let me help ya."

Minutes passed before either said another word. The sobs from Odin steadied and he eventually released his grip on the back of her shirt. As the embrace ended, Lilly looked Odin in the eyes.

"What happened? I found ya lying on the side of the building, blacked out. Did ya have too many with Simon?" Lilly rolled her eyes as she said Simon's name but returned them quickly to Odin. "I closed the bar so there was no one around to help me get ya back up here. Ya're not very light ya know?" She smiled at him, hoping for the same response, but didn't receive it.

Odin listened attentively while gazing into her eyes, taking in what she had said. The comfort of knowing that she had found him, possibly saved his life, helped him gain some confidence. He slowly built up enough courage to try to explain what he thought had happened to him.

"I don't know how to say this, Lilly. I don't know if what I saw was real or a dream, my mind is so confused." He stopped and dropped his face into his palms, shaking his head.

Lilly continued with her best face, encouraging him to go on. "I'm here, ya can tell me what happened. It's okay Odin. Let me help ya." She reached out and grabbed his hands, forcing Odin to look up and again make eye contact. "Go on, I'm listening."

Odin, not knowing what to believe, shared his story with her, what he was starting to remember at least. Lilly saw him leave with Simon so he started there. He retold the events that followed from there, including the scream he had heard and the strange sight that had greeted him when he had investigated it - the man in the air, the dark mass, everything he could remember. All of it seemed so ludicrous, he wondered if she would even believe him. He still wasn't sure he believed it himself.

When he finished with his tale, Odin noticed her staring at the floor. She didn't say anything or move for quite some time. Odin felt as though she was trying to understand the absurdity of the story.

Lilly raised her gaze from the floor back to Odin. She continued to hold his hands tight within hers. The mask she had been wearing seemed to dissipate momentarily, revealing her true emotions.

"This is gonna be hard to hear Odin, but... I know what ya are talking about. I've heard stories about what ya just described. My daddy used to tell me about this thing too. The people in this city don't speak of it out of fear. They call it ... The Eyes."

9

THE STORIES THAT FOLLOWED filled Odin with disbelief. He listened attentively as she described stories that she had heard from sailors after refilling their mugs several times. The more they drank, the more gossip crossed their lips.

One story suggested that this presence had been in the city for a very long time, even before the city was established. No one knows where it came from, and few even believe it is real.

Another old wives' tale she shared was from a young merchant who claimed that his father was taken by something dark while they were walking home from the markets late at night. He told this story years after the incident, though. The young merchant told her that this black thing, took his father, and he couldn't do anything to help. It was as if he was paralyzed during the attack - forced to watch, helpless and scared.

Her father would also tell her stories about this monster with red eyes that feeds off children if they are in the streets or getting into trouble. She said the tales were aimed to keep her from misbehaving as a young girl. Her mother was gone and her father worked long hours, allowing for numerous unsupervised opportunities to get into mischief.

As Lilly grew up, these tales became just superstition - there was no monster in the streets with red eyes. That would be foolishness. But here she was, sharing these stories with a man she had just met - a man that had claimed to have seen the thing in the streets with the red eyes and lived. There was still a hint of suspicion in her expression as she finished her tale. Lilly released the grip on Odin's hands and brought them closer to her chest. She eyed him thoughtfully with a hint of pity.

Is this man playing games with me? Did Simon put him up to this? She thought to herself. After choosing her words carefully, she spoke, "I know it seems like it was real Odin, but do ya think maybe Simon spooked ya by telling ya about the city's stories? Do ya think maybe ya bumped ya head or somethin' on ya way back here after carryin' Simon home?"

The two of them sat there in the corner of the room for a time, silent. Thoughts raced through their heads, causing increased anxiety.

He finally broke the silence, startling Lilly. "I know what I saw last night, and it was real. It had red eyes Lilly - red eyes! This thing, this monster, is out there preying on people, and it scares me to death!" He dropped his gaze once again to the floor. "I don't know what to do! Every time I close my eyes, I see it. It must be real Lilly, or I'm going crazy!" He got up off of the floor, leaving her still sitting. He started to pace the room, hands on his head, mumbling.

Lilly removed herself from the floor and walked towards the bed, where she sat on the edge. She watched him pacing around the room, wondering if what he was saying was true. If there was something in this city - something dark and evil - maybe this could explain what happened to her father.

"Maybe it is true, Odin. If ya say ya saw somethin', I believe ya. There are others out there who say similar things. I think we should go and talk to 'em. I'll need to lock up the bar while we are gone."

Odin halted his pacing and stared at her. He stared right through her light brown eyes. "I think there is someone in the market that we should talk to as well. I met a man yesterday that said a small boy had disappeared recently. Maybe he knows something else. He also told me to be careful because it's easy to go missing in this city. I didn't think anything of it until just now."

Lilly stared back with agreeing eyes. "Let's grab Simon on our way there. I don't think he told ya, but he knows about this thing. I never believed him. In fact, I used to make fun of him for telling this strange, horrifying story, but maybe it's true. It sounds a lot like yas." She stood up from the edge of the bed and made her way towards the brass tray that she had placed on the ground when she entered. "Come, drink ya tea before we leave. It's already getting cold."

10

THE TWO MADE THEIR way down the stairs toward the tavern where Lilly locked up for the day. She didn't seem very upset about her business not being open for the outstanding citizens of Floria City. All those coppers she would not earn and all the belligerent patrons missed for an entire day seemed to cancel each other out. She was anxious, almost excited to possibly get some answers about her father. Her strides were long and proud as she walked away from the locked doors. She stopped in front of Odin, looking at him very seriously.

"I know that it is daylight, but do ya want me to hold ya hand, just in case?" A slight smirk crossed her face as she finished the sentence, knowing that the jab would hit Odin good.

"I'm fine, thank you though," Odin replied in a sarcastic tone. "Very funny."

"Just tryin' to be a lady," she whispered as she set off down the street towards Simon's boarding house, not waiting for Odin nor allowing him to lead. "Ya comin'?"

Odin let out a long sigh, following after the woman - perhaps following a woman that was leading him to an answer that he didn't want to know. He believed in whatever it was that approached him last night. He believed that there was something wrong in the city, something dark and evil. He also believed that the only way to restore his life was to learn about it, possibly face it again. The thought of that caused him to hesitate momentarily. He never wanted to see that thing again, but he needed answers.

What is it? Why is it here? Why didn't it take me, like it took the old, thin man? After pausing momentarily with his worrisome thoughts, he followed Lilly, jogging slightly to catch up to her. "Hey, wait up barkeep, I don't want you having all of the fun without me," he yelled after her.

The two walked down the street towards the same intersection that Odin and Simon had the night before. Approaching this area felt wrong to him. He paused as they turned the corner, looking in the direction of the alley. It looked very different in the daylight. There didn't seem to be as many obstacles laying around in it as there was in the dimness of night. Even with the sun hovering above the bay, the alley had an eerie feel to it. Odin hurried along past it, taking a glance every few steps.

As they approached Simon's boarding house, a familiar sound rang throughout the courtyard on the first floor. As they entered, they saw who it was coming from. There he was, bright-eyed and bushy-tailed, as if he hadn't drunk his weight in ale the night before. Any other man would be as sick as a dog for days, given what he had consumed.

Simon was sitting on a stool, singing with his feet propped up on a crate, fingers locked behind his head. They stared in disbelief as the man finished his chorus about a whale swallowing a ship. They looked at each, shook their heads, and continued towards him.

"Simon, I thought you'd be in bed for a week, after last night. What are you doing out here?" Odin asked.

"Enjoying the beautiful sunrise, mate. Ya missed it though, should have been here a couple of hours ago. It was magnificent. I woke early to watch it rise out of the bay - that's the only way to watch it! Whatcha up to? Hey Lilly, why ya hangin' with this bum?" Simon responded, without taking a breath or acknowledging the previous remarks.

Lilly stepped up to the man, a hint of annoyance on her face. "Simon, we've known each other for many years, right?"

"Aye, sure 'nough. I've known ya since ya was a mere pup. I reck on...this big." He removed his hands from behind his head and held them in front of her, maybe a foot apart, as if trying to find the right length. One eye was closed and his tongue was sticking sideways out of his mouth a bit.

Her annoyance with him was escalating. Odin wondered why he had this effect on her. From the story that he knew, Simon had worked for her father when he was younger and had been almost like a family member, maybe even like an older brother to her. Why did he have this ability to frustrate her by a simple response or gesture?

"Simon?" Lilly paused for several seconds. "Since we have known each other for as long as I can remember, I want to ask ya somethin'. Do ya remember the story ya told me 'bout seeing that thing that haunts the streets? The dark thing that saw ya? Ya said it felt like ya was paralyzed and couldn't scream or run. Do ya remember?"

Simon's face turned from carefree to puzzled instantly. His hand lifted towards his beard, making long strokes. This was his thinking face, and he was deep in thought at this moment. "Why would she ask me that, on a beautiful, majestic morning like this? Why?" He muttered before responding to her question. "Aye, but why are ya bringing this up now, in front of Odie? We don't really know this bloke, do we?" His eyes pleaded with her for an explanation.

"I know he is new to town, and I just met him. But I trust him Simon, I really do." She squatted down next to his stool, holding his eyes. "Something happened to him after dropping ya off here last night. Something that scares the hell out of all of us, Simon. He saw it last night, IT!" Her glare was serious and a little menacing, too. Her intentions were to get Simon to stop being Simon for a second and take something serious. It was working based on Simon's next actions.

He quickly dropped his feet from the crate and sat up straight, looking at her as if wanting to say something. He fumbled for the right words for a few moments before finally addressing them.

"Aye, if ya saw it, then it saw ya. We should all consider that for a second before doin' anythin' stupid." His eyes left the pair for a moment as he glared out towards the bay. As he spoke again, he dropped any trace of the carefree sailor that Odin had known him to be. "I don't know what it is, but I saw it years ago and been tryin' to forget it since. I changed that day and I've never been the same. So, we've both seen it, what do ya want me to do about it?"

Odin stared at the man, sensing the fear rise within him again as he watched Simon's demeanor completely change. Three minutes ago, this man was singing a crude sailor's song, enjoying the morning sunrise without a worry in the world. Now, he was as serious and sober as a prisoner walking the plank. The mere mention of this thing, this dark entity, had scared Simon to his core. Perhaps Simon and Odin had something in common here. "I don't know what I saw last night, but I know I saw something. Something dark, something dangerous. It had a man, and ..."

Simon stood up and cut him off as Odin mentioned the man. "What man? What was it doin' to him?"

Odin took a step back as Simon stared at him, demanding answers. "It was an old man that was on the Blue Gypsy with us. Tall, thin, and ugly." Odin's expression oozed with grief and despair. "This thing was eating him, or feeding off of him. I don't know which. It looked like he was slowly being consumed somehow, like it was devouring him layer by layer. The man became nothing right in front of my eyes and I couldn't do anything. I couldn't yell or move, or anything." Tears were welling in his eyes as he recounted the horrible sights he had witnessed the night before.

Lilly leaned in towards Odin, attempting to give a hint of support as the two unlucky men stared at each other in disbelief and bewilderment. She eyed Simon with a sternness that she only seemed to use when he was around. "Simon, he needs to hear ya story. I need to hear it too in case my daddy's fate is due to this thing. Will ya help us?"

Simon began pacing around the crate he had had his feet on, pulling on his beard and mumbling under his breath. It was clear that he had tried to forget about his history with whatever was in the streets of Floria. Perhaps bottling the memories away and suppressing the fear for years had helped Simon recover from his experience, but it wasn't going to help Odin and Lilly, or stop whatever it was from continuing the threat.

After a few tense moments, Simon stopped both his frantic pacing and beard pulling, and faced the two asking him to do something he swore he would never do again. "Okay, I'll tell ya what happened, but remember, I don't like this. I'm doing it for ya Lilly, ya know I love ya like a lil' sis," he eyed her with sincerity.

Lilly looked back in his direction with a similar expression that said she loved him too and appreciated what he was about to do.

Simon invited the two of them to pull up some stools. "Have a seat, it's always best to sit on ya rump when ya 'bout to hear something awful. Anyways, 'bout five years ago I was workin' for …"

Simon went on for the next few minutes recounting how he had previously worked for Captain Largent aboard a beautiful vessel known as the Mistress Deep. This wasn't a fishing ship like the Blue Gypsy; it was a trade ship. He had a very similar job as he does now, as a deckhand, but instead of moving just fish, they moved everything:

imported furniture, food, apparel, spices, and other materials. This vessel's journeys were farther and longer than what he was currently used to.

He would travel across the Green Sea to Celonia and even south to Milstone, trading goods and slowly filling the vessel's hull for the trip back home to Floria. After completing a two-month-long journey, the Mistress Deep was docked in Kobalt Harbor, allowing the crew to have a little excitement and rest for a few days. He and some crewmates thought a night out would be rewarding after their work during the voyage. They had some coppers to spare at this point. Apparently, on this night, they had a very good time, hopping from tavern to tavern, chasing wenches and causing a little trouble. As they were wrapping up their drunken evening, they all parted ways. Some left for the brothels, others back to the ship. Simon and a mate named Pyke decided to journey towards the market district in hopes of finding some more fun, and some fresh baked bread.

It was very early in the morning based on his tale. The light of dawn wasn't present over the horizon yet but it was close. The two pals drunkenly staggered up the ascent towards the market, the Lemurians clearly in the distance. This is where the story almost becomes unbelievable.

Simon, with a straight face, went into very specific details about what happened to Pyke. As the two entered a street near the bakeries, Pyke had stopped walking. He was peering into the darkness and his drunken posture and mannerisms left in a heartbeat. This man was scared of something - something unnatural and threatening that should not be in this city.

Simon tried to get his attention, thinking the man was dawdling around but Pyke hadn't responded to him. He had just stared down the street into the darkness. Without warning, Pyke let out a blood-curdling scream, a sound that still haunts Simon today. The man fell to his knees, hands clawing at his face and eyes as if something was crawling on him. Simon couldn't move or speak; he was helpless and hopeless as he watched what happened next.

His old mate shot into the air, hovering about three feet above the ground. His body began to contort, and Simon could hear the sounds of bones snapping. His shoulders were forced backwards in an unnatural way and he was looking straight up towards the sky. His spine had been twisted into the shape of a horseshoe. More violent screams were coming from him during the assault, and Simon could do nothing about it.

Fortunately, the shock of what was happening to him caused Pyke to lose consciousness - that or his heart stopped right there, sparing him further agony

As Pyke bellowed his final scream, he slowly started to move forward, floating in the air. That's when Simon's attention turned towards the darkness in front of him. There was something there, in the shadowy depths of the street, almost camouflaged. He could make out a vague outline of something that had a shape and didn't at the same time. It was as if this thing, this entity, was translucent and engulfing the space around it.

His friend, already deceased, floated closer and closer to the darkness. As the lifeless body hovered near this monster, the limbs seemed to disintegrate. Flakes of matter slowly peeled off his body and shot towards the entity, disappearing as they reached the blackness. Piece after piece were removed from Pyke as he inched closer, until there was nothing. His friend was gone, not a trace of him left. Simon, petrified, was forced to stand there and witness this terrifying event, unable to do anything.

With a quiver in his voice, he finished his story. "My mate was gone, and there was this evil staring at me. I didn't realize it at first but within the darkness, there were eyes. Crimson-red eyes, and they were looking at me. That's the last thing that I remember. I must have blacked out because I woke up after sunrise, and a stray cat was licking me in the face," Simon fell silent and looked down at his feet, thinking about the event.

The three of them sat there in silence for a few moments, truly taking in the horror of what Simon had described to them. Eventually, Lilly broke the nervousness of the situation.

"Thank ya, Simon. Ya never got that detailed about it with me before. I'm sorry that happened to ya," She reached out and grabbed his hand, embracing it in her own. "Ya like a brother to me Simon. I don't want this to happen to another person. Thank ya for helping us." The two shared a long gaze of appreciation and support for one another. After the moment ended, she turned her attention towards Odin. "Does that sound much like ya encounter?"

Odin's eyes were still full of tears from listening to Simon, but he slowly nodded in her direction. He couldn't muster the right words to express his emotions, so instead he just mumbled the word, "Yes."

Simon looked up from the floor to acknowledge Odin. "Ya tellin' me that ya saw this thing last night? And it had a man? That it did the same thing to him as it did to me mate Pyke? Is that right Odie?" Concern and worry were etched on Simon's face.

Odin just nodded. "Yes, I saw it. I saw what it did to the man. Same thing that happened to your friend Pyke. I saw its eyes too. Red and evil. We've both seen it. I don't understand why we are alive."

Simon's demeanor changed a little as Odin was finishing up, more cheerful, more playful, more like Simon. "Well, I reckon we better find out before it's too late. There's somethin' in this city and it's killing people, not us though. Maybe we're too tough for it, what da ya say Odie? Let's go find some answers, eh? Where should we look first?" He stood up and extended a strong arm in Odin's direction.

Odin grasped his hand strongly while raising out of his seat. "I need answers as much as you do. I think there might be someone in the markets that we should talk to that might have more information for us. I met him yesterday while getting a feel for the city after deboarding the ship. He said something to me that I didn't think much of until this morning. His name is James."

11

THE MARKETS WERE BUZZING on this particular morning - flocks of peasants begging for scraps, merchants bartering and selling goods, and even a few heavily guarded lords were seen roaming through the alleys and streets, checking on their investments. The scents of a hundred dishes lingered heavily in this chaotic atmosphere as Odin, Lilly, and Simon approached from the slums below. As they ascended into the district, few paid attention to them. There was nothing unusual about three visitors from the docks strolling through.

The heavy population of peasants and merchants was challenging to navigate this morning. The three had to maneuver through the streets, avoiding wagons being pulled by oxen, as well as half-naked children chasing stray cats.

Once they made their way past the initial perimeter, they were swarmed by the peasants waiting impatiently for a handout. Large families approached without a care or a sense of personal space. Being overly cautious, Odin and Simon moved in front of Lilly, creating a human barricade.

An older man from one of the families pushed and shoved his way forward towards the three. The grime on his clothes brought a gag reflection from Odin. There weren't peasants like this back in Milstone. Of course, there are poor in every city, but the peasants here are of a different breed. This man was covered in filth. His hands were heavily calloused and large amounts of dirt were under each fingernail. His frail, thin arms were bruised and stained from using nightshade, an addictive drug common in big cities like Floria. He was also missing a pinky and ring finger on his left hand that had not healed properly which made the sight even more grotesque.

Perhaps it wasn't the man's appearance that got to Odin, but rather his stench. As the man approached, he began to beg for money, pleading for any help that could be given. Of the few teeth he still owned in his mouth, the lucky ones were chipped, caked with plaque and brown in color. At this point, both Lilly and Simon were holding their breath in hopes of not smelling the man or his rancid breath. The gestures by the three did not dissuade the peasant from inching as close as possible though.

"My family's starvin' sir, anything ya can spare? Some bread, or a copper?" He extended his grimy hand in their direction, palm open, expecting to receive something for his troubles.

Simon stepped forward, halting the man's advances, and forcing him to take a few steps backwards. "Do ya think we got coppers to spare? If I give ya a few, what are ya gonna do with it? Feed ya kids, huh?" He eyed past the man to look at the rest of the filthy lot. Malnourished young boys and girls were clinging to the females of the group, hiding their faces from the visitors. One little boy was missing his left arm. From behind the women, he gave Simon a slight smile. "From the looks of ya, it would probably get spent in a tavern, or on a bottle of nightshade. I can see ya arm mate!"

The man retreated with a look of indignation on his face, scowling as he slowly walked backwards towards his family. He eventually made a rude gesture with his good hand towards Simon as the family moved on, trying to haggle the next visitors entering the markets.

Simon waved goodbye to the family, followed by a rude gesture of his own, when he was sure only the man was still leering at them. "Take care of ya kids and stay off the shade, ya bugger!" His attention returned to Odin and Lilly. "Can ya believe that bloke? Mouths to feed and he's strung out on the shade. Highly addictive stuff and deadly. Bloody peasants." He shook his head in annoyance and disgust thinking about the children in the family. 'Well, we betta get a move on."

The three of them continued forward, not allowing another group or family to get near them, even though many tried. For the most part, they just ignored the shouts and pleas for help, and moved forward closing in on their destination.

Simon led the way through the streets, making sure no one got to close, until they came to the culinary district. As rough as he may have seemed with the peasant before, his toughness was non-existent with the bakers and chefs of the markets.

The scents of exotic cuisines caught Simon's attention quickly as they entered this part of the district. His focus and attention disappeared without a trace, leaving Odin and Lilly vulnerable in the street. They were forced to follow his lead, even though he was leading them away from their goal. Several vendors brought their free samples towards the group, causing Simon to step in their direction. Fried squid on a stick, crab claws, and honey glazed oysters were all that was on his mind. Before too long, he was haggling with these culinary experts on second servings and prices for items to go. He lost those verbal battles and the few coppers that were in his pocket.

At this point, Lilly and Odin were physically expressing their annoyance with the side adventures and finally Simon noticed. "What? A man's gotta eat." He popped a ripe oyster slathered in honey into his mouth, smacked his gluttonous lips, and offered the rest of his treasure to his two friends. "It's rude not to share, at least that's what my mum told me." Simon stood there, holding out his culinary delights for Lilly and Odin to enjoy with a small hint of humility in his eye.

After a few uncomfortable moments, Lilly grabbed an oyster, popped it in her mouth, and winked at Odin, expecting him to do the same. With a little reluctance, he followed her lead and they all seemed to agree to refocus.

The journey continued, this time with Odin leading the way. He led the group down a street lined with merchants selling jewelry. Their tents were covered in a bright orange and many had the sigil of the navy ray flying proudly above them. They made their way down the street without much suspicion and then turned right towards a flock of bazaars heavily colored in dull teal. In the middle of it all was a tent that no one could miss or not notice. It was twice the size as the others around it and had a large ram's skull hanging above the entrance, as if it were watching all that came near, warning those within. This was their destination.

Odin had to gather his thoughts before moving forward. What was he going to say to the merchant? Was he going to tell him his story about the monster in the alley? Was he going to interrogate him about his comments about disappearing and vanishing on his first night in the city?

Why did he say that? Was it a warning? What did it do to that man? Why did I survive? Why did Simon survive? The stress of the situation was becoming unbearable. There were too many questions going through his mind and he needed a moment to think.

Simon and Lilly noticed the uncertainty in his eyes and helped him to a pub table near the entrance of the teal tent.

"Here mate, sit. Just breath, everythin's okay," Simon guided Odin towards a stool.

"What's wrong Odin, ya can tell me, I'm here for ya." Lilly's eyes were full of caring.

It took a few moments for Odin to respond, with all the questions circling in his mind. His confidence was draining with each passing breath. Was he wasting everyone's time? Did this merchant know anything or were the comments just light banter from a man trying to sell a coin pouch? There was only one way to be certain.

With a long sigh, Odin forced himself to his feet and took two steps toward James' tent before abruptly stopping again. There were several unfamiliar voices coming from the tent. Whatever conversation that was occurring in the tent was serious and heated from what the three friends could tell. Odin didn't want to be seen or interrupt, so he swiftly led the two others towards the outside wall of the tent, making sure no one from the markets noticed.

Once in a safe area on the side of the tent, hidden behind a beautifully hand-carved armoire from Celonia, Odin knelt down, ear to the teal fabric of the tent's wall, listening attentively to the conversation from within. Simon and Lilly looked at each other wondering what was happening at this moment. They reluctantly joined him.

Simon leaned into Odin, close enough to whisper. "What are we doin'? Why are we sneakin' 'round like a banshee in the night, mate?" His eyes were wide and there was a hint of confusion on his face.

"I don't know, I heard voices inside the tent and panicked. Whoever's in there isn't very happy. Maybe this wasn't a good idea. Maybe we should just leave. What do ya think?" Odin pleaded for support from his two friends but found only bewildered faces. Maybe this was just a big mistake after all. "We should leave, let's go." He started to stand up, but found a heavy arm hanging around his neck preventing his rise.

"Not so fast. Ya led us here, let's find out what's goin' on. I'm intrigued now!" Simon's smile was devious and mischievous as he looked at Odin. "Mate, ya brought us here for a reason. We need those answers. Maybe whatever is goin' on in there will help us in the long run. What might this bloke know, Odin? Let's walk in there and find out."

Odin's jaw dropped in disbelief. "We can't just go in there now! There might be some powerful lord and his goons waiting to kill the merchant. We would be next! Don't be stupid Simon."

The whispers were elevating some at this point. "I'm not stupid, mate. Coming all the way in here and then turning around without answers is stupid. What's wrong with ya?"

"Nothing's wrong with me, I don't want to die and I think I almost did last night. I don't like the sounds from inside that tent." Odin shook his head in disagreement.

"Well, I almost died a few years ago. Ya don't see me running away with my tail between my legs."

Lilly intervened next. In a whisper, she directed their next course of action without a complaint or inquiry. "Both of ya shut it, now! Do ya understand?" Her eyes were serious and stern, causing the others to drop their gazes towards the ground. "We don't know what's goin' on in the city. Maybe what's goin' in here will help us get some answers. Quit bein' a couple of nillies and get ya head in the game! We are stayin' here and we are listening." As she concluded her speech, she spat on the ground in a triumphant display. Odin looked in awe. Simon just smiled.

For the next few minutes, all three had their ears to the side of the tent, listening to the conversation from within. There were at least four men inside. Odin made out one of the men to be James, but the other three were not known. Their conversation was political and financial in nature, with one deep-voiced man declaring that a certain merchant was not meeting quotas or expectations. Others piped in to reiterate the displeasure, stating negative terms like incompetence, insubordination, and even treason. Whatever was going on in this room? It was not light-hearted or benevolent.

"What in the bloody hell do ya think I do all day? Chase tail and hit the pints? I'm here all day, sellin' ya merch."

"It doesn't look like you are applying yourself James. Maybe I should arrange for a personal lesson from Lord Randall? He sent me as a courtesy, you know. Or do you think you might be able to perform up to expectations?

There was a brief pause that felt very uncomfortable. "My apologies, we don't need Lord Randall down here. I can get the job done. Please, make sure that he knows that."

"I knew you would understand James. Be sure to move two hundred pieces by the end of the week. I'm a very forgiving man, but Lord Randall, he's not so accommodating. Don't make me regret this merchant."

"Thank ya, I won't disappoint ya."

Silence fell upon the tent and the three friends found themselves holding their breath in fear of what was about to occur. The sound of boots hitting paved stones was certain and the sounds were getting fainter as if getting further away. Suddenly, the flaps to the front of the tent were flung open and the voices from within were now on the main street. Odin, still in a crouch, made his way around the armoire hiding the three of them and moved towards the corner of the tent. There, he witnessed three of the four voices from inside the tent standing casually. He bent his ear in their direction, with Simon and Lilly close behind him.

A very large man, at least in the mid-section, seemed to be in charge of this group. He wasn't exceptionally tall but had decent height. The majority of his girth came from his torso, which was odd to see. His arms and legs seemed to be weak or frail, but the gut? That required years of dedicated work to develop, and he didn't seem to have missed a day of practice in a long time. In addition to the impressive mid-section, he was heavily decorated in jewelry. Swooping gold chains looped around his neck and each finger was wrapped in rings of gold or precious stone. This man had a very calm demeanor to his behavior as opposed to the other two. Odin observed him very casually with his two associates, speaking frankly about their encounter with the merchant.

"Can we trust him? He's just a bloody low born merchant," a short, thin man dressed in navy and teal asked the others.

"He's always delivered, but this is how it starts. Miss one deadline and then the next one is much easier. I've seen this so many times with scum like this. We will be back here in a week taking his head, I promise that," A towering man dressed in gold and teal snarled with a hint of aggression.

The thin man responded to his colleagues' statements without any animosity. "The merchant has always delivered. I think he got our message. Let's come back in two days to see where he stands with promises."

"I'm gonna have to cut off his hand. You know that right? He's not gonna make it. I could see it in his eyes. He knows it and I know it. Jardin, what do you think?" The towering man looked to the calm man for support on their decision.

After a short pause, the man finally nodded in approval. "James knows not to cross Lord Randall. Give him the two days, if he doesn't deliver, do what is necessary."

The three men finished up their intense debriefing and sauntered away. Jardin, the bedazzled man with the gut, seemed to be whistling as he walked away.

12

THE THREE FRIENDS STAYED hidden on the side of the tent for some time, fearing what would happen if anyone noticed them crouching, lingering, or eavesdropping on a conversation. The words of the man in gold and teal resonated in their minds as they kneeled there; take his head, cut off his hand. Odin had left his homeland after experiencing similar violence.

Peering around the corner, Odin watched the threat finally vanish into the markets, allowing the opportunity to stand. They made their way back towards the front of the merchant's tent confused, frightened, and intrigued.

"What in bloody hell did ya lead us down here for Odie? What have ya gotten into? What have ya gotten us into now?" Simon's face was twisted with contempt, arms flailing with anger. He looked to Lilly for answers as well.

"I'm sure Odin didn't know anything about any of this, since he just got into town yesterday." Lilly's eyes were full of uncertainty, looking from Simon to Odin and back again.

"I know lil sis, I was on the boat too. Those were Lord Randall's henchmen. Do either of ya know who Randall is? Do ya know what he is capable of?" Simon eyed his companions with judgement.

There were no answers to the questions and the three of them just stood there in front of the tent, not knowing what their next move was. Odin's mind was racing and for the first time in several minutes he finally had the ability to express himself.

"I think it would be wise to go in and talk to James. He is obviously connected to this Lord Randall, which means he knows the ins and outs of the city. He might know something about what I saw last night, what you saw too." He looked for approval from the only two people in the city he felt he could trust. "I think we all need some answers. Maybe he can help us or lead us in the right direction?"

Lilly and Simon eyed each other as if speaking a silent language. After a few lifted eyebrows and some head tilting, they both nodded.

"Let me do the talking, I think he will remember me from yesterday. I'll even buy the coin pouch to lighten the mood. He might be spooked due to Randall's goons threatening him. Simon, give me three coppers - I only have two left."

"I only have five! I wanted to get some flatbread on the way out."

"You're still hungry? We stopped at every bloody booth on our way in, man!"

"I didn't get any flats. I want it for later tonight. They put cheese and dates in it. Have ya ever tried flats with cheese and dates?"

"No... what does that have to do with anything? I need to make a statement with the merchant before I just start asking him questions. What's wrong with you?"

"Nothin'! What's wrong with ya?"

Lilly's eyes were fuming before the two finished their bickering. "If ya two don't bloody stop yappin' ya mouths, I'm gonna put my boot in 'em! Simon, give him three coppers. Now!"

"But..."

"Now!"

"Here." Simon reached into his poet shirt and pulled out three copper coins and reluctantly handed them over to Odin. "Just wanted a flat, that's all." His eyes fell to the floor in disappointment.

"We'll get you a flatbread, okay? In the meantime, let's go try and get some answers." Odin strode towards the open tent flaps. As they moved forward, he stared at the ram's skull, thinking about his homeland.

The scent of incense was strong once again as Odin entered the tent hoping for answers, followed by his friends, eyeing each other with utter uncertainty. He quickly scanned the area within to relearn the layout. Perhaps even to see if any threats remained from the conversation that he had heard moments before. His eyes, focused and purposeful, moved from right to left, surveying the entirety of the room. Six oak tables, laid out in rows three wide by two long, loaded with accessories, pieces of apparel, and trinkets that most within the city couldn't afford. His eyes refocused. In the back of the tent, there he was - the merchant known as James, palming his chin, deep in thought with what appeared to be worry.

As the three made their way forward, Odin stopped, watching the merchant's mannerisms. Something was wrong with the man he had met the day before. James' eyes were forward while he cupped his chin. He swayed slightly from left to right looking towards the front of the tent, not blinking, or showing any emotion. He didn't even acknowledge that potential buyers had just entered his tent. He stared towards nothingness with a faceless expression. They had clearly gotten to him - he was in shock.

The awkwardness of the situation caused Lilly and Simon to take a step backwards towards the entrance, not knowing what to do. They eyed each other with weariness. Odin glanced back at them and finally broke the silence.

"James? Hey... it's me Odin. We met yesterday. Do you remember?" He looked at the man but there was no response. The merchant's worry spread out through the tent like a wave. Eyes glazed over, not acknowledging that a soul was in front of him. "I was looking at the blue suede coin pouch... you remember right?" Odin looked back at his companions for advice.

Lilly and Simon peered back with a similar gesture. No one was certain of how to deal with this or what to say next. Simon eventually whispered in Odin's direction.

"Maybe see if he needs to sit down? There's a stool over there towards the back of the tent. Couldn't hurt."

Odin cocked his head slightly at the idea and took two small steps towards the merchant. He was sure to maintain eye contact with James. "James, can I help you? Would you like to rest for a few so that we can talk?" Odin quietly made his way up to the man and gently grabbed his arm by the bicep. He looked at the merchant face to face, and for the first time since the three had entered, James' eyes fluttered to life.

He aggressively pulled his arm away from Odin's grasp, taking a step backwards. "What the bloody hell ya doin' in here? Who sent ya?" His eyes were dangerous and dark as he spoke. "Who are ya?" Without warning, he reached for his hip and unsheathed a knife, brandishing it towards Odin and his friends.

Odin's instincts started in a blink of an eye. He jumped backwards keeping his distance from the deadly blade pointed in his direction. Two quick paces were taken with grace, watching the threat before his eyes, trying to register what was happening. In an instance, he reached into his boot, removing a blade of his own to counter with the one pointing at him and his friends. "James! You know me! I was here yesterday!" He eyed the man with concern, looking for recognition. "I'm here to buy the coin pouch!"

The two leered at each other for a few moments before the merchant finally dropped his blade to his side. His face became solemn, full of regret and despair. After taking several deep breaths, he whispered with confusion, "What do ya want?"

The threat seemed to subside, so Odin dropped his blade as well, although he never took his eyes off of the merchant. He raised his freehand towards the man in a gesture of peace. "I'd like to talk to you James, if that's alright. Me and my friends." He looked back towards Lilly and Simon for a split second. They looked back for an explanation to his actions. He gestured towards them with a nonchalant shrug.

The bewildered merchant dropped his eyes, listening to Odin plead for a minute of his time. "I've had a rough day boy. I think I should rest. Whatever ya want to talk about, make it quick." James' eyes swayed from the floor back to Odin, looking for agreement.

"I understand... I really do. I just want to talk." Odin's eyes filled with hope as he spoke to the merchant, searching for answers. He walked over to the table where the suede pouch laid, picking it up. "While I was here yesterday, you said something strange to me."

The silence between the two seemed to last for minutes. Lilly and Simon watching on in awe, not knowing what to expect.

The merchant's eyes were fierce, yet defeated at the same time. "What did I say to ya boy? What could have been ..."

Without waiting for the merchant to finish, Odin answered. "You warned me not to disappear on my first night in the city. What did you mean by that?"

James' eyes shifted to the right momentarily. His posture seemed to weaken at the words, shoulders slowly rolling forward. "It didn't mean anything, it was just...." Further silence continued as the merchant slowly turned away from Odin and his friends.

The three friends looked at each other in confusion, bewildered looks on their faces. With a little reluctancy, Simon finally broke the silence.

"Sir, please. We just need some answers. We might be able to help each other, maybe answer some questions that ya may have, too. Please sir, stay and talk with us." Simon's eyes did most of the talking, pleading with the merchant for a few more moments.

The merchant turned back, face full of doubt and gloom. He locked eyes with Odin. "Whatever ya lookin' for boy, stop before it's too late. There's a lot that goes on in this city - a lot that is unexplained and strange. Starting with all the disappearances. I remember ya now - ya seem like a kindly fellow. Ya tried to lowball me on that pouch ya holding," a slight smile crossed his face for a split second. "I said what I said because too many like ya go missing." James gave him a solemn look.

"James ... I saw something last night - something that I cannot explain, but it frightens me like nothing else. I fear closing my eyes because I know I am going to see it again when I open them. My mate Simon here," he gestured in Simon's direction, "had an experience like mine years ago. What do you know about this ... thing?"

The merchant's eyes boomed to the size of saucers at the question, jaw dropping open with uneasiness. "What'd ya see, boy?"

"I don't know what it was, honestly, but it wasn't human. It wasn't like us. It was dark in color, yet almost clear. You know, like a pond in the twilight?" Odin stated these words very slowly. "It killed a man. Do you know anything about this?"

The look of sheer terror across James' face answered the question with confidence. "Aye, I know what ya are describin' boy. I do." There was a long pause and it looked like James' lip was trembling as he began to speak once again. "What else did ya see last night?"

"The whole experience has a lot of holes to be honest. My memory isn't exactly perfect, but there is something else." Odin eyed his colleagues behind him and then turned a pleading look towards the merchant. "I lost consciousness as I watched whatever it was. Before I did though, I noticed something that terrifies me. Something that ..."

Before Odin could continue, the merchant cut him off abruptly. "Boy ... I don't know how in bloody hell ya stand here speakin' to me right now after seeing it. I've heard a few stories about this thing - this evil that preys on the city. Sailors and pirates have told their tale of survivin' witnessin' it. Scum lookin' for handouts most likely, but they always ended the story the same way." James paused and gazed at Odin with wonder. "Tell me boy, this thing that terrifies ya, this monster that haunts ya every thought. What color were its eyes?"

13

AN HOUR HAD PASSED by before any of the four felt like enough questions had been completely answered. What was happening in this city? As the three discussed matters, they revealed their personal knowledge about what they understood and were gossiping about the mysteries of Floria. Except for Odin, who had just landed in the city, they had very valuable information to share about folklore, legends, and first hand experiences about whatever it was. Odin had his own horrifying first hand experience. Together, they attempted to make sense of the madness surrounding them.

From their deep, and sometimes very personal stories, the four found a very similar idea behind the legend of what had plagued Floria City for years. This entity had been lurking in the streets for centuries, maybe longer. Stories, both written and oral, passed down from father to son or lord to servant for generations, deeply woven into the fabric of the city itself.

Lilly spoke of stories that her father told her as a child. Like most cultures, her story was meant to frighten and warn children about misbehaving or following rules. Hers told of the monster in the streets that looked for children after sunset. Based on what her father had told her, if a child was out in the streets late at night, a monster - dark and hideous and dangerous - would come and find them to devour their souls, leaving no trace for their grieving parents. Lilly heard these stories from a very early age, believing them for many years.

She also heard wise tales from drunken sailors and merchants visiting her pub, claiming to have seen the evil lurking in the streets and lived just long enough to tell the tale. It was all rubbish in her mind as the men spoke, a humorous story meant to gain a free ale or two. But now, hearing the tales of the men with her, she thought maybe it wasn't rubbish after all.

Simon's stories were the best of the crew, however. As a child, his mother would tell him a similar story as Lilly's father told her, with one striking difference. Based on this legend, the monster was sent to deal with children who had disrespected their parents. This could be for a variety of reasons: not following rules, disobeying orders, or mischievous behavior. Apparently, if a child's behavior in any way disrespected their family name, then a mighty lord would summon the dark monster and set it free on the streets to find the boy or girl. As Simon grew up, he stopped believing in the monster because he had put himself in many situations that were probably considered disrespectful and the thing never came after him. His mother would threaten him sometimes daily but he would just shrug them off.

Being a sailor and working with men from all races and cultures, he brought many useful pieces of information to the group about the legend. He shared one tale from his early days while working for Lilly's father at the tavern. Based on his memory, he was clearing tables late one night of empty mugs and glasses. He approached an older sailor sitting alone in an alcove staring out of a window towards the docks. As he approached the man, Simon asked if he needed anything else, with his everyday friendly nature. The old man did not answer for a few seconds before he turned and spoke. As the man spoke, Simon recalled the look on his face. It was as if he wasn't alive. "Why would a dead man need anything, boy? There's something out there and it's coming. I've seen it! Make sure that ya don't see it, okay?"

This was the only thing the man said to him. He then turned back towards the window and leered out of it for the next hour. The event was odd, so Simon periodically glanced over towards the alcove but he never went back to check on him again that night. Eventually the man got up and left the tavern. Simon never saw him again.

Another story came when Simon was a bit older and already had a few seasons under his belt sailing the Green Sea. This story involved a woman though - a beautiful woman that he had met at a different tavern, The Spider's Web. Simon went into great detail about meeting this woman and buying her pints of red wine throughout the night. Based on the story, the two were getting very friendly as the night went on and at closing time, Simon offered her a place to sleep for the night. She agreed and the two started towards his flat.

As they were slowly strolling back to his place, arms locked and affectionately nudging each other, they heard a blood curdling scream from a street over. Neither were in great shape due to the ale and wine, but Simon decided he wanted to investigate. He asked his lady friend to have a seat on a bench near the docks so that he could find out who the scream came from. He ventured a street over but didn't find anything or anyone in need.

As he was telling the story, you could tell that he knew that scream now. It sounded a lot like Pyke's. As he returned to his lady friend, he found her passed out asleep on the bench, snoring loudly. Even though there are countless explanations for the scream, he told this story for a reason and he deeply believed that it had something to do with the thing in the streets.

The final tale out of Simon's mouth was about a group of mates that he used to gamble with. Late one night, aboard the Blue Gypsy, a group of sailors were playing cards, telling jokes, and boasting about their own unique heroics. One sailor, a salty old deckhand missing two fingers on his right hand, vividly described encountering something in the streets after leaving a pub after a night of drinking.

The man said that a black figure with glowing red eyes came out of an alleyway and attacked the group of friends that he was with. This figure had the ability to control their actions and thoughts, paralyzing the group as it drained them of their lives. Apparently only three of the five survived the incident. Simon never truly believed the words; he figured it was just a wise tale to get the others' attention or respect. But now, he wasn't sure. The man wasn't the most honest, but perhaps there was something there after all.

Eventually Simon cut himself off from the stories and tales, allowing the others to continue with theirs. Maybe it was the juicy figs that James brought out, or the cubes of cheddar cheese. Either way, Simon's attention shifted towards the small table at the back of the tent full of snacks. This opportunity allowed James to lead with the legendary tales of the thing that haunts the streets of Floria.

James began with an emotional story from his troubled youth. When he was fifteen, his father, also a merchant at the time, hired a new shop hand to help during the peak business days. This hand had a great personality and was magical with socializing. His easy-going persona translated to selling merchandise without any effort, which frustrated James. Apparently, he had the ability to sell anything to anyone that stepped into James' father's bazaar.

One day, after working from dawn until dusk, James' father Michael, a heavy set, balding man originally from beyond the Lemurians, was counting his coppers and silvers, and inventorying his merchandise. James had already called it a day and returned home to spend an evening with friends. The new hand loitered, offering assistance at any moment, perhaps to gain trust or acceptance, James never really knew for sure.

After asking if he could help a half dozen times, James' father finally gave in and offered the new hand an after-hours job. This job entailed shining all the blades in the inventory. A big job, and not very prestigious based on the numbers. At the time, they had three tables and a wall full of bladed weapons. It would have taken James at least three hours to do it correctly, but for a first timer it would take at least four and a half. The new hand jumped at the chance, which showed much promise and loyalty. Michael appreciated the willingness and demonstrated the task firsthand.

After showing him the steps repeatedly, James' father felt like the young man had control of the situation and thought that he could leave for the night. Boy, was he wrong!

Upon returning the next morning, James and his father didn't find exactly what they had expected. A section of their inventory gleaming with newly shined and polished blades was not there anymore. Every one of the blades was gone. James' father immediately thought of a robbery, but James knew what really happened. The new shop hand took the entire inventory for himself and was probably halfway around the world by now looking to sell them.

Eventually, Michael came to realize what really happened when his new employee never showed up again. After three days, Michael went for help. When you have been deeply wronged by someone, you reach out to a lord for support, most likely for vengeance and justice.

James' family had always answered to Lord Randall of the Golden Kraken house. He was, and still is, one of the most powerful men in Floria. This was the first time that James' father had reached out for support after years of serving and loyalty.

After the third day of waiting for the man to return, James and his father marched up the hill towards the Manors where the rich and powerful reside. No one can just walk up to a lord's keep without being interrogated by the guards. Undesirables are turned away immediately unless there is a legitimate reason to be there. Michael demanded to speak to Lord Randall about justice as he approached the North Gate. He walked right up to the first commanding officer that he saw.

"I'm here to see Lord Randall. I am the victim of a premeditated theft by a young lad that worked for me for a short time. I have served the Lord my entire life and seek justice." There was much pride in his voice as he spoke but also a sense of betrayal.

The commanding officer, sized James' father up with disapproving eyes. "You are a petty merchant, the lord hasn't the time to hear your squabbling about losing a pair of breeches. Piss off!" The officer turned away from the merchant pleading for help and continued a conversation he was in the middle of with two other guards.

The fury in Michael's eyes must have been very noticeable because the two guards dropped their eyes from the commanding officer and turned their attention towards the man with his fists and jaw clenched. The commanding officer redirected his gaze as well after seeing his guards' reaction.

"Listen here sir, I have come all the way from the market to ask for support from my Lord. I have served his Lordship well my entire life and have never sought support before. Ya will grant me access at once. Do ya understand?" The stare off between the two groups was tense.

After a few moments, the commanding officer turned to the two guards and delivered a slight nod. The two shouted orders towards additional guards behind the gate. The guards on the inside began to pull open the gates, revealing the Manors to the city below. The two towering gates, with their golden M on the left and matching golden F on the right, opened to the demanding merchant and his adolescent son.

Once the gates came to a screeching halt, and the road leading towards the manors was in full view, Michael stepped forward, with young James following reluctantly. As the two visitors passed the wall, they were approached by another guard wearing the teal and gold of house Randall. As he approached with a smug smile on his face, his dark wavy hair blew in the wind. This man came from a watch tower bearing the Golden Kraken sigil waving gently high above. When he was within a few feet of the two, he began to speak. Surprisingly he knew everything about James' father's problem already.

"Good day merchant, I've been briefed about your situation. Apparently, you hired a shop hand and this young lad stole from you. He stole a vast number of blades and swords, right? You are seeking support for this crime, eh?"

James' father was shocked that this man already had all of this information, as he hadn't told the commanding officer the details behind the theft. "Aye, that's what happened, but how did ya know about the blades? I hadn't told anyone here about what was stolen."

The escort's smugness continued as he waved off the question as if it was an annoying fly. "You would be surprised by the information and knowledge that we have, merchant. It's better to not ask too many questions though. Certainly, try not to be too forward with Lord Randall. He tends to consider actions like that disrespectful. When you are presented, state your business, and wait patiently for a response. Do you understand?" Michael nodded in agreement and accepted the man's advice. The three of them walked up the meandering road towards Lord Randall's keep.

It was the largest castle in the Manors, with towering turrets and an additional twenty-foot wall surrounding it. The sigil of the mighty house was proudly on display on the watchtowers as James and his father cautiously approached. A massive iron door, adorned with a large bronze R and black rivets the size of a child's hand, was the only obstacle left to get around.

The escort walked up to the iron behemoth, presented a brass key from his pocket, and slowly opened the door. As James and his father peered within, they noticed a long hallway leading to a banquet room that appeared to be fully lit by a blazing hearth. The escort led the two inside and down the hallway. Portraits of Randall's ancestors hung between unlit torches as the three approached the banquet room. Once they were fully in the room, the escort instructed them to stand facing a throne on the right. The escort exited the room, leaving James and Michael alone with the fear of the unknown as they waited for Lord Randall.

The minutes passed by with agonizing slowness. Finally, the escort returned. Two guards, fully armored with lances and shields, adorning the Golden Kraken, flanked a middle-aged man dressed in a teal surcoat and gold breeches. A two-toned cape flowed behind him with each long stride. His light brown hair matched an impressive square beard. Blood red rubies and green emeralds wrapped around his fingers as he walked into the room with the grace and confidence of a king. This was a man of power and strength and James' father knew it. This was his lord. This was Lord Randall.

The lord sat on a throne in front of the hearth as James and his father looked on. The escort finally introduced his Lordship to the merchant and his son after a moment of confusion and silence. "Lord Randall will hear from you now merchant. Remember what we discussed and mind your tongue."

The Lord's demanding eyes pierced straight through the two visitors as Michael began to plead his reasoning for being there. "Thank ya for seeing us, my lord. My name is Michael and this is my boy, James. I wish not to burden ya with these problems, but a great injustice has been committed against me and my family. A young lad, not much older than my son here, has stolen a vast amount of merchandise from my bazaar. I seek justice and vengeance for these crimes. Can ya help me?"

Lord Randall glared at the merchant without saying a word for over a minute, possibly taking in all of the information, or possibly as a scare tactic. Eventually he responded to the pleas. "How did this young boy enter your shop and steal all these goods without your knowledge?"

James' father's eyes dropped to the floor before he answered. "I hired the boy on as extra help during peak times. I needed help and the little bugger took advantage of me."

"So, you allowed this boy into your shop, allowed him to be around your merchandise, and he betrayed you. Is that right?"

The merchant's eyes glossed over as he answered. "Yes, my lord, that's what happened. I trusted him and he stole from me. Will ya help me?"

A sleek smile crossed the lips of Lord Randall as he eyed Michael's desperation and need. He interlaced his fingers, blazing with precious stones, as he watched the merchant. "I can help you, surely. I have the means and the desire. The question that really needs to be answered though is what are you willing to do for the help? You've stated that you have been loyal, never asking for assistance before. I admire that in a low-end merchant such as yourself. Those that I deal with in similar situations have already demanded so much of my time and energy. It's pathetic. What are you willing to offer, merchant?"

James' father was lost for words. *Isn't a Lord supposed to protect and serve? Why was this man asking for more than loyalty and obedience?* Eventually, with a rasp to his voice, Michael answered the question with uncertainty. "I... I don't know my lord. I have so little already and pay my taxes to ya every new moon." He shook his head in grief.

Lord Randall slowly stood from his seat and nodded towards the two. He held out an open palm and gestured for James' father to step forward. "Come forward merchant, I may have an offer for you, but the offer is for your ears only." He acknowledged James for a moment while waiting for the merchant to step forward. "I'm sorry son, but this offer is only for your father."

After a period of awkward silence, Michael looked at his son the only way a father could, full of pride and love. He mouthed the words, "It's gonna be okay James, I promise," and stepped forwards towards the waiting lord.

James didn't know what his father and Randall discussed or agreed upon, and he never asked his father about it either. He was sure that whatever the deal was, it was worth it because a week later most of the merchandise was returned. They were told that the young lad was arrested and imprisoned for his crimes. Years later, however, his father told him the truth.

The boy was tracked down, hiding out on a ship waiting in the harbor, apparently with a plan to cross the Green Sea and sell the goods over in Celonia. He had a young girl with him too.

As the story goes, the boy was taken into custody along with what was left of Michael's merchandise by Lord Randall's guards. He was sentenced and jailed by Lord Randall himself. James' father was content with the outcome, accepting that justice had been delivered. It wasn't until months later when Michael encountered the young girl on the docks attempting to find a vessel to flee back to Celonia.

Michael confronted the girl seeking answers to whether she was involved in the theft or not. She denied any knowledge or participation, but she also revealed some strange information as well. Her story was very different from what he was told about her boyfriend's apprehension. She was terrified as Michael questioned her, stating that there was a demon in the city. This demon had apparently entered the ship they were hiding on, and it had the ability to control her body and thoughts. Through gasps and tears, the girl painted a very violent picture for Michael. She described this demon as dark and menacing, seeking vengeance and pain.

Michael was in disbelief as he stood on the docks listening to the deranged memories spilling out of the girl's mouth. He didn't know what to believe, but one thing was clear. He needed to forget the entire experience, so he left the girl there sobbing for help, hysterical. He never approached her again, even though she lingered near the docks for a few years after the incident. Eventually, she disappeared too.

As the story concluded, Simon reapproached the group, wiping his mouth with the back of his hand, a pleasurable expression across his face. "Are ya trying to say that this thing has been here for decades? I mean, if it attacked some kid when ya were a lad ... No offence mate but ya not exactly a young buck anymore, ya more like a ...."

James responded without allowing Simon to finish, "Okay, okay, this happened years ago, and yes, I'm a little long in the tooth, sailor. I still don't know what to believe. It's just really strange that my father would tell me about the girl if it didn't have something to do with all of this." He looked at the three, gesturing with his hands. "I've always told myself that it wasn't real, but deep down I always knew the truth. There's something in this city and two of ya have already seen it. I think it has something to do with that bugger Randall, too." James looked down, apparently deep in thought, his lips moving slightly. "How was my father involved in this?"

Odin eyed the merchant with concern, "Perhaps he knows something that he hasn't told you yet, James. Is it possible to ask him?"

A look of mourning crossed his face and James' eyes filled with tears before answering, "It's too late for that boy. My old man's been missing for nearly twenty years. Disappeared around my twenty-fifth name day. No clue as to what happened to him either."

Odin dropped his gaze to the floor, "I'm sorry to hear that, James. Maybe he could have answered some questions. I'm sorry I brought it up. That can't be easy."

"It was a long time ago and I've moved on with my life. I inherited his business. I've done alright for myself throughout the years, too." James cupped his chin in his hand with an expression of annoyance. After a slight sigh, he continued. "I'd be doing a lot better if it wasn't for these taxes and that bugger Randall."

Lilly, who had been very quiet during his story, intervened suddenly. "James, when did ya say ya father disappeared?"

"Um, oh...around my twenty-fifth name day, why do ya ask?

Lilly's mind wandered far away from the tent as she furrowed her brow. "Just curious, I guess. I'm sorry about ya loss, James." She glanced in Simon's direction with a strange look on her face, as if she had just discovered something. She nodded to James with a gesture of farewell and stepped outside.

Simon and Odin looked at each other, wondering what had just happened. After a few seconds, Simon followed her through the flaps of the teal tent, giving James a simple wave. "Thanks mate, see ya soon."

Odin felt the need to follow them but lingered a few additional minutes to finish his discussion with James. The four had shared several stories and gained valuable information about the legend of the creature that had plagued the streets of Floria. Now they had to figure out what they would do with it. Odin said his goodbyes and thanked James for all the information, stories, and snacks that Simon had eaten. "James, I need to join my friends. Thank you for everything. I'll be in contact if I learn anything else. Oh, and let me take that coin pouch off of your hands, you know, the blue suede one?" He walked over to the table and picked it up. He approached James while reaching into his old one for payment.

"Nonsense lad, put ya coins away. After what ya have been through, ya deserve at least a decent coin pouch. I mean, look at that pathetic thing strung around ya waist." James eyed it with disgust. "Take it, I insist."

"Thank you, James, for everything. We'll be back, I promise." As he was walking towards the flaps of the tent, James called after him one last time.

"Odin, before ya go, I forgot to ask with all the storytelling. I remember ya asking about work yesterday. Did ya ever make it up to see the baker yesterday? Ya know Derby, the Celonian?"

Odin's jaw dropped with surprise and embarrassment. With everything that had happened on the last day, he had completely forgotten about the job the baker had given him. What time was he supposed to have been there, sunrise? With a sigh Odin answered the merchant. "Yes James, I did. Thank you, I don't think that is going to work out, though." Odin gave the man a final wave goodbye and stepped out of the tent to join his friends.

14

ODIN JOINED SIMON AND Lilly outside to see why she had left so abruptly. He walked up to the two and found that neither were speaking. In fact, they weren't even looking at each other. Lilly stood there, arms crossed over her chest, chewing on her bottom lip as if she was concentrating on something. Simon's attention had already been diverted to the vendors down the street in the markets once again. He figured he would at least try to pry something from her, even though she appeared hesitant.

"Um, Lilly? Is everything okay? You just ... sort of walked out on us in there. Is all of this becoming too much? I understand if it is. I'm kind of a mess myself." Odin's eyes were pleading for answers and understanding.

Lilly stopped chewing on her lip for a second and refocused her attention on Odin. "I ... I don't know. When he said his father went missing, it just reminded me of my daddy. He's been missing for a few weeks now, and I don't want it to turn into decades like James.

"Did ya hear him when he said he lost his father around his twenty-fifth name day? What could have happened to him? Why did he disappear? Why did he leave me, Odin?" Tears streamed down her cheeks, as the uncontrollable sobs began.

What was he supposed to do in a situation like this? He didn't really know her, not really. But there she was, laying out all her emotions on a silver platter for him. Why? Odin did what came naturally, or what felt like the right thing.

Odin walked up to her and embraced her, cradling her head in his hand. As she wrapped her arms around him, the sobs began to flow heavily. She had waited a long time to let out these emotions. She held him tighter than anyone had in a long time, and it felt good.

Eventually, the sobs lightened and Odin was able to pull back just far enough to make eye contact with her. "We are going to find out what happened to him Lilly, we are. I promise!"

With a shaky voice and eyes full of tears, she nodded in agreement. "I know, and we are going to find out what that thing was last night, too. For ya and Simon, and even James." She gave a slight chuckle at the end, realizing the absurdness of what they were discussing. "Thank ya."

After a few more moments gazing into each other's eyes, Simon interrupted. "Um, are ya two done? Ya said we were gonna get a flat when we left, remember?"

The two had just shared an intimate connection with each other. Slowly, they both turned towards him and shook their heads in annoyance. Finally, Odin said, "Okay Simon, let's go get that flatbread."

As the three of them walked away from James' tent with Simon leading, Odin reached down and grabbed Lilly's hand as they walked. He felt like she was someone very special. He had lost someone very special back in Milstone and didn't want to feel that loss again. Her bright red hair still haunted his dreams and thoughts but maybe Lilly could help with that. Was he jumping into something too fast or was this fate? Either way, he felt good strolling next to her.

15

THE THREE OF THEM meandered their way through the alleyways and streets of the market for nearly thirty minutes before Odin felt the need to stop. Responsibility snuck up on him, even with everything that was happening. He had to go and talk to the baker and explain himself for not showing up this morning.

His pace slowed, eventually coming to a standstill and dropping Lilly's hand, causing a sudden glare in his direction. Would she understand the need to explain himself? He eventually got Simon's attention too, after several shouts, even though the sailor was a good ten paces ahead of them whistling a familiar tune. Simon reluctantly returned to meet the two, cursing under his breath about food or something.

Odin addressed the two with forgiveness in his eyes, "I'm sorry but I have something that I have to take care of here in the markets. There's someone that I need to talk to. It shouldn't take too long but I need to do it alone. I hope you understand." He looked back and forth between the two, hoping for compassion from the only two people he considered a friend in this new city.

Simon slightly cocked his head and looked up into the sky, surveying the sun's position, "Well, make it quick, because it's past midday and we need to get back. I need to check in with Balfour, we might sail tonight for the first catch of the new moon."

"I will, I promise." Odin questioned the words as they exited his mouth.

Lilly eyed him with suspicion but also suggested that he hurry with a look of urgency. "Are ya sure ya have to do this alone? Maybe I can help. I'm great at talking to people. Remember when ya came in yesterday morning? I could tell that ya were nervous about talking to me, but look at us now. I think I can help."

Odin's shoulders dropped slightly as he expressed his need to do this independently. "I know you are great with people, but please just give me a few moments. I'll be back as soon as possible and we will get back to the tavern. I'm sure the fine citizens of Floria are establishing a line already." His smirk as he said the last part was very weak.

Lilly's eyes drifted towards Simon, expressing a sense of sarcasm. "Well, I guess it's just ya and me bro. This one needs to be alone. All by himself without any help." She rolled her eyes at the end, sending a nonverbal message to Odin.

Odin sensed the frustration in her tone. He grabbed her by both hands and looked her right in the eyes. "I'll be back soon, and I'll explain later. Please, trust me, Lilly."

"I know, just be careful and hurry. Simon and I will go get that bloody flat he's been crying about all day, while waiting for ya, I guess." She looked towards Simon knowing that was the only thing on his mind.

"Thank you for understanding. I'll catch up with you soon. Make sure he behaves himself." Odin gestured to Simon who was already licking his lips, most likely thinking about food again.

Odin pulled Lilly in towards his body, still holding her hands gently. He studied her light brown eyes with encouraging nods and mouthed the words, "Trust me." With that being done, Odin left the two standing there and headed off towards the east.

"Well Simon, I guess it's just the two of us for a while. Should we go get a flats? I'm ravenous."

Simon's eyes were bigger than a silver coin as soon as she said those words. "I thought ya'd never ask sis, let's go!"

The two turned towards the intoxicating scents of the markets that had lingered in the air all morning and afternoon. It's no wonder why Simon's attention had been so distant during their trip today. The figs and cheese from James were okay at best, hardly even appetizers compared to the exquisite concoctions that awaited them nearby. Simon, of course, led the way as the two made their way into this part of the district.

"Remember how I said I wanted to get a flats with dates and cheese?" Simon's words stated honesty but his expression altered from the truth. "Well, I did, and I also wanted to try ..."

Lilly cut him off, in order to derail the monologue. "Simon, it's okay, we have time to shop, whatever fancies ya. We don't have many coppers though, so keep it cheap. And make sure ya get me one too, whatever ya buy." She nonchalantly reached into the low-cut part of her dress between her bosom, without an inch of discrepancy, and pulled out a small, black pouch. She opened the pouch and removed a handful of coppers and one silver too. She then held out the coins for Simon with a look of understanding. "Got it? I want one of everything."

"Well, if ya put it that away. Sounds good, be back in a few."

As he was walking away from her, she grabbed his arm, "Oh, I forgot, get some sardinja too. I haven't had any in ages. The really good, spicy kind, okay?"

Simon looked at her in annoyance. "Did ya really think I wasn't going to get some? I mean, come on Lil."

As Simon strode off, Lilly had a moment to think about all that had occurred during the past day. She also had a lot of questions too.

Who was this new man that just turned up in her tavern, rented a room, and turned her life upside down? What had really happened to him last night in the walkway on the side of the bar where she found him unconscious? Why did Simon have the same story from five years ago? How was the merchant James involved, or Lord Randall for that matter? What about her father? Where was he?

The unanswerable questions were causing a splitting headache and she needed a minute to try and contemplate all the events and how they were connected. She found a bench nearby and slowly took a seat, taking deep breaths as she attempted to focus on her thoughts. The worries in her mind were not going away any time soon, so she decided to try and forget about them for a while. She was good at that, putting things off to the side, especially emotions.

The breathing exercise helped because she started feeling better almost immediately. Comfortable, confident, more like herself. She turned sideways and reclined on the bench, feet up and hands placed behind her head, trying to relax. This was just what she needed, a moment to forget everything and everyone.

After about ten minutes of uninterrupted silence, with her eyes closed and not a thought or worry in the world, the sound of footsteps and the whistling of a familiar tune were approaching.

Without opening her eyes, laying almost horizontal on the bench, she acknowledged the approaching person. "Simon, that was quick, bro. Hey, I've been meanin' to ask ya whatcha think of our new friend. I don't know what it is about him but I think I really like him. I don't usually spend time with men like him, ya know? Kind, gentle, and caring. I've always attracted such idiots like O'Doyle.

"He's got great hair too, so thick, dark and wavy. And his body! When we hugged earlier, I couldn't help but feel the muscles in his chest and arms. Oh, and he smells so good too." She shifted a little on the bench and licked her lips in a seductive way. "I wonder what he tastes like? If ya got some of that sardinja, maybe I'll find out later." With her fingers still interlaced behind her head, she slowly opened her right eye and then her left revealing that the person in front of her was not Simon.

"Thanks, I guess?" Odin's expression was utter embarrassment as he attempted to keep eye contact with her.

"Odin! Why didn't ya tell me ya were there? What the bloody hell man?" Her face expressed more than her words had - eyes as big as saucers and her tan skin turning pale. Embarrassment and shame exuded from her as she tried to hide her face.

Odin did his absolute best to try and recover from the situation. "I'm sorry if I startled you. I should have announced that it was me approaching. Everything is okay, and I didn't hear anything that you said." He could tell that this wasn't making anything better based on her body language and decided to change the subject. "Where's Simon anyways?"

She didn't answer. She just laid there, with her hands covering her face, wanting to run and hide from the embarrassment. Could she ever look him in the eyes again after this?

Odin did his best for the next few minutes to leave her be and pretend that he was looking for Simon. He glanced to the east and then the west, hoping that the sailor would return soon. Maybe that would break the tension. Eventually, after several awkward minutes, Simon came strolling up to the two with several items for taste testing.

"Well, I don't know 'bout ya, but I'm hungry, and I bought a lil' bit of everythin'." He eyed Lilly laying on the bench still holding her hands over her face. "Move ya feet so I can put this stuff down Lil. I brought everything ya asked for. Don't be rude!"

Lilly looked through her fingers and gave a slight smirk. She swallowed her pride and decided to sit up. As she straightened up, Simon laid down a platter full of exotic cuisines: baked goods, salted meats and fish, oysters, and even pink and purple fruit that resembled a berry, but was three times the normal size.

He then reached into a back pocket and pulled out a flat bread, baked with dates and cheese. He broke the bread in half, eyed each piece to make sure that they were equal, which they weren't, and handed her the smaller of the two. "Here ya go sis, enjoy."

Lilly and Odin both looked at the goods presented before them and then finally at each other briefly before averting their eyes once more. They could get over this and they both knew it. Lilly let out a brief sigh and then tore a piece of her flatbread off and handed it to Odin, catching his eyes for a moment. "Here's the flat this idiot has been blundering 'bout all day."

He slowly mouthed, "Thank you," in return, and the three of them started their little feast, there on a bench in the middle of the markets.

Odin had never experienced the delicacies of the market and he savored every moment. Perhaps it was the exotic cuisine, the company, or both. All that he knew was that in this moment, he was happy. He wasn't thinking about home, or last night. All he was thinking about was the moment, and how alive he felt.

After scraping the platter clean of all the oils and sauces with his final piece of flatbread, Simon glanced towards the heavens momentarily. "Sun's going down soon, betta get a move on." As he stood, his glare remained overhead and a nervous expression crossed his face.

The uneasiness of his expression must have affected Odin and Lilly because they stood as well, looking upward.

Before the others could respond, Simon attempted to take control of the group and the situation, "Ya two, get it together." He stared at Odin and Lilly while nodding, expecting them to nod in agreement. In contrast, they looked at each other in confusion. "I've gotta get back to port and see Balfour, we need to move now! Do ya understand?" As he eyed the two, they looked at each other and a slight smile crossed their lips.

"Okay, okay Simon, let's get moving. I think we have all seen enough of the markets for one day." Lilly looked from Simon to Odin with a flirtatious smile. "Let's make sure that everyone gets home safe and sound, and tucked in. What do ya think Odin? Is it time to leave and head back towards the docks?"

As the words were coming out of her mouth, Odin found the look on her face very inviting and beautiful at the same time. *Where did this angel come from and why was she interested in me?* he thought to himself. These were the only thoughts moving through his mind now. *Why did she come into my life?*

Instead of answering her questions, Odin simply stared upward as well and stated, "Let's get home. I think I've had enough of the market for one day."

Simon was already three steps ahead of the other two as they started their journey back to the docks.

After a few minutes of walking side by side, Lilly leaned in and asked Odin a question with a hint of sarcasm in her voice, "I forgot to ask, how did it go with the baker?" Her eyes were full but there was no seriousness to them. She expected that it didn't go well.

Odin's disappointed expression said it all. "I got fired before I even started working for him. I tried to fabricate a lie about not being there this morning, and told him that I had an emergency with my new landlady." He smiled at her. "He didn't believe me though. Called me irresponsible and dishonest," he paused for a few seconds while thinking. "It's not like I could have told him the truth, right?" Odin faced her hoping for assurance to his question.

"Of course not, nobody would believe that tale. Especially from some fresh-faced lad just off the docks. Even if he is good on the eyes." She winked in his direction causing a mischievous smile to cross his face. "Oh well, ya can always do some work around the Whisky Dip. I already told ya, there's always mugs to clean and windows to wash. I could use the help too."

Odin didn't respond to her comments. He just strolled along beside her, smiling as he walked. He slowly reached down and gently grabbed her hand, once more embracing her company. They walked together, hand in hand, all the way down the slope of the market until they reached the entrance. They took their time, casual with each step. They were in no hurry.

The moment ended suddenly however, as Simon shouted back towards them with a sternness to his voice. He had come across something he had to address. "Ya two wait here, I gotta take care of somethin'." He walked towards a family of peasants, the same family that they encountered upon entering the markets.

As Simon left, Odin noticed Lilly slightly sigh and roll her eyes in annoyance. Odin found the gesture odd but didn't inquire further.

The frail, filth covered man that was missing two of fingers eyed him with suspicion, expecting a verbal exchange as he crossed his arms over his chest. Simon ignored the aggressive posture and pushed past the man; he was pursuing something else. He darted toward the rest of the family standing near the backside of a building. He stopped when he was feet away from them, their stench stinging his nose.

The women of the peasant family huddled in a group near the wall of a brothel protecting their young ones. Their eyes expected the worst as Simon stood there with his jaw clenched. The children of the group couldn't help but attempt to get a view of this man that had trespassed on their safe zone. As they stood there, eyes fixed on this stranger invading their sense of life and prosperity, one female decided to speak up and ask what Simon wanted.

With her eyes fixed and a sense of nervousness, she asked, "Sir... what da ya want? We didn't come lookin' for trouble."

Simon didn't give her a chance to continue. "Lady, come here." He pointed towards his feet with an expression of disgust and annoyance.

The woman slowly approached, reluctancy taking over her face while looking back and making sure another female from the group stood in front of the children. Her expression was uncertain and ignorant with each step forward, approaching this man with the colorful arm tattoos and long beard.

Simon stared at the woman as she inched closer. He noticed her eyes dropping to the floor as she came within a few feet of him. With a strong voice, Simon began to speak.

"Lady, I know things are tough and ya doin' everything' ya can for those youngins behind ya. I respect that, I really do. They need to be fed and have a solid role model in their lives." He slowly turned around and gave the male of the family a look of disdain, shaking his head.

After a few seconds of scowling, he turned back towards the female. "What are ya doin' with this bloke, anyways? What does he do for ya? Does he provide when he's not looped up on nightshade?" The questions were clearly rhetorical as he stood there, hovering over the woman, not really expecting an answer.

After a few moments of silence, the woman finally looked up and addressed Simon. The shame in her eyes told the whole story. "Sir, we have no protection from the other peasants in the city. They steal and rob from us daily. Brennan here keeps them at bay, as we try to survive.

He's a good man, and he protects us. I know he uses the shade, but that's only in the evenings after we have all..." Tears were welling in her eyes as she spoke.

Simon listened attentively to her explanation, nodding with a subtle agreement. Before she could finish her speech, he cut her off though.

"Listen here woman, take care of these babies and keep them fed. Get away from dead beats like this," he pointed a thumb behind him in the male's direction. "There's merchants in the markets that can give ya a decent job. Quit relying on this guy, do ya understand?" He watched her face for a sign of understanding.

He pulled out two more pieces of flatbread, wrapped in a sheer cloth. He presented the bread to her and explained that it was for the youngins of the family. "I'm serious, take care of these youngins, understand? It's not much, but make sure they all get a piece." He looked back once more towards the male, now scowling in his direction. His annoyance with the so-called patriarch was boiling over as the two held each other's stares. "He doesn't get a bite, I mean it. I'll be back to give ya more next week." Without notice, Simon grabbed the woman by the shoulders and brought her in close to his face.

The male behind him didn't even flinch at the boldness of Simon's display. His glare said everything that was on his mind as he watched the two engage. Simon's eyes, however, were solely invested in this peasant woman, hoping that a smidge of a fraction of his words were getting through to her. As he looked deep into her eyes, he finally found the assurance he was looking for.

With tears streaking down her dusty cheeks, she nodded without breaking his gaze. After some time, Simon let go of her shoulders, but the two didn't drop their eyes. Simon quietly whispered something to her that could not be heard and the woman gave him a slight smile, while wiping away her tears. She took the flatbread and turned back towards the rest of her family and Simon returned his friends, not even acknowledging the male as he passed by.

"What was that all about?" Odin inquired, staring at his friend.

Simon didn't initially answer the question. Again, he was staring at the sky, his mind distracted. After a few moments he finally responded. "Just felt like doin' the right thing mate." He left it at that and neither Odin or Lilly had anything else to say about it. "Well, let's get a move on." Simon eyed his two friends and again chose to lead the group, obtaining another disdainful glare from Lilly.

With the sun nearly set, they continued the descent out of the market. With Simon a few paces ahead, Lilly and Odin again had an opportunity to walk side by side, exchanging playful looks and whispering under their breath.

16

"I HAVE TO GET a few things from my room real quick," Simon stated as he left the two standing in front of his boarding house. "Be right back."

Prior to this, Lilly seemed to be having a pleasant time taking a stroll while the sun was setting. Her demeanor changed quickly as Simon walked away from them however. Staring holes through him as he walked away, Lilly asked, "How many times is he going to just leave us standing around waiting for him?" With a roll of her eyes, she let out an exasperated sigh. "He never changes, ya know?"

Odin didn't know what to say. He was just having a great time with her, strolling down from the markets, wistfully walking next to her. Her behavior and attitude changed so rapidly. Was she really that annoyed with Simon's actions? "I hardly know the guy, but he seems like his heart is in the right place most of the time. He'll be right back Lilly, I'm sure of it."

As he spoke, he noticed that her stance stiffened even more, as she lightly shook her head in annoyance.

"Ya don't know him like I do." There was a long pause as she stared off into the distance towards Simon's boarding house. "Eventually ya will though, if ya spend enough time with him. He'll end up letting ya down." She gave her head another light shake as she stared at the gravel road, lightly kicking the small stones.

Neither spoke for the next few minutes until the familiar sound of Simon's whistling caught their attention once again.

"Alright then, got what I needed. I'm headed to the Blue Gypsy to meet with Balfour. Ya two goin' back to the tavern?" Simon looked at the two waiting for a response. "The tavern, guys?"

Lilly's annoyance suddenly burst out of her without warning. "What do ya care Simon, plannin' on meeting us later or somethin'? Probably won't even show up, like always!"

Simon was heavily caught off guard and didn't understand what had just happened. "What the bloody hell is the matta with ya Lilly? What did I do?" He stood in front of her with his arms stretched out wide, palms facing up, gesturing with a look of astonishment on his face.

Lilly returned the gesture and glared at him. Slowly she muttered, "Nothin, nothin' is wrong with me bro. All's great, isn't it? Maybe we'll see ya later after ya done takin' care of business." She held his eyes with a look of disappointment.

"Whateva Lil." He blew her off and turned his attention towards Odin. "I'll see ya later tonight, alright. Ya should probably get back before the sun sets ya know? Before dark."

Odin nodded in agreement. "I'll see you tonight, friend. Stay safe alright?"

"I'm always safe, the safest bloke ya probably know, Odie."

With that, Simon set off towards the docks and the vessel known as the Blue Gypsy. His counterparts turned right passing the alley, on their way back to the Whisky Dip.

After passing the alley and getting to the main road adjacent to the docks, Odin finally decided to break the silence. "You want to let me know what's really bothering you, Lilly?"

With some hesitation and hostility, she finally responded. "I hate how he just lives his life without a care in the world. It's so annoying, ya know?" She stopped and looked deep into his blue eyes, looking for assurance. "I mean, my daddy's been missing for a while now and he doesn't even seem concerned. He practically raised Simon, gave him a job, treated him like he was his own son." As she mentioned her father, a slight nervous crack occurred in her voice. "I don't know. I'm just so scared that I'm never going to see him again. It just hurts when he doesn't seem to care at all."

"You have to admit that he kinda showed he does care back there with those peasants. He didn't have to do that. He wanted to do it because it was the right thing to do. That's what he told me, Lilly." He held her stare and noticed her eyes welling over. "I'm sorry about your father, but maybe you are taking it out on Simon?" His look was hopeful but inside he was trembling.

The awkward stare remained for several moments before Lilly's demeanor changed. Looking away down the road, she finally mumbled, "Ya don't know anything Odin, but maybe ya are right. Let's get home." With that, she turned the corner towards the Whisky Dip, leaving Odin standing there confused.

"Hey Lilly, wait up. Let me walk with you, if that's okay?" As he quickly turned the corner, not paying attention to what was in front of him, he collided into what felt like a brick wall. Solid, strong, and powerful. The collision caused him to fall backward to the cobblestones, landing on his back. Stunned and shocked, he stared up at the mass that now looked down on him, with terror and surprise in his eyes. This can't be happening. Not again.

The mass slowly leaned down, hovering over Odin. The thickness of its torso blocking out the setting sun past the bay. Surprisingly, it let out a loud chuckle, and then it spoke. "Well, well, well. Hello there, boyfriend."

PART 3

DISCOVERING THE TRUTH

17

THE SUN HAD ALREADY set by the time anyone found them.

A dark-haired peasant girl, carrying a wooden pail of water fresh from a nearby well nearly tripped over Lilly as she returned to her crude, makeshift home near the docks. Startled and afraid, she began to scream at the sight of Lilly lying face down on the cobblestone street, and ran as fast as she could to her waiting family. The shrillness of her scream brought Lilly back from the darkness of unconsciousness, and she slowly opened her right eye, grimacing in pain.

With a sigh and groan, she slowly lifted her cheek off of the cold stone beneath her. Her vision, fogged and blurry, gradually focused after several blinks. "What ... What the hell happened?" she mumbled under her breath as she made her way onto her hands and knees.

With her eyesight returning to her, she started looking around for answers. Without notice, however, Lilly's head began to throb, causing her to bring her hand to her forehead. There, she felt a mild laceration still wet with blood dripping down the side of her head. Intense pain rushed to her head, as she finally lifted herself completely off of the street. While holding her bloody temple and grimacing in pain, she continued to scan the area with her eyes.

There in the distance, some thirty paces away on the weathered wooden planks of the docks, was something. Or someone. With reluctance, she started to approach, anguish crossing her face with each step. Once she was within ten paces, the mystery slowly deteriorated. It was Odin. He too, was laying facedown, motionless. She blocked out the pain of her injury and ran towards him, throwing herself on the wooden planks beside his still body. Turning him over and staring at his pale face, she began to panic.

"Odin ... Odin, wake up! Wake up, Odin!" Gentle taps became harsh slaps to his face as she tried to awaken him. With her voice cracking and anxiety setting in, she began to yell. "Odin, wake up! Don't ya leave me! Odin! Odin!"

As quickly as the hysterical behavior started, it ended. With his head in her lap, Odin suddenly let out a gasp for air. He was alive, but what had happened?

"Breathe... just breathe. I'm here. Just breathe, Odin." Her voice slowly lowered to a whisper as she gently stroked his dark brown, wavy hair away from his eyes. "Just breathe."

Rapid breaths turned into violent coughs in the matter of seconds as Lilly attempted to control Odin's flailing movements. Once the initial coughing spell ended, he opened his eyes and found the warm comfort of her embrace and the matching gaze of a loved one.

"What's wrong? Why are you crying?" He asked in an exasperated voice.

She didn't answer him immediately, she just embraced the moment, cherishing the fact that they were both alive, and for the most part in one piece. "I'm fine, it's nuthin'. I don't know what happened, I just found ya here, lying on the docks." She suddenly started looking around, mumbling to herself, searching for answers.

Without notice, Odin sat up, looking around the dimly lit docks himself. He reached out to his left where his dirk lay on a rotted plank of the dock. As he brought the weapon back towards his body, he could vaguely see a dark, saturated smear along the length of the blade.

It was blood. He could smell it as he brought the point nearer for a better glance. But whose?

"Is that ... blood, Odin?" The fear in her voice was obvious and alarming.

Holding the blade and examining it, Odin responded, "I think so, but it's not mine. Did I hurt someone? Why can't I remember what happened?"

As he lifted himself off of the docks, Lilly began shaking her head. "I can't remember anything either. What happened? I woke up over there," she pointed aggressively towards the cobblestone street dividing the taverns and hotels from the wooden planks of the docks, "... and I found ya here. I don't understand?"

"I don't either Lilly, and I don't like it. Let me think, I just need to think for a few minutes." He sheathed the dirk, still moist with the mysterious blood.

With both of his hands on top of his head, Odin began pacing the area trying to search for answers within his own mind and memory. He had felt this same way earlier in the morning after awakening in his boarding room, confused and shocked. *Why can't I remember what happened?* The thought continuously looped around in his mind.

"Did ya ... kill someone Odin?" The fear and uncertainty of her question caused Odin to stop and stare at her.

"I don't know, I really don't. God, I hope not." Panic sunk in as he continued to ramble in her direction. "But what if I did? Am I a murderer, Lil? Did I hurt someone?" There was a long pause as he stared straight through her, not expecting an answer. "This can't be happening again Lilly, it just can't. Not again, not again ..." He continued to say those two words over and over again as he shook his head in disbelief.

With concern in her voice, Lilly intervened. "Hey, hey... it's okay, I'm here Odin. Talk to me. What do ya mean ... again? What happened?"

As he met her eyes, he eventually spoke. "I've never told anyone about this, but something happened in my hometown. There was an accident ... someone died."

She nodded in his direction encouraging him to continue, "Go on, keep going. What happened, Odin?"

After releasing a long sigh, he slowly continued. "There was a girl ... my girl at the time. We were engaged and planning on getting married and ..." He couldn't continue, shaking his head in disgust.

"Okay, okay, okay. It's fine, we don't have to talk about it. Let's just try to figure out what happened here." As she nodded at him, looking for agreement, he finally nodded back. "What's the last thing that ya remember?"

Once he thought deeply about the question, he answered. "We left the markets and ... you were upset at Simon for something. He left, remember? To the ship to see his captain ... and then... bloody hell, why can't I remember?" The frustration in his voice was boiling over.

Again, Lilly stepped in, calming the man's nerves and helping him refocus. "Yeah, yeah that's right. I remember that. Simon pissed me off, acting all bossy and tryin' to tell us what to do. Leavin' us standing around waiting for him. I remember! And then ... What happened, what ...?" The confusion on her face was clear as she bit her lip, pleading for help with her light brown eyes.

Odin jumped in without letting her finish the sentence. "I tried calming you down, that's what happened. I remember. And then you walked away, going home towards the bar. I remember now! I ran after you and ..."

The two looked at each other in disbelief knowing the truth.

In unison, they both cried out the name, "O'Doyle."

"I remember too," Lilly whispered.

18

THE ENSUING CONVERSATION BROUGHT back memories from before the blackouts. The two of them were able to recall most of the events all the way up to their encounter with O'Doyle. A towering, thuggish brute, with a tendency for violence and mayhem. Odin's previous encounter with the man was not pleasant, as he recalled the previous night in The Whisky Dip. Fortunately, his new mate Simon had intervened and diverted what could have been a disastrous, or even worse, deadly moment. However, after literally bumping into O'Doyle, their memories were still unclear and incomplete about what happened next. Was it his blood on Odin's dirk?

After clearing up most of the confusion with Lilly over the next few minutes, Odin turned his attention towards the fact that they were alone in the streets after dark, which made them even more anxious to get indoors. "Lilly, we need to get out of here and back to the tavern. I think ... with some more time, maybe we will remember more of what happened. I don't like being out here, I feel like something is ..."

"I know, I know. I feel it too." She looked around the docks from south to north with a facial expression of uneasiness. "Come on, let's go. Let's get home,"

Without answering, Odin agreed and they both started walking south towards the tavern, praying to get there without an incident. As they walked, the distinctive somber sound from the bay created a slight feeling of comfort, even though the truth of what may be around the corner, still haunted their every thought. Step by step their pace quickened, scanning the area in front and behind them until...

"Hey, ya two!"

From the docks on their right, they heard something - someone, actually. Not a voice that was recognizable, or unrecognizable for that matter. Whoever it was, he had the Florian accent much like Lilly. Someone was there, in the shadows near the ships lazily swaying under the moonlight in Kobalt Harbor.

"I saw what happened!" The voice rang through the silence of the early evening once again, causing Odin and Lilly to freeze, not able to take their eyes off of the docks. "I saw it, ya know!"

Fear was escalating through them as they tried to focus their vision and pinpoint where the shouts were coming from. Lilly, now shaking slightly, grabbed Odin's arm pulling herself as close as possible to him, seeking protection from whoever was out there.

"Ya know it took the big guy, right?"

Without hesitation, Odin unsheathed his dirk, pointing it towards the docks, while keeping Lilly behind him with his freehand. After a short period of silence, Odin shouted into the darkness, "Who are you? What do you want?" Odin waited for a response, still trying to learn the whereabouts of the mysterious person.

Immediately, he received a response, but not what he was hoping for. Whoever was lurking in the shadows started laughing maniacally. Then, the laugh stopped suddenly, causing a shriek from Lilly.

"What's wrong with you? What do you want?" Odin again attempted to find out what the person wanted, still pointing his blade towards the docks.

"I saw it, ya know. The thing."

The fear and frustration from within rippled out of Odin in an instance. "What are you talking about? Where are you? Who are you? What do you..."

Odin could see a figure stand up between two foundation poles of the docks. The light of the moon glistened off of its eyes, like a candle in a window sill, and Odin watched as the figure left the darkness and swiftly approached. As it got closer, Odin could see that it was a man - a peasant, based on its ripped, soiled attire.

"Stay back, don't come any closer. You hear me, stranger?" Odin started taking a few paces backwards, still keeping Lilly behind him. As he shouted commands, the man surprisingly stopped. Without taking an eye off of him, Odin again asked, "What do you want?"

After an awkward silence, Odin observed the man take three long blinks and then look up to the moon. Once he looked back down in Odin and Lilly's direction, he finally responded but didn't answer the question. With an eerie smirk across his face, he again let out a quick laugh, followed by another statement of his own. "I think the big guy was dead before it took him, ya know."

Searching for an explanation, Odin again demanded some answers. "What the hell are you talking about? Who are you?" As Odin glared in the man's direction, he could see how malnourished the man was. Rips in his shirt exposed a bruised and battered ribcage. His frail legs were caked with silt and grime. As he smiled, Odin could see that the man was missing several teeth.

As Odin watched the man, Lilly slowly leaned forward and whispered into his ear, making sure the peasant couldn't hear her words. "Do ya think he's talking about O'Doyle? He keeps saying the big guy."

Odin momentarily turned and faced her, taking his eyes off of the peasant and gesturing with his freehand. "I don't know what the hell this guy is talking about. I think he's crazy. We can't listen to a crazy person Lilly! We have to get off the streets!"

Instantly, the peasant was within a few feet of them, startling both Odin and Lilly. The shock of the close proximity caused Lilly to shriek in surprise and Odin to jump backward, waving his dirk at the peasant. "What the bloody hell man? What are you doing?" Odin's voice was full of shock and fear.

The peasant just stood there, not making eye contact and not really looking at them. It was as if he didn't even acknowledge their presence in front of him. The smirk on his face resurfaced once again followed by a short chuckle. "Why did it take the big guy? Why didn't it take the two of ya?"

As the peasant spoke, Odin and Lilly could tell that something was frightfully wrong with this man. After a brief pause, Lilly responded with dread in her voice.

"I ... don't know? Do ya know why?"

The response caused Odin to stare in her direction in disbelief. As he stared at her in astonishment, he mouthed the words, "What are you doing?"

She gave him an awkward look that clearly stated, "I don't know." Then, without warning, she came out from behind him and faced the peasant, causing another frantic gesture from Odin.

She tried to make eye contact but the man just stared in her direction without an emotion showing, until the smirk appeared once again across his face.

"I don't think you have the mark."

Lilly could not restrain herself any longer. "What mark? What do ya mean? Help me understand what happened."

For the first time since the encounter began, the peasant actually looked at them, truly looked at them and made eye contact. After a brief chuckle, the peasant whispered, "It only comes for those with the mark. Ya don't want to know what happens when ya have the mark!"

Lilly responded immediately, "I think ya are right about that. How does someone get a mark?"

"Ya are marked by someone. Someone powerful, with enough strength to control it."

"I see ... thank ya sir. Did ya see what happened to me and my friend here?" She gestured back towards Odin with a thumb. "Did the big guy attack us?"

"I saw everything. I saw a struggle. I saw the big guy pull a knife and ..." The man paused, then looked up at the moon once again.

Lilly intervened, "Go on, tell me what happened."

Odin immediately interrupted, "Lilly this is stupid. Why are you even listening to this lunatic? He's ..."

Lilly abruptly turned back with a look that immediately stopped Odin. She then faced the peasant again and continued. "Please tell me, what did ya see?"

The peasant momentarily looked at Odin, then redirected his odd gaze to Lilly. "The big guy held ya, hand aroun' ya throat. Ya weren't screamin' though. Ya were sleepin.'"

Lilly was in awe as she attentively tried to comprehend what this man was saying. Even Odin was leaning forward now, mouth hung open in disbelief, trying to remember the events.

"I was sleeping, and the big guy was choking me. Is that right, sir?"

"Yeah ... and then he stabbed the big guy in the back." The peasant pointed in Odin's direction with that eerie smirk returning. He held his bony index finger extended at Odin for several moments while Lilly turned around in shock.

As she faced Odin, face full of dread and fear, she whispered, "I'm pretty sure ya killed him. I think ya saved my life though."

"That can't be possible. I didn't kill anyone. I'd remember some-thing like that. This isn't real! There's no way any of this can be real! He's just some crazy guy loaded on nightshade, Lilly. That's all." As Odin spoke, the uncertainty in his voice could be felt. He didn't want to believe any of this, especially with his past creeping into his thoughts.

"Ya said it ya self that it was blood on ya blade. Where did it come from Odin? Whose blood is it then?" The questions were clear-ly rhetorical but she continued to glare at him, expecting an ac-knowledgment. "I know it sounds crazy but maybe ... maybe that's what happened. I was unconscious and ya fainted after running him through with ya dirk."

"Where is he then? Where's O'Doyle? Where's his body? He'd be pretty hard to miss. The guy's the size of an ox, Lilly." Odin scanned the docks looking for any signs of a fallen man but found nothing. Even in the dimness of the early evening, there was no dead body to be seen.

"I don't think we're gonna find him. I think he's gone."

"What do you mean gone? Where does a three-hundred-pound monster like that go?" Odin's eyes shimmered with disbelief.

"I think it took him. That's what this man just said, remember? It took the big guy. What else could that mean?"

"This is madness, Lilly. I don't know what happened but I'm going to find out. We need to get off the streets and indoors, fast. I hate being out here. I feel like I'm being watched from every direction." After a brief scan of his environment, his gaze caught the peasants' eyes. "... and we need to get away from that crazy lunatic." Odin pointed towards the peasant with an expression of disgust.

"Hold on Odin. Let's use our brains here. We know there was a confrontation between O'Doyle. We know that because we both remember seeing him once we got down here. I found ya here ... after waking up over there." She pointed towards the cobblestone street running parallel with the docks. "There was blood on ya blade, and then this peasant came out of nowhere explaining step by step what happened. I don't think it's a coincidence."

"I'm telling you Lilly, he's just fabricating some crazy event inside his demented, maniacal mind. Something happened for sure, but what he's saying makes no sense. Let's get back to the tavern and think some more, please."

Lilly knew from the plea in his eyes that he needed to get inside. She would have to drop these ideas momentarily and help him find safety. If there was such a thing, in this city. "Okay, let's go. I don't like being out here either."

Walking side by side, they began to hear the peasant once again. He wasn't talking though. That eerie, maniacal laughter began again. Slowly the laugh began to echo through the streets. With the distance increasing with each swift pace, the sounds of his laughter strangely seemed to get louder and louder, increasing the stress of the entire situation, until...

It stopped.

Odin and Lilly abruptly turned around trying to find the man in the darkness. But there was nothing there. He was gone. Possibly hiding in the shadows once again.

As quickly as they had stopped, they turned around and continued their long walk back to Lilly's tavern. With a nervous and frantic voice, Odin whispered to Lilly without looking at her. "We need to hurry, and I think I need a really strong drink."

"So do I, Odin. So do I," she whispered back.

19

"FOUR PINTS OF IRON Bros. comin' right up."

Without a thought, Lilly reacted instinctively and stepped away from the bar, making sure to sway her hips with each step. Intoxicated patrons seem to be loose with their coppers when around an attractive woman. A little bit of wisdom from her father, as she remembered. With her subtle, flirtatious actions, she quickly made her way towards the casks of ale and began to pour. "Odin, I need clean mugs! We're almost dry."

In the back of the bar, behind the casks of ale, Odin worked frantically to keep up with the number of mugs coming in and going out. Two brass tubs, filled with water, were in front of him. One for cleaning and the other for rinsing. As he finished rinsing this batch, he carefully placed twelve, somewhat clean mugs on a wooden tray and carried them back to the front of the bar where Lilly impatiently waited. "Here, here... sorry, I'm still catching on." He looked out towards the numerous patrons filling the tavern on this night. "You didn't have to open tonight, you know? Why did you let them all in? We really need some peace and quiet so that we can talk."

Lilly glanced at Odin for a split second and then back to the casks to continue filling mugs. "What was I supposed to do? This is my livelihood Odin - it's all that I have. This is the only thing that my daddy had and I'm the only person left to make sure it doesn't crumble into the ground."

The words resonated within Odin for a moment, as he thought about all of the events that had transpired recently in his life. Deep in his mind, images of O'Doyle, the thing that he saw in the alley behind this very tavern, along with a beautiful redhead, haunted his every thought. Which one was the worst though? Back in Milstone, everything was taken from him - Not by choice but by tragedy. Was he being selfish, asking Lilly to think about their situation instead of her whole life? After a subtle sigh he responded, "I'm sorry Lilly. I know how much this place means to you; I really do. I just think we need to..."

She cut him off before he could finish. "I know, I know. Just... let's get through this initial rush. A few ales and they will leave us alone for a while, I promise. How could I turn all these people away? Who knows how long they were waiting outside for me to open up, too? I think the coppers we earn tonight might help us answer some of our questions." As she looked at him, hope crossed her face and he could see it.

Without a rebuttal, Odin simply nodded, left the tray of mugs near the cask taps and slowly strolled back near his dirty water filled tubs. Once he got back there, washing and rinsing mug after mug, he had the opportunity to observe Lilly in her natural setting as a barkeep. This had to be her destiny. Look at all those sailors, gawking and flashing their best smiles, trying to grab her attention.

He had been on the other end of it the day before, ordering an ale and trying to make small talk with her. The awkwardness had been clearly noticeable at the time. He was never good at talking to girls, let alone a beautiful woman like her.

He never expected to meet her, let alone fall for her. But here he was, silently scrubbing ale mugs and watching the woman he was falling in love with do what she was destined to do. As he stood there, transfixed on this woman, this beautiful woman, the only thought in his head was *Is any of this really happening?*

Reality slapped him upside his head quickly, with the sound of glass breaking. Without noticing, a mug had fallen through his soapy hands onto the stone floor below. The sound of shattering glass was deafening in his ears. He quickly dropped to one knee, heart racing, attempting to grab the larger pieces of what was left of the mug, hoping that the sound did not alert anyone else, especially Lilly. Those hopes flew out the window as he stood, however, making eye contact with Lilly.

She wasn't scowling though, nor was there a look of disappointment on her face. There was a look of concern at first and once she realized he was okay, she gave him a wink and a shrug of her shoulders, gesturing that accidents happen. With his heart rate slowing down, he swept up the last fine pieces of glass and went back to cleaning his mugs at the back of the bar, shaking his head in amusement.

The next hour flew by without incident. The patrons of the bar found their seats in the alcoves and stools around the tavern, Lilly was able to meet all of their needs and requests with drinks, and Odin failed to break another glass or cause a disturbance. With a free moment in sight, Odin finished with his last tray of mugs and approached Lilly as she playfully mimicked an older sailor on the right side of the bar.

"Wow, there's a lot more to this than I thought. Do you need anything else?" His brow furrowed with the question as he wiped sweat off of it with a soiled rag.

She looked around the tavern, observing the smiling faces and listening to the laughter amongst those indulging in the night in her tavern, her daddy's tavern. With a subtle sigh, she responded, "I think we're good. I hope we're good. I don't need any more surprises."

"You're right about that, Lilly. One hundred percent."

The next few minutes were blissful - neither said a word or acknowledged what had happened. No one bothered them either. Not a single request for a drink. They embraced the moment, appreciating the fact that they still had opportunities like this after the events of the past few days. They knew that death could have easily grabbed them.

The moment wouldn't last long though. A loud clatter occurred near the entrance of the bar, grabbing the attention of all of the patrons - Odin and Lilly too.

"Hey mates, did I miss anything?'

20

"Do ya really think the thing took O'Doyle?" Simon's words were filled with intrigue as he sat in a stool at the bar, discussing the events that he had missed with them. "I mean, ya got all of this from some crazy peasant, right?"

"I know, I know... it sounds nuts, but it's all we got. What other explanation is there?" Lilly looked between the two, hoping that they would see her logic.

"I've already told her that we can't trust what that lunatic was saying. I mean, you should have heard the way he was laughing Simon. It was bloody creepy."

Simon sat there, pulling on his long beard, contemplating what had been said. "Well, my mum always told me to never trust a peasant. They tend to lie, steal, rob, fight, and beg. Oh, yeah, did I mention lie?" His eyes were full and wide, as if he had just stated the obvious.

"My daddy always said the same thing, and ya know what, they are both right. Peasants do lie, all the time. I can't tell ya how many times I've had to run a few off from here, making empty promises to get a free drink." She eyed them with contempt, only the way Lilly could. "But..."

"Lilly, come on, ya don't actually..." Simon's words were cut off before he could finish.

"Don't interrupt me!"

With a balled fist, she struck the top of the bar, getting many of the patrons' attention momentarily. After a few seconds, they went back to their conversations.

"Sorry Lil, go on. That was rude of me."

With a cold stare in Simon's direction, she continued. "As I was sayin', what if it was true? What if O'Doyle attacked both of us?" She dropped her head for a few seconds, thinking about her next words. "Maybe this thing came after him because he was marked, like the peasant said. And maybe that's why we can't remember it -because we shouldn't have seen it."

The two men sat there not knowing what to say or how to react. They certainly didn't want to upset her again. Eventually, without too much awkward silence spent, Simon eyed Odin and gave him a slight shrug with his shoulders.

With quite a bit of reluctance, Odin responded. "Now that you mention it Lilly, do you recall how hard it was for me to remember what happened in the alley when you brought me tea this morning? My whole memory was filled with holes and it was so hard to fill in those gaps. I barely remember running into O'Doyle earlier. Maybe there is a reason why my memory is so fogged. Yours, too." He looked to Simon for a little support.

"I don't know what to believe, ya two. Maybe he was just a crazy lunatic. But I know that something happened, and ya had blood on that sheathed dirk behind ya, Odin."

Odin turned and looked at his blade laying on the bar behind him. With a long sigh, he turned back to Lilly. "I know I do. I can't explain it any better than you can. Something definitely happened, and maybe I ..." He shook his head in disbelief at what he was about to say. "Maybe I killed him. Maybe I stabbed him in the back like that lunatic said. I don't want to believe that, but ..."

She could sense the frustration and terror in his voice as he said the words and intervened. "Odin, let's not think about that okay. Let's just focus on this instead. This thing, this darkness, haunting the city, came and took him before he could have hurt either of us any further. That's what happened, okay." She waited until he nodded in her direction. "And because we were not on its list, or marked, we shouldn't have seen it." She quickly turned to Simon, who was still staring at the floor stroking his long beard. "What do ya remember 'bout the night ya saw it?"

Without looking up, Simon answered. "For a very long time, I couldn't remember anything about it, other than those red eyes. The morning after it happened, my mind was so foggy. It was like I had spent a very long weekend in Barbasos, and not the nice part either." He looked up at them with a slight smirk. "I mean, it took a while to fill in all of those gaps, just like ya said, Odin." After a brief pause, he continued. "Do ya suppose that this thing can fog up our minds? I know it has some evil powers, but maybe that's another one - to sort of protect itself from those that weren't supposed to see it."

Both Lilly and Odin took a few moments to think about his theory behind the mystery. They eyed each other and then redirected back to Simon with baffled expressions.

"None of this makes any sense. I don't know what to believe." Odin just sat there, shaking his head.

"Neither do I." Lilly looked at him with empathy. She wondered if he would ever tell her what really happened in Milstone. She wanted to know. No, she needed to know. Feeling the responsibility to lighten the atmosphere, she decided to change the subject. "Well, the rush has been over for a while now. Are ya ready for that drink, Odin?" She waited for a response.

For the first time all night, a smile crossed his lips. "Oh, please! And something heavier than an ale, too."

Like clockwork, Simon joined in, "Now we're talkin', mates! I'll have what's he havin' Lil." He stopped himself before getting carried away though, wearing an awkward look of concentration. Eventually, he continued, "On second thought, make mine a double, sis." A toothy grin followed.

Lilly just rolled her eyes as she strolled towards the cabinet with the bourbons, shaking her head slightly. "Bloody Simon," she whispered to herself.

The mahogany cabinet centered behind the bar was by far the nicest piece in the entire tavern. Behind two stained glass doors were displayed the treasures of any drunk or connoisseur. There were labels from local distilleries, branded with the common D.O.F. (Distilleries of Floria), as well as less common brands from other territories around Aileran. These were in abundance throughout the cabinet, but that is not what Lilly had her mind on. She ignored the bottles on the bottom four shelves and cautiously reached for an iridescent, cyan colored bottle in the center of the fifth shelf.

Based on the dust surrounding the bottle, it had not been touched in months. Maybe years even. As she wrapped her nimble fingers around its slender neck, she brought down the bottle and gently rubbed the blue label with her thumb. She read the words under her breath. "Optimus semper futurum esse." With a bewildered look her only thought was, *Why was this so important, daddy?*

After filling three small tumblers with the finest whisky in the tavern, she made her way back to the two men that had caused her so much trouble recently. these were the only men in her life, the only people she had. Without her father around, she didn't have anyone else. Even with the annoyance of her so-called brother, she managed to bring a slight smile to her lips as she walked back to them and delivered the drinks.

"Bottoms up boys, the finest in the house." She handed each a short tumbler easily filled with five coppers worth of golden delight.

"Is this what I think it is Lil?" Simon's expression was pure euphoria. "He never let me try it before. He never let me even touch the bottle. Are ya sure?"

Lilly's expression was stoic as she listened to Simon ramble on. Once he finished, her response was subtle, yet filled with conviction. "Well, he isn't here, and I'm in charge. I think we all deserve it." Lilly looked at the two, nodding her head with approval. "Regardless, I don't know if my daddy will ever be back, and not one bloody patron has ever even asked about it. Not like they could afford it anyways."

After a brief check for assurance through eye contact, the three of them lifted the tumblers and drank deeply, enjoying the finest bourbon any of them had ever had the pleasure of sampling.

After a long, gluttonous sip, Odin broke the silence. "Hey Lilly, you said earlier that maybe all the coppers that we make tonight might help us later. What did you mean by that?"

She dropped the tumbler from her lips momentarily, but didn't look directly at Odin. "If we are going to get to the bottom of this, we are going to need to talk to some powerful people. That'll take some bribes. No lord is going to accept us, let alone talk to us, without a little premeditated favor, ya know." She wrinkled her nose as she looked out into the tavern and all of her patrons' smiling faces. "I didn't open up the tavern tonight just to please them. All the coppers they hand over tonight is going to get us a little closer to meeting with one of the lords, and hopefully getting some answers." The sincerity in her voice told the whole story.

"I see. That makes sense." Odin in turn wrinkled his nose as he watched a small group of sailors clink their glasses together. "How much of a bribe are we talking about here?"

"I really don't know. I've never had to even think of bribing someone before. I've never really had to do anything, except help out 'round here. I bet my daddy bribed a few in his day though. Ya know, along with all the taxes."

"Your father had to pay taxes? To whom?"

Lilly turned away from the patrons and once again made eye contact with Odin. With a sarcastic tone she answered. "Lord Randall, the one and only. He owns half of the city, ya know? Been takin' money from us every month for as long as I can remember." She shook her head in annoyance.

"How much does he take each month?"

"A hundred coppers, two hundred ... I really don't know. I never had to deal with any of that. None of his goons have been 'round neither to collect since my daddy's been missing. Maybe he's got a kind heart and is takin' pity on me."

Simon almost fell off his stool as she finished. "Are ya kiddin' us Lil? That man doesn't know what pity is. From what I've heard 'bout the bastard, he doesn't even have a heart, let alone a kind one. Lord Randall's a monster, full of gluttony and greed. Ya not that foolish, are ya?"

"Don't call me foolish! We have to do somethin' and Randall is the most powerful Lord in the city."

"Everyone knows that, but I think ya might be gettin' in a little over ya head here Lil. I mean, ya just a woman."

Lilly didn't really respond, she just stood there and looked at him, as she brought the glass tumbler to her lips once again. When she finished with her drink, she lowered the glass and placed it down on the bar in front of her, still holding Simon's eyes, but not making a sound.

The awkwardness of the silence and the stare caused an involuntary swallow from Simon. "That came out wrong, Lil. I didn't mean that." He broke her gaze momentarily and stared at the floor. "I know ya've heard stories 'bout that man. The things he has done, or sent his men to do. Da ya remember what we heard those goons saying outside of James' tent earlier? That happens all the time in this city."

Lilly eventually broke her glare and nodded slightly. "Yeah, I've heard. I know. I just don't know what else to do. Who to talk to, or who not to talk to. If anyone in this city knows something 'bout what has been goin' on, it's Randall. This is probably our only choice." Her confidence in the idea seemed to diminish as she finished.

Odin decided to break the tension between the two. "So, let me get this straight. Your daddy paid a few hundred coppers in taxes every month to this Lord Randall guy, right? That's a hefty fee even for an establishment like this. It shouldn't take nearly that much just to talk to him, if my logic is right."

"Let's hope not. This pathetic lot is almost out of coppers, and we've only earned a little over sixty tonight." She scanned the room filled with drunken sailors and merchants, living life the only way they know how to. "I don't know if it will be enough for all three of us."

"So how do we contact this Randall guy? How do we let him know that we want to meet?" Being so new to the city, Odin didn't understand the city's politics or inner workings.

"I think I have an idea. But we'll have to go back to the market and talk to the merchant James again. Seems like he has had quite a few run-ins with Randall recently. He'll know something, I'm sure of it." The confidence from earlier was returning to Lilly's voice as she spoke.

"We'll head up there tomorrow morning." It wasn't a question - she was taking charge.

Odin and Simon looked at each other, both delivering a single nod. Tomorrow morning it was then.

"Sounds like a plan, Lil. I'll meet ya two here in the morning. I'm gonna head back to my room and get some rest. I'm sure tomorrow's gonna be another full day."

As Odin listened, he thought the same thing. The past two days had brought so many emotions out of him. What could he possibly expect from tomorrow that hadn't already happened? He knew they weren't close to finding the answers that he wanted - no, needed. There was no way that their adventure in the morning was going to be easy, he realized. "I think I'm going to do the same, Lilly. I need some rest after the past few days. Thank you for the drink." As he stood, Lilly reached out and grabbed his hand.

"Are ya sure ya going to be okay? I mean after all that happened..." She gave him a playful wink.

"I'll be fine. I'm just going upstairs. Nothing can happen up there, right?" Odin looked at her with a playful smirk.

She gave him a slight nod and released his hand. "Okay, be careful on ya way up there though. If ya need anything, and I mean anything," her wink was a little more flirtatious, "I'll be right here." She tapped the bar top in front of her as she raised an eyebrow.

Odin's eyes widened at the response. He wasn't expecting her to be so forward with him. He still couldn't believe that she was interested in him, let alone nonchalantly propositioning him. The idea of being with her for the night would almost make up for all the terror that he had been through since stepping off of the Blue Gypsy in this forsaken city. It sounded amazing in fact.

However, the more he thought about it, the more melancholic memories of Milstone returned. Deep within his consciousness, a beautiful face started to slowly appear. A very light complexion with a few freckles on the cheeks, ruby colored full lips, surrounded by long flowing red hair. Her green eyes contrasted with the fair skin and red hair. As the face became clearer and clearer, Odin mouthed the name, "Mia."

Lilly couldn't quite make out what he had just said. "What was that Odin, I didn't hear ya." She leaned forward on the bar, exposing her figure.

As she spoke, Odin returned from his slight dream, confused and a little startled. "Uh ... nothing, it was nothing. I'm fine. I just need some rest, Lilly. I'll let you know if I need anything, I promise. I'll see you in the morning." He waved slightly in her direction and started to walk towards the two swinging doors with Simon right behind him. As he pushed the doors open, he stopped and looked back at Lilly, delivering a final nod.

With a look of bewilderment, she nodded back slightly, but he could tell that she was confused by the sudden nature of their departure. "What the bloody hell is wrong with you, idiot?" he whispered to himself as he walked through the doors.

Simon walked up beside him and gave him a slight nudge in the ribs. "Ya know she was flirtin' with ya, right? I mean, it was pretty obvious, Odie."

With a long sigh, Odin acknowledged that he was aware of her advances. "Yes Simon, I know that. It's just ... I don't know. I really like her, I do. But ..."

"But what? She's a keeper mate. I've watched her date a bunch of losers heaps worse than ya. Give her a chance! Ya won't regret it, I promise. Plus, I won't have to worry 'bout her so much if she's hangin' out with a big softy like ya self." He slapped Odin on the back as they turned the corner towards the stairs to the second floor above the tavern. "I know ya like her, I saw it in the market with all the bloody hand holdin' earlier." Simon rolled his eyes at the thought.

Odin stopped on the first step, looking down at the much shorter sailor. "I do like her, she's amazing. And so beautiful too. It's just..." He paused and took in a deep breath, balled fists resting on his hips. "There was a woman - back home I mean. Back in Milstone. We were to marry and ..."

"Mate, she's not here, is she? I don't see her if she is. Besides, ya not planning on returning home anytime soon are ya?" His mocking glare suggested what he was saying was obvious. "Tell ya what, get some rest. A little sleep will help pump some clarity into that empty skull of yas, mate."

Odin knew Simon didn't understand the complexity of his situation. How could he? Odin hadn't told a soul the truth about what happened back in his homeland- let alone anything about the love of his life or the tragic accident that turned his entire existence upside down. His tone as he spoke was emotionless. "You're right Simon, a little sleep will do me wonders. Thanks for everything, friend." He extended his hand out towards the sailor in a gesture of friendship.

Simon grabbed the outstretched hand and nearly broke it in half, squeezing with all of his might. "Okay, okay. That's enough." A slight grimace of pain crossed Odin's face as he tried to pull away. "You win, Simon..."

"Told ya. Ya big Softy." With that, he released Odin's hand and let out a bellowing chuckle. "See ya in the morning, Odie. Get some sleep." With a quarter turn, Simon made his way north back to his meager boarding house. A familiar tune came from his lips as he strolled away, without a worry in the world.

Odin watched him until he was out of sight. He slowly chuckled to himself while shaking his head, and his hand too. "Bloody Simon."

The steps of the stairway were gone in seconds as he quickly unlocked and made his way into room 206, locking the door behind him. As he looked around his bare residence, the feelings of anxiety and terror that he expected to take control as soon as he was alone were absent. He felt calm, comfortable even. The bed in the back corner screamed his name in silence. As he approached the mattress in the back of the small room, he removed one boot while hopping on one foot and then the other before he sat on the edge of the bed.

With a hefty sigh, he collapsed backwards onto the mattress, sinking into the meager padding. Finally, he could forget about all of it, for at least a few hours. The last thought that ran through his mind before sleep finally took him was of a face. A woman's face. Her face. Mia.

21

I KNOW THIS ALLEY. It looks so familiar but I can't quite place it, he thought to himself upon entering.

He slowly stepped forward, glancing from right to left, searching for a clue to where his current location was. The stone block buildings lining the alley were heavily weathered, as if hundreds of years old. He cautiously approached the left side, carefully observing the salt crystallization on the base of the building as he touched several blocks, feeling the grooves and holes that had been formed over decades of slow dissolution. He had been here before, acknowledging the dull red coloring of the blocks used for this building.

As he continued walking down the alleyway, he noticed a specific pattern to the color of the buildings on both sides. Red, beige, and white repeated over and over again, without a mishap in pattern. With the exception of the color, the block buildings were nothing alike however. Multi-storied inns looked down on single-storied markets or taverns. In addition to the levels, no two buildings were built of the same size blocks. The variation in block size was exceptional, from a small brick to a cubic ton.

After clearing a rusty, beige awning over-hanging half of the alleyway, he found himself in the middle of an intersection where a new alleyway crossed his. Four multi-storied buildings boxed him in as he looked up into the clear blue sky, observing a single gull flying overhead. As he stood in the middle of the intersection, contemplating where he was, a decision had to be made - continue forward along the patterned buildings of the alleyway, or turn left or right. His first instinct was to continue down the path that he had started, following the salt weathered buildings and their odd repeating colorization. But something caught his eye to his right as he looked down this new alley. All of the buildings to his right were the same color - that dull, weathered red. In addition, they were all two-storied, windowless and doorless. Observing the alley from his point of view made it seem as though there were two dull red walls that continued on forever. There was something in the middle of the alley, bright white as if glowing. It was so far away it was hard to tell what it was. His inquisitive nature got the better of him and he turned right.

Walking along the left side of this new alley with his hand gently sliding against the textured stone blocks of the wall, he noticed the bright, white object move slightly. The shock of the movement caused him to halt his progress, with squinted eyes fixated in front of him. He decided to call out and see if a response would be returned.

"Hello! Who's there?"

The object didn't respond, but a series of movements subsided due to his loud shout. Whatever it was, it knew he was there, watching from a distance. Intrigue continued to pulsate through his veins as he marched forward at a steady pace. What was this thing in the distance and why was it here?

Moving swiftly down the alleyway now, he noticed that the object wasn't getting any closer. How could this be possible? Was it moving away from him, perhaps because it felt threatened by his presence, thus keeping its distance? Or was it toying with him? There was a need burning within him that had to be met, at any cost. He had to find out what this thing was. His steady pace turned into a jog abruptly while keeping the object in his sights. Still, he was not gaining any ground. The steady jog became a sprint within seconds. Building after building zipped past him as he chased whatever this thing was at full speed.

"Who are you, what are you?" He demanded with an exasperated shout. Still, this thing, this mystery, kept its distance with no response.

Panting heavily from the sudden burst of speed and feeling drained of energy, he was forced to slow down and stop. Hunched over, with his hands on his knees, he made one last effort to reach out to the white thing in the distance. "Stop... wait ... I'm not going to hurt you." He paused for a few moments to catch his breath. "Who are you, what are you?"

As he was pleading for this thing to stop and his breath slowly returning to him, he noticed something unusual. Whatever this thing was, it didn't seem to be keeping the same distance any longer. In fact, it seemed to be approaching him, growing larger with each passing second. He couldn't look away as it slowly came into focus, the bright white contrasting with the dull red of the buildings around it. Watching in awe as the thing's true identity was revealed, he realized something. It was a person after all - a woman.

Her gown, stitched of cotton and lace, seemed to glow as she strolled forward with bare feet. The iridescent glow of the gown created a haze in the space surrounding her, obstructing a clear view of her face. It wasn't until she was within a few feet that he was able to see her features clearly.

Her bright red hair was pulled back tightly, exposing her beautiful details. He noticed that the light complexion of her skin was sprinkled with freckles, and the green of her eyes shone through the haziness surrounding her. These features seemed so familiar to him but he couldn't quite make out where he had seen them before. "You look so familiar. Do ... do I know you?" he asked with a dropped jaw, praying for a response.

She observed him with curiosity for several moments but never responded to his inquiry. The sincerity in her eyes put him at ease as the two held each other's riveting stares. He knew this woman, but why couldn't he place her.

"She is so beautiful," he mumbled under his breath, mesmerized by the sight of her.

Suddenly, and without warning, she turned around and started to amble away from him, leaving the bewildered man alone in the middle of this strange alley, surrounded by dull red buildings that never seemed to end.

With a sense of panic in his voice, he called out to her, "Wait, where are you going? Who are you ... why are you leaving me!" Without notice, powerful emotions came over him, both sadness and anger. He couldn't allow this woman to get away from him, his desire for an explanation to where he was and who she was too strong. "Stop ... Now!"

Surprisingly, this mysterious woman with the long braid running the length of her back did stop. She paused right in the middle of the alleyway, her white dress gently blowing in the breeze. But she didn't turn around to acknowledge the man roaring at her from behind. Her gaze remained in front of her and she seemed to be frozen in place. Instantly, dread struck the man thinking that he had offended this woman.

"I'm sorry... but I need to know who you are! Why were you running from me earlier?" Tears started to well in his eyes as he pleaded for some explanation. He dropped to his knees with both arms outstretched towards her, begging for her to acknowledge him. "Please ... you have to help me understand! Please speak to me!"

The woman in white never turned around or spoke to him though. She remained perfectly still, stoic in nature even, facing away from this beseeched man.

A final desperate plea was coming forth from the man when he noticed something that halted any further episodes or emotional rants. The haze seeping out from around the woman in white seemed to be growing as if alive. It was then that the man realized that he wasn't looking at a woman alone in this strange alley. There was something else there too; something that he couldn't explain.

As his gaze fixated on the haziness of the presence surrounding the woman, trying to make sense of what his eyes were showing him, a sudden blast erupted in the sky above in the alley. The thunderous eruption in the sky forced his gaze towards the heavens where the impossible occurred.

In a split second, the sky was as black as night, stars twinkling in the cosmic distance. Disorientation took over as the man dropped his eyes from the dark sky back towards the woman in white and whatever else was there with them. Even more perplexing was the fact that he was no longer in the same alley. The dull, red stone walls of the buildings had changed in the blink of an eye, replaced by blues, yellows, and whites. These buildings had windows and doors. He was somewhere else, but he knew this alley too. He knew where he was because he had been here recently.

Looking into the alley at the two figures from his knees, he couldn't understand what his eyes were showing him. The woman in white hadn't changed at all, but the bright, white haze around her had significantly changed its presence. The haziness of its being was still present but the color had changed. It was as if it was made of nothing but darkness. He realized the confusion and awe of the situation wouldn't allow for a moment to clearly think. He was a spectator in this, and for some reason, he couldn't take his eyes away from what was occurring in front of him.

The woman in white, still frozen as if paralyzed, suddenly no longer had her bare feet on the cobblestone floor of the alley. She slowly levitated up into the air a few feet off of the ground, legs buckled, arms lightly swaying at her sides.

Then, he heard the first abnormality. It was a sound that was both intriguing and terrifying at the same time. A heavy hum or buzz filled the air in all directions. This was when he witnessed the black mass surrounding the woman begin to pulsate. From the center of the dark object, he observed a single ring form that grew outward. As one ring formed and left the center of this darkness, another quickly formed behind it. Instantly the entire mass of this black presence was in motion. Within seconds of watching this, he heard the second sound.

The woman in white began to scream. This wasn't a frightened or shocked scream. This was the sound of true agony and pain that no living soul should ever endure. The man wanted to help. He needed to step in and save this mystery woman that he knew nothing about, but he couldn't move. Much like the woman suffering in front of him, he was paralyzed. All he could do was watch as the black mass of nothingness lifted the woman higher into the air and towards it. Terror and shock struck the man's haggard face as he watched the woman rise.

The humming sounds emanating from the creature became deafening as it slowly seemed to disintegrate the woman in white. As she floated forward, strips of flesh began to peel off of her body, revealing saturated muscle underneath. These strips moved rapidly towards the mass and disappeared as if becoming a part of it. The muscle and tendons of the woman began to peel away from her body as well. Within seconds, a torso and head were all that remained of the woman.

For all of the effort he expelled, trying to get up off of his knees, he knew there was nothing he could do. No one could survive what he had just witnessed, no one. He knelt there, tears streaking the sides of his face, as he was forced to watch this murder, this execution, this ... *feeding* occur. Then, to his astonishment, what was left of the woman in white turned around and faced him.

Throughout the agonizing screams and terror of being ripped slowly apart, the woman's face still appeared intact. Her expression as she looked at the man didn't show fear or pain; it was calm and serene. This is when the immobile man noticed the real differences in her appearance. Her hair was no longer the bright red color, though it was still tightly braided. It had changed to a dark brunette. The green of her eyes had changed as well to a light brown. The fair complexion and freckles were absent, replaced by smooth, flawless, tanned skin. This was not the same woman that he had chased in the strange alley minutes before. This was someone else, someone special, and he knew who she was.

"Lilly!"

As he shouted in her direction, the deafening sound emitting from the black mass suddenly stopped. The ripples and spirals pulsating throughout it stopped as well. He watched as the torso housing Lilly's face opened its mouth to speak. One word came out of her mouth, but she repeated it over and over again. "Odin ... Odin ... Odin."

Suddenly, with a shrieking gasp, Odin sat up in his bed, dripping wet with sweat, confusion grasping his every thought. "Lilly ... Lilly!" A few moments passed while the confusion subsided and he realized where he was. "What the bloody hell was that?"

Outside his door, there was a vigorous knock followed by a familiar voice full of panic. "Odie ... Odie ... Get up mate, get up. Lilly's gone, she's not here!"

22

WITHIN SECONDS, ODIN WAS up, trying to comprehend the vivid, terrorizing dream and what Simon had just said about Lilly. He stood outside room two's white door, bare foot, palms on his head, trying to process all of it. "Just hold on! Hold on a second Simon. What do you mean she isn't here? Where would she go?"

The worry on Simon's face spoke volumes about his concern. He had always thought of Lilly as a little sister and with all that they had gone through in the past few days, dread and fear leaked out of every word spoken. "I don't know mate, she's just ... just gone. It's not like her to go somewhere without leaving a note or telling me. Especially since Mitch disappeared."

"Who's bloody Mitch?" Odin demanded.

"Her daddy, dummy ... have ya not been paying attention?" Simon eyed Odin with indignation, shaking his head. "That's not the point mate- she is not here." He pointed to the floor expressing the obvious of his statements.

Odin was searching for an explanation, trying to come up with a reason why she wouldn't tell anyone where she was going. "Maybe, she just needed some air... you know, some alone time just to ... you know, think." At this point, Odin's worry was showing as well, regardless of his statements as he paced back and forth along the second floor decking.

"I'm tellin' ya mate, something isn't right about this. Lilly's not the type to just be alone, or go for a walk, or whateva ya tryin' to say. She doesn't do stuff like that Odie. She's gone, and I'm worried, and..." The more Simon spoke, the more Odin realized something wasn't right about this situation. His mind immediately returned to the dream, attempting to block out the terrorizing visions and feelings that remained.

Why was her beautiful face on that that thing? Odin halted his frantic pacing and dropped his head, gazing at the wooden decking. "Okay, okay ... Let's think, Simon. Did she say anything last night? Anything that sounded odd or out of character for her?" He grabbed Simon by the shoulders and held his stare. "I need you to really think now."

Simon halted his shifting, dropped his eyes and started pulling on his beard in successive strokes. After a few stressful moments of silence, his look again returned to Odin's bright, blue eyes. "Last night was normal, nothin' out of the ordinary or different. She was being Lilly, all bossy and hostile. That's how she always is, mate."

"I see, well ... Do you remember her saying anything that would hint at her taking off, or leaving without us?" His grip on Simon's shoulders strengthened with each word.

It took Simon over a minute to answer, as he reflected on all that he could remember from their conversations at the bar the night before. He looked up with warily eyes, "Don't know. Everythin' was normal. We were just talkin' 'bout makin' coppers and goin' to see Randall. That was it."

Odin was attentively listening, while his mind also reflected on the previous night's conversations. *Remember, remember, what did she say to you?* he thought to himself. *What was it about taxes and bribes?* With the second question fresh in his mind, something magically

clicked. With a poised expression, he began. "Simon, listen to this."
He paused for a moment to make sure he had the sailor's complete
attention. "Remember when she said that we might not earn enough
coppers to meet with Lord Randall. She said something like...sixty
might not be enough, right? For all three of us to meet with him."

"I don't know, maybe. What does that have to do with this?"

"What if sixty wasn't enough for all three of us to see Randall, but it
was enough for one? Do you think she would try to get to the bottom
of this by herself?" He lifted his left eyebrow in a gesture, hoping that
Simon would understand.

"I think ya are getting ahead of yaself mate, she wouldn't try somethin' like that. She's as tough as nails and by far the bravest woman
I know, but to go and see Randall, alone?" He shook his head in
disagreement. "I just don't think she would do that. He's a monster
and she knows it."

"Well, I don't know what else to think, Simon. If you really think
she is gone, it's a possibility. That, or..." He didn't continue with the
sentence. He just looked at Simon with a mournful expression.

"Don't think about stuff like that mate, she's fine. She has to be."
His tone got very serious and assertive. "She probably ran off and did
somethin' stupid like ya said, Odie. That's all."

Odin shook his head in confusion, "I don't know. Maybe. If she was
going to do something like that, wouldn't she leave something behind
to let us know what she was doing? It makes doesn't sense to me now
that I think of it."

Simon was already nodding frantically agreeing with the thought.
"Like I said mate, she doesn't just leave without letting me know.
She always does, ever since Mitch disappeared. That's what makes me
think somethin' ain't right here."

Odin cupped his chin, wondering if she could have slipped out in the night, trying to solve so many mysteries for all of them. "Well Simon, we are not going to find out standing around here. Give me a couple of minutes. I'll come downstairs and we can go and find out where she is." His eyes were strong and confident as he looked at Simon, passing on a little reassurance.

Simon didn't reply, he merely nodded and went downstairs where he had to deliver the bad news to a group of salty sailors waiting for access to their favorite watering hole, even if it was mere hours after sunrise.

Odin was a man of his word. After a few minutes, he came downstairs and the two started off towards the markets. Their first stop in the quest to find Lilly was to see the merchant James, and hopefully get some information on how to get to the most powerful man in all of Floria, Lord Randall.

23

THE TWO MADE THEIR way through the markets with ease at this time in the morning. Without the hustle and bustle of the afternoon crowd obstructing them, they approached the merchant's tent in a matter of minutes. Even the scents of exotic delicacies flowing through the air couldn't alter their journey at this point; they needed to find their friend.

The flaps to the teal tent had yet to be opened, which caused some nervousness in both men as they stood outside, shoulder to shoulder. Visitors are the livelihood of any merchant; it was strange that James had yet to open up for the day.

Simon leaned in and whispered, "Everyone's already open 'round here. Why isn't this bloke? I think somethin's wrong."

With wary eyes, Odin delivered his theory. "I don't know? Maybe he overslept. He's probably in there right now, getting ready to open up for the day. I mean look around. It's not that busy yet."

"Well, there's only one way to find out. Go on, take a look." Simon gestured towards the tent with his right hand and a grin. "Go on."

Odin faced the sailor with an expression of disbelief. "Why don't you take a look? Why do I have to do it?" He gestured back towards the closed tent.

"It was ya idea to come down here. That means ya take the first look, mate." He gestured again, with an even more annoying grin.

"What?" Odin's jaw dropped, trying to rationalize Simon's words. "You were every bit a part of the decision too, Simon. Tell you what, let's go together, okay?"

Simon's expression was full of uncertainty. He immediately started to shift a bit from his left to right, while stroking his beard anxiously. After a few paces, he finally remained still for a moment. "Mate ... what if somethin's wrong though. What if ... ya know. He's gone as well? Or ... worse."

Odin cocked an eyebrow, "If he's gone too, I'm still in the middle of my nightmare. Regardless, you said it yourself - the only way to find out is to go and check." He again gestured in the tent's direction. "Together, Simon."

With a wrinkled nose, Simon responded. "Ya still have nightmares? What are ya, like ten?"

"I'll tell you later, it's not important. Are we doing this or not?"

Simon let out a long sigh, followed by more shifty paces. "Alright, alright. But ya lead, okay?"

The approach was very cautious, but they finally made it to the flaps of the tent. Odin's gaze lingered on the massive ram's skull hanging above the entrance, as the two stood there not knowing what their next move was. "Should I just call for him? Maybe he'll respond and we can go in and talk."

"Worth a shot." Simon whispered while shrugging.

Odin leaned in close to the fabric of the tent's two flaps, still down and dragging on the dirt floor. It smelled of incense and leather as he got within inches. After a deep breath, he called out. "James! James, are you in there?" After not receiving a response, he looked at Simon for advice. "Maybe he's not in there. What should we do?"

"I think ya should go in. I don't think ya have another option, Odie."

"Wait. What happened to us? Why should I just go in?" The frustration of the moment could be heard in his voice. "You said you'll come if I lead, remember?"

"Ah mate, well that was before ... ya know... there was no response. What if ..."

Odin cut him off in the middle of his excuse. "Stop being a child, and get yourself together. We have to find out what's happening in this city. We have to find Lilly, Simon." The honest words had an immediate impact on the sailor as Odin looked him in the eye, hands tightly gripping his shoulders. "We can do this. Together."

After a few deep breaths, and a long swallow, Simon convinced himself that he was indeed ready. "Alright mate, I'm right behind ya. If that's okay?"

Odin shook his head in annoyance but firmly grabbed the left tent flap. He slowly pulled it away from the right flap revealing total darkness from within. He decided to call out once more. "James! It's me, Odin. Are you there?" Once again there was no response.

The two looked at each other, tense expressions crossing their faces. Odin decided to call out one last time, praying for a sound, a voice, anything in response. "James, it's Odin. I'm coming in, okay?" After a period of silence, Odin stepped into the tent, followed reluctantly by his sailor friend.

24

"Bloody hell Odie, I can't see a thing in here." Odin turned around and faced his friend abruptly.

"Shhhh! Be quiet. Just look around and see if we can find anything."

"How are we supposed to look 'round and find somethin' in pitch blackness, mate?"

"You know what I mean. Feel around, listen for something. There's got to be something here that will help."

Odin turned away and, step by step, made his way into the center of the room. A small opening remained in the tent flaps allowing for a sliver of sunlight to penetrate the darkness. The bright light illuminated a single tentacle of the Golden Kraken painted on the fabric of the back wall, which Odin was slowly approaching. One of James' tables, full of goods, prevented him from getting close enough to truly admire the detail of the art piece. He placed both hands down on the table, trying to make out the rest of the intricate, painted creature.

Why do they always choose strange creatures as their sigils? Odin thought to himself.

With his hands still touching the edge of the table, he cautiously moved around the left side until his foot struck something. Odin immediately froze in place, not sure what he had just bumped into. The streak of light hitting the painting did little near the ground. He cautiously took one step backwards away from the table, and whatever was on the ground near it. The entire area within the tent was dim but Odin turned his focus to the ground where he could vaguely see the outline of something.

What is that? He thought to himself. He turned around to try and find Simon who was still in the front of the room. "Hey Simon, open up the flaps and let some more light in here. Something's here on the ground near this table."

The sailor turned around, facing the entrance, grabbed the right flap and pulled it open, instantly flooding the left side of the tent with sunlight. As he did, a sudden gasp and shriek could be heard from Odin.

"Bloody Hell! James! It's James!"

Simon was in the back of the tent in less than a second, peering down at the merchant alongside Odin. "What happened to him? What the hell is this? What the ..."

"I don't know! I just bumped into him! He was just here. I don't know!"

"Look at his face! What the hell man. Is he dead?"

"I don't know! He looks dead! Oh no, Simon, where's his hand?"

"Who cut off his hand? What is this? Oh no mate, this is bad, really, really bad..."

"I know, I know! What the bloody hell happened here?" Odin leaned down near the lifeless merchant. "James! James! Can you hear me?"

"He's dead mate, he has to be. Oh my, look at him!" Simon began to pace frantically from left to right, hands wrapped around the back of his neck. "This is bad!"

"Settle down, we need to think. What happened? What happened here?" As he was mumbling to himself, crouched down near the ground, the merchant suddenly let out a saturated cough.

With a shriek, Odin jumped back in surprise, putting distance between himself and the merchant, pushing himself back with his hands on the dusty floor. "What the hell!" As the coughing continued, Odin again approached the man lying on the floor of the tent. "James! James, can you hear me?"

Simon was already on his knees near the merchant as well. "Mate, it's us. Simon and Odin. What happened here? What happened to ya?"

The coughing subsided momentarily, but the two watched as blood trickled out of the corner of James' mouth. His right eye was so severely swollen he couldn't open it. The left eye, now eyeing the two hovering over him, had several broken blood vessels within. His nose appeared to have been broken and a thick laceration streaked his left cheek. This man received the beating of his life and it was a miracle he was alive. With every ounce of energy, he had left, he said one word. "Water."

"You want some water? Okay, okay James! Simon, give him your canteen."

Simon reached for the canteen on his hip, rapidly unscrewed the lid and gently poured some of the contents into the merchant's waiting mouth, causing another series of violent coughs. Bloody spittle sprayed the dirt floor as James convulsed on the ground, trying to control himself. "Just breathe James, just breathe. We're here for ya."

"James, what happened here. Who did this?" Odin's voice was full of worry.

The merchant wasn't able to respond, but he gestured for another drink of water. Simon obliged immediately, carefully pouring a smaller portion into James' waiting mouth. Far less coughing occurred from this round and the merchant seemed to catch his breath momentarily.

Odin leaned in once again and began to inquire about what had happened. "James, what happened? Who did this to you?"

The merchant's left eye scanned the room quickly but returned to Odin. More blood trickled out of the side of his mouth as he attempted to speak. "Jardin. It was Jardin."

Simon and Odin locked eyes at the news of who was responsible for this.

"That's the bloke that was here the other day threatening him, remember? The one with the gut." Simon began to stroke his beard nervously.

"Yeah, yeah, I remember," Odin answered. "He works for Randall, right?" He turned his attention back to James. "Why did he do this, James?"

The merchant swallowed vigorously and then slowly responded. "I was ... helping."

"Helping? What do you mean? Who were you helping James? Why did this happen to you?" Odin leaned in even closer to the man so that he could hear him.

"I was helping ... her."

Odin's jaw dropped in confusion. He instantly knew who the merchant was talking about but asked the question for assurance. "Her? James ... Did Lilly come here this morning? Were you helping her?"

"Yeah mate, was Lilly here? Help us understand."

The merchant didn't respond, he merely nodded his head acknowledging they were both correct.

Odin turned to Simon once more. "She was here Simon, early this morning."

"What happened to her? Where is she now James?" Simon's voice cracked as he demanded answers. The worry in his eyes was escalating.

The merchant began to cough once more, even more forceful this time. More blood spewed from his mouth causing a rattling sound in his throat. It was very clear that he was not going to make it. He will die here today, very soon too.

They kneeled there, shaking their heads at what had happened to him. The brutality of this act had never been seen by either of them before. This was the scene of a nightmare.

Odin needed more time, and he needed more answers. "James, did they take her? Did they take Lilly with them?" His eyes were beginning to well up.

So much had been taken from him in his life. He didn't know if he could handle another tragedy like this. Mia's death was an accident, but he continued to blame himself fully for her loss every day. His mind wandered to that day in his father's shop. He could still vividly see the thief, and the knife. Why did he unsheathe his dirk? Why did he confront him?

"Please James, I need to know what happened to her. Do you know anything?"

The merchant's breathing had slowed steadily in the few moments they were communicating. The rattling sound coming from deep within his throat had slowed as well. His time was limited and everyone in the tent knew it. With all the energy in his body, he spoke his final words. "Randall ... Randall has her." As the last word came out of his blood-stained mouth, he exhaled for the final time.

Simon and Odin were in disbelief. How did all of this happen? They sat there, on the dusty floor, thinking about all that had transpired. Looking at James' lifeless body and the brutality that he endured, brought on emotions of sadness, fear, and anger. This was not right.

They still hadn't found their friend, but they knew where to look for her now. Why did she come here alone? Why did she try to find the truth without them? So many questions remained unanswered. What was going to be their next move?

After a moment of long silence, Odin let out a deep sigh and got up off of the ground, dusting off his pant legs. His appearance was stoic, but on the inside, a thousand emotions were bubbling to the surface. Eventually, he broke the silence. "Simon, get up! Let's go get Lilly. We have a Lord to kill!"

PART 4

VENGEANCE

25

A STEEP INCLINE LED the two towards the castles and keeps of the city, once they meandered their way out of the market and all of its distractions. The road was paved with cobblestones, which made for sure footing, but the grading made it a laborious hike. As they cleared a hilltop, panting and perspiring, the impressive wall came into view. There was no plan to get inside, and this seemed like an impossible task, but they had to confront Randall and get Lilly back.

There are only two gates that lead into the Manors, the north and the west. They stood on the street, loathing the colossal size of the west gate that looked down on them and the rest of the city. The gate was a grand portcullis, made of iron and steel, twenty feet high and nearly that wide too. Its vertical bars, thick as a man's arm, were spaced out in rows less than a foot apart, making penetration nearly impossible. If the sheer, menacing appearance of the gate wasn't enough of a deterrent for those brave enough to ask for admittance, the guards on duty would do it.

Emotionless, trained killers manned the wall and the gate every second of the day. Pairs of two, adorned with plated breastplates and helms, patrolled the perimeter, armed with lances and shields. Their orders were to use whatever means necessary to keep those within the wall safe and segregated, with death being the preferred method, so the lords didn't have to deal with the trials. In addition to the patrol teams, eagle eyed archers were stationed at the wall's watch towers, which reached high into the sky every 100 feet or so along the perimeter. No one was getting in. A battalion from the Aileran Army would have trouble forcing their way in with all of the security.

The roadway along the wall was littered with merchants and their wagons or carts filled with goods for sale. This was the best place to sell their product because the Lords of Floria always have the most coins to throw around. Indulgence and gluttony were a daily appetizer up here, high in the hills.

As Odin and Simon approached, they kneeled down behind a large wagon parked a distance away from the gate. From this vantage point, they observed another wagon parked closer to the gate's entrance that seemed to have a broken wheel. The merchant, and what the two assumed was his son, were struggling to lift the axel off of the ground to remove the broken wheel. The man seemed very strong, but something was off with the boy.

"Hey Odie, I've got an idea. Let's go help those blokes. Maybe they know something about how to get in there. Maybe they can help us get in." Simon's words were confident and strong. The only person alive that he considered a part of his family needed him.

"Look how close they are to the gate - the guards will see us."

Simon cocked his head in irritation, "Look at ya, look at me. They don't know us. They'll just think we are with the merchants. Those guards aren't gonna worry about a couple of fellows helping to fix a wheel. It's not that close anyways, Odie."

"I don't know, Simon. What if they figure something out? What if they take us just like they took Lilly?" Odin's hesitation didn't even begin to show how much he hated this plan. Even if they did help them out, what were they going to say to them? How were they supposed to get intel on how to get inside? He hated every part of this, but what else could they do? At least it was something. After releasing a deep sigh, he nodded towards his friend. "Are you sure about this?"

Simon held Odin's eyes for an awkward amount of time until finally answering. "No ... not really. But what else are we gonna do?"

Neither were prepared, but they had to try something. Either this would work or it would be a colossal failure. Lilly's life may be in jeopardy and they were willing to risk theirs to free her. The decision had already been made.

"Follow my lead." Simon abruptly left his crouch and the concealment from behind the parked wagon.

Without a worry in the world, he proceeded right up the cobblestone road towards the two merchants straining to repair their broken wheel. Odin followed a few paces behind, mumbling under his breath.

"Hey mate, need a hand or two with that?"

The father, attempting to lift the carriage up while his son removed the broken wheel, halted his onerous efforts at the sound of Simon's voice. The wagon came back down to the road with a crash, and a strenuous sigh from the overworked man.

The man turned around and sized up Simon, observing the muscles on his tattooed forearms. "Ah, that would be great. Three of the damn spokes splintered once the wheel hit that hole there." The merchant pointed behind the wagon at the street where a visible stone had been dislodged from the road, exposing a deep cavity. "Aye ... ya look strong enough. Come on in here and help me lift the carriage. Pip, get that damn wheel off this time, boy!"

Simon hustled over to the side of the carriage and got a steady grip on the underside. He observed the merchant's rough, calloused hands as he filed in next to him. More of a working man than a salesman, obviously. Blacksmith maybe? The two lifted with their might, clearing the wheel off of the street and holding it in the air. Odin quickly scurried over and supported the son, allowing for easy access to the bolts behind the axle. In mere seconds, the wheel was removed and the wagon was gently placed down this time.

With the first step in the process complete, Simon started some small talk, in hopes of getting some minor intel from the merchant. "Bloody hell that thing's heavy. What's in the cargo?"

The merchant slowly wiped his brow with a cloth he removed from a pocket, as he eyed the sailor. "Goods for the manors, Supplies for the soldiers." He began shouting orders to his son. "Pip, get the spare spokes from the wagon and start repairin' the wheel. We need to get inside."

The boy, 14 or 15 at the latest, looked at the man with a puzzled expression. There was something different about him, something odd. His mannerisms and demeanor didn't match that of a young teenager, he seemed much younger through his actions.

"Boy! Get the spokes! Now!" The man's shouts caused the boy to cower slightly, flinching with each spoken syllable, but he received the message loud and clear. He was in the back of the covered wagon searching for the materials that his father demanded in an instant. The man faced Simon and Odin once again, shaking his head in disappointment. "I swear, if it wasn't for his mother, I'd have sent him off years ago. Can't add two plus two but he knows machines. He can fix anything." A slight smirk crossed his face as he finished his sentence.

"He can fix anything? Well, that's quite a talent. Probably comes in quite useful, I would say." Simon looked at Odin, nodding his head.

The merchant nodded back. "It does, that's true. Especially in our line of work." The man walked over to his black ox, still attached to the dismantled wagon, and began to stroke its thick neck with affection. The animal was casually grazing on a patch of grass poking out between two stones in the street. "He means well, but ... It just takes him a little longer to understand stuff, ya know? Been like that for years too, never speaks either. Don't know what's wrong with 'im."

Simon slowly shook his head, attempting to appear as genuine as possible. "Bloody shame mate, bloody shame."

"Well, it's not all bad, ya'll see soon 'nough. He'll have that wheel repaired in no time, promise." He paused for a few moments, almost admiring the sight of his son. "Want to thank ya two for helpin' us out. The name's Marshall." He extended his open hand in a friendly direction in Simon's direction.

Simon greeted the man with a tight grip, knuckles whitening as he acknowledged the man's gratitude. "No worries, ya would do the same, Marshall. I'm Simon and this is my mate Odie."

The man released Simon's hand and nodded in Odin's direction. "What ya two doin' up here anyways, sellin' or tradin'?"

The man's questions caught Simon off guard. He hadn't thought that far ahead and didn't know how to respond or what to say. He couldn't be honest, he had to think of something, and fast. "Well, um, ya see …"

"We're picking up a few chests to take down to the docks. Full of old merchandise that the lords don't need anymore. Taking them across the Green Sea to sell." Odin interjected just in time, nodding his head. "Thing is friend," He started approaching the man with a look of need in his eyes, "We forgot the orders back at the ship. Do you know how stern those guards are about letting merchants in without the proper papers?"

Marshall's expression was contemptuous as he looked at Odin with a smirk on his face, followed by a chuckle. "Ya must be new to Floria, eh? See those guards over there," he turned around and pointed towards the west gate, "They'll kill ya just for not havin' the papers. Ya not gettin' in there without written or verbal approval friend. I suggest

ya go back and get 'em before walkin' up there and catchin' a beatin'
or far worse."

Odin looked to Simon for support but the sailor simply shrugged
his shoulders, not knowing how to intervene or engage further. *Bloody
Simon*, he thought to himself with a slight shake of the head. He
turned away from his friend and refaced the merchant, knowing that
he had to get some more information. Lilly's life possibly depended
on it. "I understand. Thank you for your candidness, Marshall. That
wouldn't be wise of us just to walk up there empty handed, not having
the proper papers for admittance."

With a nod, Marshall continued. "Not a problem. I've been comin'
up here for years deliverin' goods to these damn soldiers. They know
my face well enough, but I still wouldn't try gettin' through without
mine." He patted a leather pouch hanging from his hip. "I knew a
man that tried it once." He stopped momentarily and made a face of
grimace, "Poor fella left the gate with two less fingers. If there was ever
an idea to try it, they flew out of my head the day I saw his mangled
hand." He shook his head as he thought about the man and his missing
digits.

"They cut off two of his fingers for not having the right papers?"
Odin shook his head in disgust at the thought of the man's story. The
act that he was portraying was non-existent now as he thought about
what could happen to him and Simon. He had to search deep, within
his core, to gather the courage to continue this facade. He had to, there
was no other choice. "Well, I don't know what to do then. Simon?"
He eyed his sailor companion and subtly gestured for help.

"Um, well ..." Simon started stroking his long beard thinking about
the situation. After a few seconds, he seemed to garner an understanding of what Odin was trying to accomplish. "If we go back to
the ship for the papers, we won't be back in time. The captain might

cut our fingers off, mate. I happen to like my fingers, too." He flashed that toothy smile of his while holding up his hand to admire it. His attention returned to Marshall and then back to Odin.

"You think the captain would be that irate with us, Simon?" Odin's words were sincere, as if genuine.

"Aye ... I reckon he would. These old goods are worth a fistful of coppers, and I am sure ya know that coppers are coming harder and harder to earn, Marshall."

Odin looked to the ground, kicking a rock near his feet in disappointment. After a few moments, he looked up and locked eyes with the merchant, face full of worry and despair. "Marshall, I hate to even ask, but do you know any way that we can get inside?"

The merchant contemplated the two friends' dilemma, thinking about the situation that they were in. He had been in their shoes before, stuck and out of options, and felt obligated to pay it forward, given how they just relieved him of his misfortune minutes before. After a moment he gave a slight nod in their direction. With a confident voice, he answered, "I'm goin' in there to drop off these goods for the soldiers. It's not uncommon for me to come out with some that need repair. If I get ya inside, we should be able to load up the chests ya're picking up without anyone questioning a thing. Once on this side of the wall," he pointed to the ground and tapped his foot, "I'll get ya two down to the docks for departure. What do ya think?"

Odin and Simon locked eyes as they thought about the man's proposition, wondering if this plan would work. Could it really be this easy? This man just solved their entire problem in mere seconds, with the simplest of ideas. Maybe helping the merchant with his broken wheel was a good plan after all. Simon's grin was contagious as he began to nod in Odin's direction, signaling that he was onboard with the plan. Odin smiled as well and nodded back. It was worth trying. What's the worst that could happen?

Odin redirected his attention back to the merchant, thanking him for his efforts with his kind, blue eyes. "Wow Marshall, that sounds like a great idea. I understand the plan about the merchandise, but, how do Simon and I get in there? Do we just walk in with you?"

The merchant didn't respond immediately, he was checking on his son's progress with the wheel. "No boy, flip the spoke 'round, then insert it. There ya go, just like that. Keep it up." Once feeling more confident about the wheel's situation, he turned back to engage Odin. "What'd I tell ya, right. Wheel's gonna be good as new. I'm sorry there, what were ya sayin'?"

"I was just wondering, Marshall, how do we get beyond the wall?" He pointed to himself and Simon. "We don't have clearance."

"Ah, try not to worry 'bout that." He cupped his chin in his hand while nodding slightly. "I'll vouch for ya. Tell 'em ya workin' for me, new shop hands. With all of their menacing looks and skills, they ain't the brightest bunch, those guards. Just stay on ya toes and don't say a thing. I'll do the talkin'."

"Seems like ya takin' a big risk for us, mate. Ya sure 'bout this?" Simon's concern was genuine, given the information that had been provided regarding approaching the gate without the proper authority. Losing a finger or two was one thing, being detained for a treasonous conspiracy against the Lords of Floria was something much bigger. Either they were all in or they weren't, regardless of who else could possibly get hurt.

"Yeah, I'd hate to burden you like this Marshall, given that we just met and all. It does seem like you are doing a lot for us." Odin's feelings about the plan were similar to Simon's. He knew the ramifications if this whole scheme didn't work out for any of them. Were they willing to risk another's life as well as their own just to get inside?

"Well, if we get up there and there's trouble …" He paused for a few seconds while staring up at the sky. "If there's trouble, I'll send ya back. Tell 'em we forgot somethin'. They'll buy it, I'm sure of it." As he spoke, the confidence and optimism from before vanished. He wasn't as sure about this idea the more he thought about it.

It was true that he had been coming up to the Manors for years and the guards knew him by face and name. It was also true that he had never had an incident or misstep with his transactions of goods with these men. Still, these are ruthless killers who enjoy their profession. One part of this goes awry and that could be it for all of them, even Pip.

Simon and Odin could see that the man had doubts, now that he had more time to think about his idea. Without saying a word to each other, they both agreed that he shouldn't have any part of their scheme to get into the Manors to confront Randall. They couldn't stomach the idea of something happening to an innocent soul, because of their vengeful emotions. Eventually Odin spoke up. "Marshall, thank you for the idea and for trying to help us. I think it's too big of a risk though. We're just going to have to go get the papers and deal with Captain."

"Yeah mate, thanks, but I don't want anyone to lose a finger, know what I mean?"

The merchant seemed both relieved and disappointed at the same time while he listened to their reasoning. He knew deep down that his plan would work, but maybe they were right. He couldn't put his son in danger like that, even if he was trying to help a couple of fellow merchants out. He appreciated their honesty and the fact that they weren't being selfish about their needs. "Well, if ya don't feel good about it, we won't do it." His attention quickly turned to his boy who was rolling the repaired wheel towards them and the wagon. "Ahh, look at that. What did I say? The boy can fix anything. Ya fellows care to help us get this back on so I can deliver my goods?"

"Yeah, of course. No worries, mate. Let's get ya up and runnin' again."

Simon walked over with the merchant and went through the same routine as before when they took the wheel off.

Lifting and heaving while Odin and Pip worked on fastening the wheel to the axel. It took a little longer, but the wheel was back on in no time and Marshall was out of the jam that halted his delivery.

"Well, I have to thank ya two. I wish I could do somethin' for ya, but I understand ya concerns about walkin' up there. Those guards are monsters. To be honest with ya, I was a little worried it wouldn't work either." He let out a bellowing laugh and slapped Simon on the back, and the two shared a moment of humor about the whole situation.

Odin approached the man and extended his hand in a friendly gesture, expecting to grimace in pain from the man's grip. "You'd do the same Marshall. Thanks for trying to help us out." He was right about the grip, he had to pull free after a few seconds, concealing his pain inside.

"Well, alright ya two. Hopefully I'll see ya 'round." He climbed aboard the wagon and averted his attention towards his son. "Pip, let's go! I don't have all day, boy!" He waved farewell and snapped the reins, causing the ox to move forward pulling their covered wagon full of merchandise towards the west gate.

Odin and Simon watched as the man steered the wagon right up to the towering gate, slowing the ox with a slight tug of the reins and a whistle. Marshall carefully reached into the leather pouch on his hip and pulled out a yellowing parchment, the papers for admittance. One of the guards, possibly a patrol captain, due to the decorative crest adorning the top of his plated helmet, walked over and snatched the parchment from the merchant.

This was all a formality, these two knew each other, based on the nonchalant conversation that could be heard as the patrol captain held the papers, not reading a word that was on them. It was obvious that this was just protocol for admittance. As they watched the captain hand the parchment back to Marshall, they realized that the plan probably would have worked. They could be walking through the gate right this moment, just as Marshall was steering his wagon through. Failure hit them severely, as they watched the portcullis close. Was there another way in, or had they already failed Lilly?

26

THE TWO HUNG THEIR heads as they walked down the street away from the gate and its menacing guards. They needed some time to think, and most importantly, to discuss what they were going to do next. The one plan that could have gotten them inside the walls fell through and they hated the idea that they failed. There must be another way to get to Lilly.

Simon's arms were flailing as he expressed his emotions about missing out on their chance. "Bloody hell Odie, what are we gonna do now? That was our chance, and we blew it."

Odin stopped walking and grabbed Simon by the arm. "We don't know for sure if it would have worked, Simon. That plan had some risks to it, I know. There's got to be another way inside."

Simon ripped his arm away from Odin's grip. "How Odie? Just how are we gonna get in there? Those guards must have seen us while we were helping with the wheel. There's no way we can just walk up there, pretending to be traders or merchants now. There's no way in."

"There has to be something we can do. We just need to think and come up with a plan. We have to do this Simon. Just think man, please."

Simon let out a long sigh, and then hunched over, hands on his knees. His eyes were distraught as he scanned the area, trying to think of a new plan. "Mate ... there's just no way in. We can't try to scale it; the archers or patrols will kill us for sure. We can't waltz right up there either - they'll cut off our fingers or worse. I don't know what to do. But I have to do somethin' Odie, I have to." Simon stood back up straight, locking eyes with his friend. "If anythin' happens to her Odie, I just ... I just don't know what I would do. She's all the family I have left."

"I know Simon, I know." Odin paused for a few moments, thinking about how much he cared about Lilly as well. "We have to find a way friend, we have to. She's counting on us to find her. I know she is."

Simon wiped a tear from his left eye. "Well, what are we gonna do? Grow wings and fly over the bloody wall?"

Odin let out a slight laugh. "No, I don't think that is an option, Simon. I'm sure the archers would hit us mid-flight anyways. Let's just try to focus and come up with something, okay."

The sailor nodded slightly. "Alright ... if we are not going to scale it, fly over it, or walk through it, what's left mate? Is there another option? Dig under?"

"No, the patrols will see us for sure." He placed his hands on the top of his head and started to pace back and forth thinking. Eventually a detail came to him. "The original plan that Marshall came up with probably would have worked, right?"

"Aye, I'd say so. Some risk though."

"Yeah, definitely there was. But there's no way that we can try that now because some of the guards probably noticed our faces, right?"

"I know they did. As I was lifting the bloody carriage up, I looked over and saw two of them eyeing us and whispering. Who knows what they were talkin' 'bout though."

"I thought I noticed something like that when I glanced over too. So that part of the plan is out. But ..." Odin paused momentarily, looking at the ground. Something just occurred to him and maybe a part of the original plan would still work. "But, do you remember how easy going the guard with the feathered crest was with Marshall? He didn't look at his papers or inspect the cargo."

"Aye, they knew each other, that was clear mate. There was some trust there. Where are ya goin' with this Odie?"

"I don't know if it's trust with those men. From the stories I've heard, it sounds like they like to maim and kill. Savagery like that seems to be an addiction. Anyways, I'm sure Marshall isn't the only regular coming and going. The one in charge is probably nonchalant with everyone he sees - it's just routine for him."

"Okay, I agree there, mate, get to the point though."

"Think about this Simon, we know that we can't be seen because they will know something is off. But what if we are not seen? What if they don't even know we are there?"

"What are ya talkin' 'bout Odie? Turning invisible?"

"No, no, nothing like that. What if we get inside a covered wagon and sneak into the Manors without anyone knowing, including who-ever is driving it?" A series of nods came from Odin as he smiled lightly at Simon hoping that the sailor understood. "Well?"

"I'm listenin' Odie, go on."

"Think about it Simon. We sneak into a covered wagon, and hide in the back behind the cargo. The merchant doesn't know we are there, so there's no risk on his end. They won't even look in the back. Once we get through that damn gate, we sneak out of the wagon when it's safe and go find Lilly."

Simon was already stroking his beard before Odin finished with his pitch. He was thinking hard. A smile slowly started to form across his face. "This might just work mate, it just might."

"It has to work, there's no other option."

"But what if they search the wagon, and they find us. That's the end mate. There won't be a finger or two gettin' hacked off for what we're attemptin'."

"We can't worry about that right now. We have to be confident that they won't search it. If we worry, we're going to talk ourselves out of going through with it, like before. This is going to work Simon; I know it will."

Simon took a few moments to truly think about what they were about to attempt. If you approached the gates without the proper papers, it would be much harder to hold a pen going forward, but sneaking into the Manors of Floria and confronting a lord? There was only one answer to that question. Execution. He had let Lilly down many times in his life, but this was not going to be one of those times. He had to do this, for her. "I know it will work too, mate." Simon extended his hand. "I'm in."

With confidence and pride, Odin gripped Simon's hand, hard. The two locked eyes, trying to see who would pull away first, not allowing a hint of pain to be revealed. After a few moments however, the smirk Odin was previously wearing vanished, replaced by pain and grimace. "Okay, okay Simon. You win, again! You win!"

Simon released Odin's hand and smiled from ear to ear. "Alright ya big softy, how do we choose our wagon?"

Odin, trying to revitalize his hand through a series of shakes, answered the sailor. "Leave that to me."

27

"What 'bout that one mate? It looks big enough," Simon nodded towards a caravan approaching from down the steep slope. The lead wagon, pulled by a deep chestnut-colored ox, rocked back and forth over the cobblestone road.

"It's definitely big enough for us to hide in, but how would we get inside it? Look," Odin pointed towards the caravan. "One, two, three... four, there's four wagons behind it. One of the other waggoneers would see us. The only way we can do this is to stow away in the last one."

Simon began stroking his beard once again, understanding the dilemma, stealth being the only answer. "So, the last one. Okay, I like the idea." Laying on his stomach, he peered over the granite outcrop that he and Odin had been hiding behind while observing the wagons. The tall, yellowing grass encompassing the outcrop added extra cover. "The last one's not as big, but I reckon we can fit. Get in there, tucked behind the cargo."

Odin looked over at the sailor. "If we do this, there is no turning back. Committed to the end, whatever that is, right?"

Simon didn't answer; he just gave a nod signaling that he was committed to their plan. His eyes were fully focused and determined.

"Alright, follow my lead. As the third wagon passes under us, we start our descent down the slope. Stay low and close, Simon. No one can see us."

"Aye, got it. I'll be right behind ya."

Odin was fixated on the caravan now rolling over the road below them. He counted under his breath as the first three past them, "One ... two ... three." The fourth wagon had fallen behind the few in the front of the caravan. Once it neared, Odin gave the signal in a hushed tone. "Now!"

The two remained on their stomachs and dragged themselves down the side of the hill towards the street, keeping as low as possible through the tall grass. As they slowly made their way down, Odin continued to count, "Four's past." Odin continued to slither down the side of the hill, watching as the fifth wagon approached and passed him, Simon right on his heels. He looked back and delivered a nod to Simon, "Let's go."

Instantly, the two popped out of the concealed grass and made their way behind the fifth wagon, making sure no one else was coming up the road that would notice them. Moving swiftly, Odin gripped the tail of the wagon and pulled himself inside. Once his feet were stable, which was challenging due to the constant rocking, he turned around and grabbed Simon's outstretched hand and quickly pulled him inside the back of the wagon as well. This was the easy part of the plan.

The tan bonnet covering the carriage bed blocked out most of the sunlight, making visibility poor. Its low ceiling also caused difficulties maneuvering from within, with all of the cargo. As the two peered inside, they could vaguely see three rows of pine chests, stacked two high in the center of the bed. Looking beyond the chests, crates labeled with the Golden Kraken, and the White Gull were in front of the waggoneer's seat.

Odin slowly moved to the outside of the chests, back against the inside wall of the bonnet. He sidestepped his way back towards the crates, Simon mirroring his actions right behind him. Once they reached the crates, the two slid in between the crates and the last row of chests, concealing them from anyone that may potentially glance in the back of the wagon.

With a stream of sweat trickling down his brow, Simon leaned over and whispered, "What now, mate? Do we just wait?"

In a whispered voice, Odin responded. "If this is going to work, we need to get past the gate and into the Manors. Let's just pray no one looks in here."

The next few minutes were agonizing, as the two slowed their breathing in order to provide utter silence. They rocked back and forth with the cargo as the wagon made its way up the slope towards the portcullis gate on the westside of the Manors.

Around them, they could hear the wooden wheels scraping against the stones of the street with each turn. The confined space, dimness, and fear of what would happen if they were found caused this five minute journey to seem like a lifetime. Soon, a whistle came from the front of the caravan and the wagon slowly halted. They were in front of the gate, and voices could be heard in the distance. The sounds were muffled but they could make out the conversation going on at the head of the wagons.

"What ya bringin' in today, Mooney?"

"The normal merch. Some spices and salts from the other side of the mountains for Lord Stone. Who knows what the bloody hell he does with all that stuff? Got some new gear for ya men, too. There's a few crates for Phillip and Randall in the back. Don't know the contents though. Don't ask, don't tell, right?"

"Words to live by. Smart man. How many in the caravan?"

"Five in all, each loaded with goods."

"Any ale? I hate going down to the taverns with all the scum of the docks, begging for scraps."

"Let me check my records but I think there are four." A brief pause occurred between the two men. "Ah, yes. Four casks. Should be in number three back there."

"Quality stuff or the piss they serve in the taverns?"

"Only the best for the lords, Adams. Ya know that. There's a few cases of bourbon from across the sea in a crate too. The best this side of the Lemurians."

"For a meager merchant, ya make bold statements, Mooney."

"Hell, when ya've been doing this as long as I have, there's no boldness - only confidence and experience."

"Ya got the papers?"

"Yeah, it's here, hold on a second." There was another moment of silence followed by the creaky sound of a hinge opening and then closing. "Here Adams, it's all there."

After another brief pause between the two, the conversation continued. "Did ya say there were five in the caravan?"

"Yeah, five wagons. Loaded and full. Why?"

"Ya always bring in four. What's with the new wagon?"

"Ya know the lords, always wanting more. Couldn't make four work anymore. It'll be five going forward."

"Alright. Which one is the bourbon in? Five?"

"Yeah, I think so, in a crate back there. Hey, don't go poking around in there. I'm not going to be responsible for any missing bottles."

"Mind ya business, Mooney! I just want to see what's coming in, ya know? Get a feel for what to expect later this evening. I'm not gonna take anything."

The conversation between the two unseen men halted, and footsteps could be heard getting closer to the back of the caravan. With the sound of each step, sheer panic began racing through Simon and Odin as they listened to the clack of wooden soles hitting the stones of the road. Slowly and silently, Odin unsheathed his dirk, holding the blade at his side. Simon, already with a boot knife in his left hand, prepared for the worse, trembling at the sound of the footsteps. Suddenly, the footsteps stopped right outside of the wagon concealing the two friends.

"Damn Mooney, ya weren't lying. These things are loaded top to bottom. I can't see anything though. Those crates, are they in the back?"

Another set of footsteps passed the side of the wagon and stopped at the rear. "Yeah, I think so. Behind all of those chests."

Without notice, the wagon rocked a little from left to right, but steadied quickly. The patrol captain, Adams, was inside the covered wagon, leering at all of the chests and crates. Holding their breath now, back against the chests, facing away from the patrol captain, Simon and Odin prayed to get out of this alive.

Adams grabbed a hold of the first chest in front of him, unhinging the hasp and drawing the bolt. With the daylight shining down on the back of the wagon, it was easy to see the contents from within the chest. He opened the lid, reached inside and pulled out a leather jerkin.

Merch for the soldiers. He thought to himself. "Anything interesting in the rest of these chests, Mooney?"

"No, not that I am aware of. Remember, don't ask, don't tell?"

"Yeah, I remember. I want a good look at the liquor though. Crates in the back, right?"

"Yeah, in the one with the kraken imprinted on it. Not that ya'll be able to see back there though."

After returning the jerkin and closing the lid, the man made his way to the side of the chests stacked two high in the center of the wagon's carriage. He carefully squeezed himself between the side of the chests and the tan bonnet, inching closer and closer down the length of the wagon where the two partners waited, blades out and ready to kill if necessary. He cleared the first set of chests in seconds.

Odin looked over at Simon. The sailor was shaking his head from side to side, knuckles whitening from his grip on the knife. The fear in his eyes said everything about the moment. He had never killed a man before, was he ready to do it now?

There was no way out of this situation - it was kill or be killed. Still, if he put his blade through the man's heart, how long would it take for the rest of the guards to overcome them, in the back of the wagon or outside on the cobblestone street? He was going to die today, he understood that now as he stood there, shaking with his back against the crates, tears streaking down his cheeks. He had failed her again, and he knew it.

Adams shimmied himself past the second chest, mere feet from the two stowaways, ready to seize the spoils of bourbon that he knew awaited. Unfortunately, the only thing waiting for him in the back of the covered wagon was a six-inch boot knife, and a terrified sailor committed to seeing their plan through to its end.

Simon brought the knife up to the side of his head, ready to plunge it into the unsuspecting man the moment he saw him or felt his presence. The patrol captain continued to slowly make his way down the side of the carriage, inching closer and closer to the crates holding the treasures of distillery, when...A voice rang out from outside the wagon. It was the waggoneer, Mooney.

"Hey Adams, I made a mistake. The bourbon is in number four, not five. I don't know what I was thinking."

The patrol captain let out a disgruntled growl as he turned towards the opening of the wagon. "Damn Mooney, why the hell am I in this one then?" He began to sidestep away from Simon and his deadly boot knife, not realizing how close he came to seeing all the faces of those he had put in the grave. "Bloody waggoneers!" he mumbled to himself as he hopped off of the back of the wagon.

Instantly, Odin let out a muffled sigh, followed by deep breaths. He realized how close they were to failing, and possibly killing a man. Not that it wasn't a small part of their overall plan, but Randall was their target, not the guards. Once his nerves were calmed, he looked over at Simon, still holding the boot knife against the side of his brow. "That ... could have been really, really bad. Were you going to kill him?"

Simon didn't respond, he just stood there, back against the chests, staring forward with a slight shake still. His breaths were rapid now that he wasn't holding them any longer. Deep within, his mind was working faster than ever before.

Thousands of thoughts and emotions were hitting him all at once. He had lived a relatively carefree life up to this point, void of responsibility or commitment. The actions that he almost had to take would have changed everything. Was he ready to die for this cause? Was he as committed as he said he was? Were his actions and words during this entire voyage a mere facade? He didn't quite know the answer to those questions. What he did know was that his only family member in all of Aileran needed him. Eventually his head stopped spinning and reality set back in. "I ... I really don't know. I don't know Odin."

The response caught Odin by surprise. He cocked his head inquisitively. "Did you just call me by my real name? You've never done that. Are you okay Simon?"

Releasing a sigh, Simon answered. "No, I'm not okay, mate. None of this is okay, none of it. But I think I've realized somethin' here, somethin' important." He slowly sheathed the boot knife and turned to face his friend. "I told ya I was committed to the end, whatever that is right?"

"Yeah, you're committed. You've always been committed."

Simon gave a slight shake of his head in disappointment. "Mate, I don't think I truly understood what that meant at the time, but I do now." He paused momentarily and exhaled deeply. "I want ya to know ... I want ya to know that I will die for ya, Odin. I will die for Lilly, too if I need to. Ya can count on me." His eyes were sincere and wide as he spoke. Something had changed within.

Odin's reaction was subtle yet supportive. "I've never questioned your loyalty, Simon. We are in this together, alright. You and me, until it's over. Until we have Lilly back. Whatever that means, friend."

Simon nodded his head in agreement, accepting the words of encouragement. "Until it's over mate, until it's over. Whatever that means."

Suddenly, a whistle broke out near the front of the caravan, and seconds later, the wagon began moving once again, rocking back and forth. In the distance, the sound of chains turning through a pulley signaled that the gate was opening. The colossal portcullis, raising its iron teeth high above the cobblestones and the insignificant minions seeking passage, opened wide, ready to swallow those that pass through its gaping mouth. Odin and Simon had made it; soon they would be inside. They had penetrated the Manors of Floria.

28

THE FAMILIAR WHISTLE FROM Mooney the waggoneer sounded out minutes later, halting the caravan and the powerful oxen pulling the wagons. Still lost in the darkness from within wagon five, Odin and Simon were unsure of what to expect next. Would the guards immediately start unloading the wagons or was there logistics before breaking apart the new inventory.

Simon leaned in and whispered, "Mate, where do ya think we are?"

Odin responded with a similar whisper. "I think we are beyond the wall, near the manors. There has to be some type of staging area, large enough to house all of the wagons. We're not the only caravan inside today, remember?"

"Aye, that's for sure. Heaps came in before us. What in the bloody hell can they do with all of this stuff?" Simon responded with a shake of his head.

"I don't know, but ... Quiet! someone's coming."

The two stood there in the confined space of the wagon, between the chests and the crates, listening to footsteps approaching from the front of the caravan. Along with the footsteps, there was a familiar voice and a new one. The accent was foreign to them, even with all of the ethnicities and dialects flowing daily through the port city. The speech was proper, each syllable accented directly. The two listened attentively trying to discover who was outside of the wagon.

"As ya can see my lord, all five are accounted for, stocked as full as I could get them."

"I see, thank you for your competence, Mr. Mooney. The other lords will be most pleased with your efforts."

"I appreciate that sir, I really do. Thank ya."

"I am sure that by now you have heard of the banquet scheduled for tomorrow."

"Aye, I figured that is what all of this stuff was for, sir."

"You are not entirely incorrect Mooney, most of these goods are for the banquet; however, some are for personal use. Do you know why a lavish banquet, such as this, is on the agenda for tomorrow?"

"I can't say that I do, sir. Celebrating something?"

"It is a celebration, yes. A grand festival of the coming of a new age. A new age for the city and for all of its inhabitants."

"A new age sir? What's this now?"

"You will learn soon enough. Thank you for not disappointing me, Mooney. My men will be here soon for the dismantling and distribution of goods. In an hour's time, you can be on your way. In the meantime, please come and enjoy the courtyard. Bring a few companions with you."

"I will, thank ya my lord."

The familiar footsteps that had quickly approached moments before, vanished from sound in an instance, moving in the opposite direction. As far as Odin and Simon could tell they were alone, but would they be able to get out of the wagon and find Lord Randall's keep without being seen? What about the waggoneers?

"Well mate, we got this far. What's the next move?"

Odin's attention was focused on his surroundings, trying to gauge if anyone was near. He knew that if they were caught now, this entire dangerous journey would be for nothing. They hadn't come this far to fail now.

"We need to get out of this bloody wagon, look around this place, and find Randall's keep. I'm going to take a look outside and see if anyone is out there." He wedged himself out of the tight space between the chests and the crates, and began to sidestep his way back towards the opening of the bonnet.

After passing the second set of chests, he unsheathed his dirk once again, holding the point out in front of him. As he reached the edge of the tan bonnet, he paused, listening for any indication that someone was nearby. Utter silence was all that he heard, giving him the assurance that maybe this was their opportunity to sneak out.

Carefully, and with modest reluctance, he inched his head out of the back of the covered wagon. With a brief glance right to left, he noticed countless other wagons parked in an empty lot. They all seemed to hold similar merchandise as the one that he and Simon had just stowed away in, chests, crates, and trunks. There was not a person to be seen or heard anywhere. The sight was beautiful to his eyes, knowing that they may just pull this off.

Odin returned to the safety of the tan covering, sheathing his dirk once again. He slowly looked back towards the area where he had once hidden and whispered for his friend. "Simon, come out here. I don't see anyone. We're alone."

"Are ya sure? Maybe they're just sleeping ya know. Gettin' a wink or two in."

"There's no one out here, now's our chance Simon. Hurry." Odin could hear the stout sailor struggling to release himself from the tight grip of the confined space. It was the combination of mumbles and curses just loud enough to hear. Eventually though, Odin could vaguely see the outline of his friend in the dimness of the wagon approaching, sidestepping towards him.

"Where'd they go? Where's Mooney?"

"I don't know and I don't care. We're getting out of this bloody wagon right now Simon. Are you with me?" His voice had conviction in it.

The sailor was close enough for Odin to see now, slowly coming up right beside him. "Till the end right, whatever that is."

With a slight nod, Odin hopped off of the back of the wagon, landing in a crouch, hand near the hilt of his dirk, just in case. Simon landed a mere foot behind him, crouching as well, scanning the area for threats or obstacles. The lot was empty, not a soul could be seen or heard.

"We are all alone, mate. Where did everyone go?"

"I don't know, but I don't want to wait and find out either. Come on, let's get moving. Follow me." Odin stood and swiftly paced towards the east end of the lot, Simon right on his tail. This area was occupied by a long column of wagons. To the right of the wagons was a gray stone wall, ten feet or so high and as long as the lot itself, providing them with cover as they got their bearings.

In a crouch once again, shielded by the wheel of one of the parked wagons, the two now had the visibility to truly see this staging area. Rectangular in shape, the area was massive, littered with wagons of many different sizes. The wall between them and the wagons ran the entire perimeter from what they could tell. It bent to the left in front of them and to the right behind them. At the North end of the wall, there seemed to be the only break where traffic could enter or exit. This break in the wall was wide enough for three wagons, but there was no other way in or out. In order to find Lilly, they first had to get out of this staging lot without being seen.

"Simon, do you see that opening in the wall? All of the Manors are beyond that." He scanned the horizon where the castles and keeps could be seen, sigils blowing in the wind.

Simon brought his hand above his eyes to shield them from the sun. "Aye, ya reckon that will get us out of here?"

Odin looked back at the sailor, still in a crouch. "There's only one way in or out. Unless we scale this thing." He pointed his thumb behind him at the stone block wall. "Who knows what's on the other side though. I think if we just stay low, keep hidden behind these wagons, we can get out of here. We can go find Randall and Lilly."

"I'm with ya, lead the way mate."

Staying as low as possible, the two made their way down the east corridor of the lot, scurrying from wagon to wagon. As they neared the bend leading towards the opening on the north side, they paused briefly. Peering around the last wagon to the left, once again they noticed that there was no one around.

With this artificial corridor clear, they quickly made the left turn and started their journey towards the opening in the center of the wall. At this point, they both had their blades extended in front of them, just as a precaution.

Inching closer and closer to the opening in the wall, Odin stopped and held up a fist, signaling for Simon to stop as well. "Let me take a look first. Make sure everything is alright." Keeping as low to the ground as possible, back against the wall, Odin approached the wide opening. Slowly, he peaked around the corner and found it empty.

"See anything?" Simon whispered. "Anyone?"

Odin shook his head. 'No, it's clear. There must have been fifty merchants here this morning, even more waggoneers. Where is every-one?" He shook his head in confusion, attempting to understand what had happened to all of the people that had entered the gate before and after them.

Simon caught Odin's eyes. "Somethin's wrong here mate, I don't like this. How do hundreds of people just vanish in minutes?"

Odin looked at his friend, trying to calm the man's nerves. "Maybe no one vanished, maybe they're just in a meeting or something. Getting ready for the celebration like the lord that was talking to Mooney said."

"I don't know Odie. It just feels like somethin' isn't right. Let's just get out of here and find Lilly. The sooner all of this over, the better."

"Let's hope we can find her. We still need to find Randall's keep and get inside." His words were cautious, hopeful still.

Simon delivered a nod in Odin's direction. "I'm right behind ya mate. Ya've gotten us this far."

With the nervousness of the situation dissipating, they both sheathed their blades and started walking along the opening's right wall. They noticed that the two walls lining the opening were nowhere near as long as the lot's sides. As they slowly sauntered along, they observed the wall's height decreasing, getting shorter and shorter with each step. At the end of the opening, the height of the stone block wall was mere feet above the ground. Beyond this though was a sight that they did not expect. A series of streets meandered throughout the hills beneath the Lemurian mountains. These paved streets led their way to the numerous keeps and castles. Their journey was almost over - they were standing in front of the Manors of Floria.

29

THE VIEW FROM THIS side of the wall was even more impressive than what they had seen countless times looking to the west from the docks or market. The castles themselves were tremendous, made of stone blocks in a myriad of colors. Each magnificent structure occupied a portion of the land here, layered with their own looming walls, turrets, and defense towers. This is where the rich and wealthy lay their weary heads at night. The Manors were the crown jewel of the city, if not all of Aileran.

Gazing up at the unbelievable sight, Odin and Simon had to make some difficult choices. With all of the meandering roads leading their way up the slopes of the hills, how would they select the correct one to get to Randall's? Unfortunately, there were no signs or directions. If you were invited to meet with a lord, you knew how to get to his keep.

The only chance that they had for success was to follow the Golden Kraken sigil's swaying in the breeze from the top of Randall's many turrets and towers. The problem was that the Golden Kraken was not the only sigil swaying freely. The skyline was dominated by the many symbols representing the great Lords of Floria.

The kraken, with its long, spiraling tentacles, was heavily represented, especially on the North side of the Manors; however, the White Gull of Lord Phillip and the Blue Ray of Lord Stone were dominant as well. In addition, lesser lords flew their sigils - an orange crab, a blue dolphin, and surprisingly a black spider. They could be seen proudly bustling in the wind from smaller keeps along the lower half of the Manors.

There were three possible roads to take that seemed to lead in the direction of the Golden Kraken. Three roads, three choices, and three chances at saving Lilly. Neither friend cared for those odds.

Simon eyed the three roads, stroking his beard slowly. Making difficult choices or decisions was never a skill that he felt comfortable or confident about. This was very important and he couldn't make a mistake now. One wrong turn and their journey could be compromised, leading to their death. Eventually he spoke up about the choices. "Which do we take mate? Left, right, or center?"

"I don't know for sure but I'm leaning towards the right. It seems like the majority of Randall's sigils are on the North end. Maybe his keep is on the fringe of the Manors. Then again, it looks really big from here. Maybe all three of them will lead us there."

Simon stopped his routine beard grooming and looked over at Odin, eyes full of wonder. "If that's the case mate, any choice is a good choice. We can't go wrong right?"

"Good point. That's just a theory though, Simon. I really don't know if they all lead there or if only one does. What I am wondering is where are all of the guards? Why was the outside so heavily guarded, but inside there's no one?"

With a nod Simon answered. "I said it back there in that lot with all of the wagons. Somethin's not right, mate."

"That's an understatement, my friend. Something is bloody wrong with this whole city. All of it starts right up here, with these damn lords. They know something about that thing haunting the streets.

They might even be responsible for what it does. When we get in there, I'm going to find out what this Randall fellow knows about all of it."

"Like I've said, I'll be there. Right beside ya until the end." Simon paused for a few moments, gazing at the three roads. "So, are we still leaning towards the right? It looks promising."

Odin looked over at the sailor, appreciating his charisma and glass half-full mentality. This situation was bloody hell; he knew it and Simon knew it. Any of the choices could lead them right to the gallows or worse. Chances were that none of them would make their way out of this alive, but he wasn't ready to die yet. He had been hiding, scared for months now, running away from his past. Was he going to run and hide forever or was he going to face the demons lingering in his heart?

Mia's death wasn't his fault, he knew that deep inside. He didn't plunge the knife into her gut, it was the damn thief trying to steal some bread for his family. Still, her fate seemed to haunt his every thought. He was ready to face the demons and give her the peace she deserves. He had torn himself apart over the events of that dreadful morning for long enough.

With tranquility in his voice, Odin responded. "I like the right one too Simon. I think it's a great choice."

Unlike the uneven, rough cobblestone streets throughout the city, the roads leading to the many opulent Manors were paved in thick, strong red brick. The road swayed back and forth up the slope through several switchbacks. Like the streets outside of the wall, tall yellowing grass bordered the road on each side, which presented cover if the need presented itself.

After clearing three switchbacks, Simon looked down on the rest of the city. From this height, the wall that they so creatively penetrated could barely be seen. The view beyond it was breathtaking. The markets were fully in bloom with their teals, oranges, and yellows. The expanse of this part of Floria was tremendous, but to see all of it from this vantage point was something of awe.

Beyond the markets, the parallel rows of businesses seemed to kiss the bay from where he stood. Few ever have the opportunity to observe the city like this and he wanted to cherish it, just for a moment.

Odin slowed down as well to take in the sights. The ships in Kobalt Harbor seemed like tiny white stars dancing in the Green Sea below. There was no wonder why the lords wanted to keep all of this to themselves. It was truly beautiful.

But he hadn't come this far to sight see. He came for answers, and possibly vengeance. After a brief moment to take it all in, he rallied Simon and the two continued their journey up the switchbacks leading to the Manors.

Two more switchbacks and they reached a plateau opening up to an amazing sight. In front of them was a colossal castle. Its heights were magnificent and the scale of the structure would engulf an eighth of the markets. The stone blocks used to construct this masterpiece varied from a light grey to a dull and weather worn teal.

Odin and Simon knew these colors quite well. James was a victim of the ruthlessness behind the colors. These were the colors of a powerful lord in Floria, one that happens to use the Golden Kraken as his sigil. The road to the right had paid off after all. Lord Randall's keep was half a league in front of them.

The two stood in the middle of the road gazing at the metaphorical monster that they had agreed to infiltrate and vanquish. They had finally reached their destination. The journey up to this point had not been easy, it had been down-right hell. They had overcome so many obstacles trying to find Lilly, the one person in each of their lives that really mattered at this point.

She had come into Odin's life spontaneously upon his arrival to the city. Before setting his eyes on her, the thought of love or a relationship seemed like it would never happen again, after the tragedy or course. For Simon, she had always been his little sister, regardless of anything else. The love for a sibling is not something that can be replicated. Lilly was all that mattered and they were going to fulfill this quest to free her, in triumph or death.

Simon brought his hand above his eyes once again to shield from the blazing sun overhead. "That's it, mate. That's bloody Randall's place. There's the kraken. We made it."

There was no response from Odin. This fortress didn't have a front door or a window that they could simply crawl through. Each manor had its own wall or fence, and Lord Randall's was the largest wall of any of them. Surprisingly, the sight of this next wall didn't hinder Odin. "Yes Simon, there it is. Now let's get over this thing and rescue our Lilly."

The two crept forward, keeping low and cautious with each step, listening to their surroundings. Upon reaching the wall, they gazed at this next test of their allegiance with confidence. This one was far less menacing, with no hired assassins on patrol or pin-point archers watching from above. In fact, there didn't seem to be any security anywhere.

Odin began inspecting the wall, feeling the stone and its imperfections. The stones were of different sizes, stacked high and mortared together. The crevices between the stones were deep and wide, creating ideal footing and space for grip. They weren't going to smuggle themselves through this wall; they were going to scale it. "How high do you think it is Simon? Fifteen, twenty feet?"

Simon shielded his eyes from the sun as he observed the wall from the base to the top. With a slight nod he answered. "I'd say so, it should be fairly easy to climb mate."

"I agree. What ... what do you think we are going to see on the other side?"

Simon began stroking his beard once more. Thinking about the question and the countless answers. "Well, I hope we just see his castle. It would be pretty nice if the door was wide open too. That's what I'm counting on, but ya never know, right?"

"That would indeed be very nice. Hopefully there won't be any surprises though. Do you think one of us should look first to get a feel or should we both look together?"

Simon eyed Odin. The look of uncertainty surrounded him like an aura. "I ... I'll climb to the top and take a gander. It would be smart for just one of us to do it, in case something happens. In case something isn't right, ya'll still have a chance to figure out another way in." He paused and looked at the ground, kicking a small stone. "But everything's going to be fine mate. Ya'll see soon enough when I call ya to the top." His positive words didn't match his tone.

Odin gently grabbed Simon by the arm. "Of course, everything's going to be fine. Hey, until the end, right?"

"Yeah, yeah mate. Until the end. Let me get up there and I'll call for ya in a second."

Simon faced the wall and outstretched his right arm as high as he could. His fingertips barely touched the cavity between the third and fourth stones, but he was able to get a grip with a slight jump. Hanging on the wall with just one arm, he lifted his body and found a minor footing to brace his weight, allowing his left hand to grab the crevice as well. He pulled himself up the side of the wall with tremendous effort, where he found a new abnormality in the stone which provided some strong footing. With his body outstretched, he continued to alternate arm and leg as he slowly ascended up the wall

The view from below resembled a lizard scaling the vertical face of a rock. Odin called up from below, checking on the sailor. "Simon, you are doing great. You are halfway up already my friend. Keep going."

The words of encouragement seemed to do very little because all he received from the sailor were curses and mumbles as the man continued his ascent. Odin realized how difficult this was going to be. He was in decent shape, adequate muscle tone, but watching Simon struggle made him nervous. The stout sailor wasn't the tallest man in the city but he made up for it with strength.

Simon was nearing the top of the wall when he suddenly lost his footing. The spontaneous action caused his body to crash into the face of the wall and he dangled there, stunned, hanging on by his two strong hands. After the sudden shock of the situation dissipated, and he realized he was okay, he reestablished his footing and continued to pull himself up. The scare hadn't hindered him and he was more driven to see this through.

With pebbles and dust raining down, Odin shouted up once again. "Simon, you okay?"

Simon resisted the urge to look down and talk to his friend. His eyes were held upward towards the top of the wall which was a few feet away now. He shouted his response hoping that it would travel down below. "I'm alright. Just lost my footing for a second. All's good, mate."

With a final stretch, Simon reached his fingers farther than he knew was possible and gripped the top of the wall with his right hand. He pulled his left foot up and searched for solid footing, finding it almost instantly. With that established, he pushed upwards and grabbed the top of the wall with his left hand, and then pulled with all of his remaining strength until his torso was firmly resting on the top of the wall. He swung his legs up and turned over face up, laying on the wall's top face, staring at the clear blue sky. Attempting to catch his breath and relieved that he had made it, he called out to his friend below. "I made it, I'm up here."

Odin cupped his mouth, hoping his words would travel to the top of the wall. "Simon, what do you see?"

Simon had yet to look over on the other side, he was still trying to recover from the difficulties of the climb. He slowly turned his head in the manor's direction, trying to see if there were any threats present. But there was nothing.

The castle was there, but there were no guards, no archers, nobody. There were no threats at all. This might be easier than either of them figured. They could possibly climb down the other side of the wall and walk right into the castle, demanding for Lilly's return. Still looking at the motionless castle, he sat up, smiling. He braced himself with his hands and quickly stood, admiring the castle and all of its glory.

Simon turned to deliver the great news to his friend impatiently waiting on the ground, but his eyes caught movement on the road some thirty feet away. Six heavily armed guards, adorning the teal and grey of Randall were approaching fast. Before he even had a chance to think or warn his friend below, an arrow pierced his shoulder causing him to lose his balance and take two steps backwards.

Odin, looking at his friend from below, witnessed the shot fly over his head and strike its target squarely. "SIMON!" Odin quickly turned to face the oncoming forces.

Stunned and confused, he glanced upward for a split second to see where Simon was, but the sailor was gone. The momentum of the arrow driving into his shoulder had caused him to rock backwards and he was no longer on the wall. Not having a choice, Odin turned once again to face the oncoming threat. He instinctively unsheathed his dirk, holding it towards the men with death and anger in their eyes. In an instant he was boxed in, three guards brandishing ten-foot spears pinned him against the wall while three other guards equipped with crossbows aimed their deadly arrows at his heart.

How did this turn so quickly? What was he supposed to do now? Without a second thought, he threw his dirk to the ground, issuing his surrender. They had failed her.

PART 5

A NEW GIFT

30

THE DUNGEONS BELOW RANDALL'S castle were what one might expect. Each cell in the dungeon was lined with three walls of limestone, while the fourth was thick black iron bars. There were six cells in all, three on each side of a wide corridor. Torches were staged between the cells to provide faint lighting. The dirt flooring provided little resistance from moisture or pests. There was no privy, or even a bucket for that matter. This was Odin's home now while he recovered from the beating he received from the guards before they took him into custody.

Laying on his side in the damp dirt, protecting his broken ribs, Odin was quickly awakened by the loud clatter of wood striking iron. Each morning, day after day, the gaoler came down the steep stairway and entered the corridor lined with cells, rattling each iron bar with his wooden club.

After making sure all of the prisoners were awake, the gaoler delivered a single scoop of slop for nutrition, presented in a wooden bowl without a spoon.. Odin had refused to eat the filth the first two days, but he knew he needed the energy to heal his many wounds. When the bowl was slid between the iron bars, he crawled over to it, nursing his side, and began devouring the contents ravenously. This was the only food source until the next morning, he had finally realized.

After the slop was delivered, the gaoler would then make his rounds to interrogate or terrorize the prisoners, depending on what he had already discovered. Interrogation was for those with tight lips, and terrorization was for those that had already confessed to their crimes.

Despite the pain he was suffering, Odin continued his defiance when being questioned. He had demanded to speak to Randall every time he was questioned and would not say anything more. With all that happened, he was still not giving up on the plan to save Lilly, and find out what was happening in the streets. He had already accepted the fact that Simon had perished from the fall off of the wall outside. This rebellious behavior was not favorable to the gaoler, and he had made that very clear each day.

"Speak maggot," the gaoler demanded, spittle flying from his mouth. "Why were you inside the walls?"

Odin leaned against the unforgiving stone of his cell, clutching his ribs with his left hand. He turned and faced the menacing man pacing the length of his cell. "I've told you. I want to see Randall. Take me to him or bring him here, I don't care."

The man growled and spat at Odin, missing him by a foot, the glob of phlegm sticking to the dusty floor of the cell. "So, it's the hard way once again I see. Don't think that your bravery will last much longer, peasant."

Odin observed the man carefully, praying that he was bluffing but knowing what was really coming. "Let me speak with your lord. I can explain everything once I see him. Please! I came to see Randall! Listen to me!"

The man looked at Odin with indignation, scowling at every word he heard. "If you are not going to talk, you know what will happen. So be it."

Odin quickly stood up pleading with the man for mercy. "No, no, no ... you don't understand. I need to see Randall. You don't have to do it. Please ... please don't do it again, please!"

The man didn't listen to Odin's pleas as he turned and walked back towards the stairway exiting the dungeon, ignoring the other three prisoners in their cells. The sounds of his footsteps got fainter with each step. The final sound was of the man unlocking the iron door at the top of the stairs. Odin was pacing his cell, still nursing his ribs with his left hand, knowing what was coming next. He had been through this the past three days, and each time was worse. His hand bore the cuts and mutilations from the actions that were about to be repeated.

The next few silent minutes were agonizing. Odin paced his cell wishing that something would happen to stop the pain that was coming. With terror streaking through his veins, his mind began to wander. He wanted to leave his body and go somewhere safe, some place where he couldn't feel the pain. His mind couldn't take the torture again.

He thought of Simon and Lilly, how they would always argue just like siblings are prone to do. He thought of his homeland, of his father, and he thought of ... Mia. Her face slowly seemed to appear deep within his consciousness. Beautiful fair skin spotted with freckles. Ruby red lips and bright green eyes. Long flowing red hair. She was perfect. As he focused on her face, the anxiety and terror of reality seemed to vanish. He was almost at peace sharing one final moment with the love of his life. But, in an instance, she was gone. The loud sound of the iron door up the stairs slamming shut brought him crashing back to reality. They were coming.

The gaoler, known as Borque, returned with friends, and they were carrying a device they referred to as Agnes. As Borque stepped onto the dirt floor, dust settling around his boot, he called out to Odin, who was now at the back of his cell, attempting to guard his injured side.

"This is your last chance maggot, why were you on this side of the wall?" His eyes shone with fury as he stalked his prey, locked behind the iron bars. He walked right up to Odin's cell and removed a silver-plated key from his pocket, toying with Odin like it was a game.

Odin watched as Borque and three of his henchmen impatiently waited outside of his cell door. Pacing back and forth like a pack of rabid hounds. "I already told you! I came to see Randall! Why are you doing this? Please ... please stop!" The hysteria in Odin's voice was haunting.

Borque cocked his head to the side and spat once again. He then eyed Odin, now cowering in the back of the cell. "So be it. You know what happens when I don't hear the truth." He looked over his shoulders at the guards behind him and smiled. "Owen, Elias, grab him. Ivan, bring Agnes in and set her up." Borque unlocked the door and the four of them entered the small cell, overcoming Odin in seconds, regardless of the kicking and screaming.

31

MINUTES LATER, ODIN NO longer had the will or drive to fight. He was secured by his wrists and ankles, gagged and strapped to Agnes. He hung his head, fists clenched in defeat and humiliation. But he knew that the worst had yet to come. The real torture would begin very soon.

Borque paced back and forth in front of his prey, eagerly salivating for step two in this process. His voice was cold, statuesque even. "Open your hands, peasant. Do it now or you won't have hands any longer. Did you hear me maggot?"

Odin had endured to this point but couldn't withstand another round. His muffled voice pleaded for the man to stop but there was no stopping Borque when the scent of blood was fresh in the air. Screams attempted to escape his mouth but the gag prevented them from reaching anyone. His only hope was to blackout and find that happy place once again. Through reluctance, he forced his fists to open and prayed that this would all be over quickly.

Borque walked up to Odin, securely embraced in the loving arms of Agnes, and pulled out his straight razor. He had already visited the index and middle finger of the right hand. Today's appetizer was the ring finger, lucky number three. Borque grabbed it, not allowing Odin to clench the hand again.

The two henchmen that strung him up applied pressure to his torso, not allowing him to move or squirm. With the precision of a doctor, Borque started his incision at the top of the finger and made his way down to the knuckle on the palm side. The muffled screams and shaking of the first cut halted his progress momentarily, but he would continue soon. He had a goal in mind.

The pain was so intense that Odin's entire body began to spasm, shaking severely. The two henchmen holding him down struggled with the ferocity of the convulsions but prevailed in the battle. Once the shaking stopped, Borque stepped back in to continue his handy work. He started the second cut at the knuckle, moving horizontally all the way around the finger, triggering another violent spasm.

"Hold him still. Dammit, hold him still!" The anger was boiling over within Borque. Lord Randall paid him well for his technical skills but it wasn't the money that motivated him.

The motivation came from inflicting pain and suffering. He was born for this job and loved every aspect of his position. "If you don't get him still, you'll be up there next! Hear me?" He eyed his two associates with contempt.

With the brief pause in cruelty, Odin attempted to gather his thoughts. The pain in his hand burned like a wildfire, reaching throughout the rest of his bound limbs. Another cut and he would blackout, he knew it. He hadn't been awake for the previous final cuts and he thanked the heavens for that. It was approaching, he could feel it deep within his soul. He yearned for its arrival, embracing the thought of not feeling, seeing, or experiencing any more of this.

Through his struggles, he was able to spit out the gag and release a final scream that could have been heard at the top of the Lemurians. The agony, despair, and torment that occupied the scream caused his assailants to stop and gaze at one another. They seemed confused, even a little unsure whether they should continue. Screams were common, but something was different about Odin's scream. Something was ... unnatural.

It took a few moments for Borque to collect himself, cautious about what just came out of his latest victim's mouth. But nothing would stop him from completing another masterpiece. As he stepped back in to complete his work, he gripped the bloody, saturated finger once again, holding it in place. He eyed Odin, waiting for another scream or spasm, as he raised the straight razor and moved it back towards the finger. Odin's head hung low, as if he was already unconscious. Slowly, and with precision, he placed the razor on the top of the finger once again. This final cut would run down the backside of the finger, stopping at the knuckle. As he prepared to make the cut, he thought he noticed movement from Odin and resisted the temptation to continue. He backed away, waiting and observing.

Odin twitched slightly, nothing like the spasms and convulsions from before. Just a minor flinch that proved he was still alive. After a few seconds, another twitch occurred though. Borque and his men didn't know what to make of it. They were still a little shook up by the scream from moments ago. Without warning, Odin lifted his head, revealing a slight smile. His eyes remained closed, shut off to the rest of the world. Had he found that happy place he so madly sought? No memory, no pain, no reality.

Borque felt like enough was enough. He pushed past his cautions and began barking orders once again. "Get in there and hold him." He eyed Odin with fury, boiling out of every word. "Ya think this is fun, maggot? Do ya? I'll show ya a really good time." With his two henchmen firmly supporting their weight against Odin, Borque held the straight razor against the side of his face and tried to approach. But he found that he couldn't move. With all of his energy he tried to take a step, but he was frozen in place, paralyzed, void of the ability to move. His eyes widened, raging with madness. The veins in his neck and forehead pulsated from the effort and straining, but he was helpless.

The two henchmen holding Odin released their grips. They slowly faced Borque with terror in their eyes, pupils dilated to the size of a copper. They tried to move off to the side of the cell but found that they could not move either. Their eyes were fixated on their paralyzed boss, or what was behind him.

Through all of this, Odin slowly started to come back to reality. He blinked his eyes several times, but his vision would not improve. The shock of the torture had effected every aspect of his body. His breathing was faint and his head throbbed. A loud, continuous buzz could be heard in the cell but he couldn't identify its source.

With a few more strong blinks, something slowly came into view in front of him, but the blurred vision made it impossible to see what it was exactly. It didn't really have a shape to it, but it was eerily dark. Odin continued to blink, hoping that his vision would improve and identify what the shape was. The entire event with Borque had been heavily stressful, and he felt unconsciousness peering down on him once again.

With a final attempt, he looked out towards the dark shape in front of him and something started to come into focus, slowly and deliberately. A color began to emerge within the darkness. Two new objects, crimson in color, began to appear. With a final blink and focus, he saw what they were. He had seen them before too. The Eyes were watching. Not able to maintain consciousness for a second longer, Odin dropped his head, allowing the darkness to take over and relieve him from this misery.

32

THE CHATTER OF VOICES filled his ears as he laid motionless, barely taking in enough air to live. His right ribs, already broken, ached even more from the latest series of violent torture. Death was the only way to escape this pain and suffering. He prayed and prayed for it, but would it be so accommodating?

The voices were near, as much as he could tell, feet away. They seemed slightly familiar, too. Slowly awakening from his deep slumber, Odin began to open his eyes and observe his surroundings. A massive limestone wall was inches away from his face. Taking in that extraordinary sight, he slowly rolled over. Through the agony of movement and shifting, he was able to see another wall made of pure limestone. Death had not been his mistress today; he was still in his prison cell.

Slowly sitting up and acknowledging his whereabouts, Odin found the iron bars at the front of his cell, where the sounds of the familiar voices were coming from. He could vaguely see what he assumed was another person. The blurriness of his eyesight made for difficulties with identifying who was outside of his cell.

With great and painful effort, he began to crawl towards the iron bars. As he was crawling, he looked down at his hands clawing at the dirt to advance his movement. Through his impaired vision, heavy bandages were noticed on his right hand. Upon noticing the bandages, memories of the torture began flooding his mind, triggering a maddening scream.

The voices stopped, and Odin attempted to control himself. The incoherence of reality was something that had plagued him since awakening on the dirt floor. Slowly, the thoughts of imprisonment filled his mind once again, along with the thoughts of Lilly and Simon ... and Mia. With great need, he continued crawling forward, spittle leaking from the side of his mouth.

The prize for all of the effort in his condition was possibly learning who was out there, whispering freely while he was incarcerated for seeking the truth. As he approached the bars, he gripped one tightly with the left hand only, favoring his bandaged right. Peering out through two of the bars, body hanging on the floor, he realized the voices weren't coming from directly outside his cell. They were coming from across the empty corridor, from the prison cells on the other side of the dungeon.

Two men kneeled at the front of their individual cells, gripping the iron bars, watching and wondering about the defiant prisoner now peering back at them. They knelt, getting as close as they could to whisper, separated by four feet on limestone between their cells.

"Did ya hear that, Mitch? That scream. He did it again, the same scream that summoned the bloody thing yesterday."

"Yeah, I heard it. How could ya not? What the hell's wrong with him though?"

"I don't know but something ain't right. Hey look." The prisoner on the right pointed in Odin's direction. "He's finally awake. Ask him what's wrong. Ask him what that thing was."

In a strong, authoritative tone, the prisoner on the left responded. "Why don't ya start, see what ya can get out of him? I'll talk to him soon enough."

"Alright, but help me if I lose him." The man on the right raised his voice, projecting it across the corridor hoping to get Odin's attention. "Hey mate, hey buddy. Can ya hear me?"

The sight in his eyes was returning with each heavy blink. Odin could see the two men now, clearly watching and observing him

"Yeah ... yeah, I can hear you."

"Bloody hell, he can still speak." The prisoner mumbled under his breath. "What the hell happened in there yesterday? What was that thing?"

Odin slowly pulled himself up into a seated position, favoring his side once again. Gazing out between the rough iron bars, he could clearly see the man he was speaking to now. The prisoner was older, probably in his mid fifties, grey streaking the majority of his black hair. From the look of his soiled and ripped clothes, he was either a peasant from the streets or he had been in this dungeon for countless years slowly rotting away. His thin frame suggested either as a possibility. Odin began to contemplate the man's questions but found that his memory was hazy once again. He couldn't recall the day before and he didn't understand the man's inquiries about the thing. Confusion and uncertainty began to set in.

"I ... I don't know what you are talking about. I can't remember anything. Did you see something?"

The man eyed Odin with bewilderment, not knowing whether to believe him or try to support him with his lost memory. "Ya don't remember what happened? Ya don't remember the ... thing?"

"You keep saying that. What does that mean? What did you see?" A bit of frustration was now mixing with the confusion. "What happened to me?" Odin looked down at his heavily bandaged hand, wondering how he received the injuries and who applied the dressings.

He held up his hand for the prisoner to see. "What happened to my hand? Who did this to me?"

The man shook his head, realizing that Odin was being truthful. Empathy began to run throughout his mind as he stared at Odin across the corridor. "Ya really can't remember any of it, can ya?"

Odin didn't respond, his eyes remained on his hand, straining to find the answers that were now haunting his thoughts.

"Ya don't remember the gaoler? Borque? What he was doing to ya?"

Odin merely shook his head side to side, stating nothing to the man.

"Well son, it's probably best that ya don't remember. That souvenir on ya hand was courtesy of that bastard. Got what he deserved though. He'll never do it again to another prisoner." The man held up his own disfigured hand for Odin's viewing pleasure. His index and middle finger were amputated at the knuckles. "See, I wear the badge too. Received them a long time ago though, boy."

Peering at the man's mutilated hand, Odin quickly averted his eyes back to the bandages covering his hand. With shock in his eyes, he finally broke away from his silence and asked the man a question. "Did ... did he do that to... to me? Are my fingers -"

The man cut him off before he could finish the question. "I don't think so, that damn thing came and stopped him from finishing. He definitely gave ya some cuts though. I'm not sure about the other two that he worked on either. I think ya'll heal up just fine."

Odin stopped gazing at his hand and eyed the prisoner once again. "What is this thing you keep mentioning? What was in my cell? What happened to the gaoler?"

The prisoner hung his head in guilt. He didn't want to be the one to tell Odin about Borque and his henchmen's demise. The news of his possibly amputated fingers was enough to shock a person into having a stroke. As he knelt there, thinking about how to answer the questions and not drive Odin completely mad, the cellmate to the man's left chimed in for support.

"Hey there boy, perhaps I can help ya with that."

Odin looked to the left, observing the other prisoner with hope in his eyes. The prisoner on the left was relatively the same age as the one on the right, now relieved that the conversation had been taken over. He had a strong build, possibly from years of manual labor. Must be new to the dungeons based on his powerful physique. His accent was local and he had dark hair greying slightly on the sides. There was a kindness to his eyes that seemed familiar as Odin watched him.

"Ya new to the city boy, fresh off the ship?"

Odin eyed the man with curiosity. "Yeah, I just landed a few days back. How did you know?"

"That's the easy part. Well, if ya just landed, then ya probably don't know much about the city and its secrets, right?"

Odin dropped his look, shaking his head slightly. "I don't know, my head is so fuzzy. It's hard to remember anything." Odin shut his eyes tight, trying to think. After a few moments he looked up again making eye contact. "I ... I remember something. Something about children. Children missing?"

The prisoner on the left took in a look of surprise, almost a look of fascination. "Ya have heard something; I can see that now. Well, ya aren't wrong about that. About the children that is. Many people go missing in this city every year. Do ya remember why or how?"

Odin stopped shaking his head, focusing on the recent memories swirling through his mind. Unfortunately, there were massive holes in each thought and memory causing further confusion and frustration. Digging deep into his consciousness, he began to remember a few things. Instantly he blurted out. "There was a man, and he was floating in the air."

The prisoner allowed a slight smile to appear across his face. "Okay, yeah his name was Borque."

Odin instantly responded, certainty in his voice. "No ... this wasn't a guard. This man was at the docks. I remember now. Something was in front of him. Something dangerous, and dark."

"Are ya saying that ya have seen this thing before yesterday, boy? Before Borque?"

"What is this thing that you two keep talking about? Why do you keep saying thing?" Odin's frustration was beginning to surface, his words quick and agitated, each word getting louder than the last.

The prisoner quickly got to his feet and gestured for Odin to calm down. "Okay, okay, calm down, lad. We don't need Jardin coming down here. He's been in a right pissy mood since Borque and his men disappeared, and I don't want to lose any of my fingers today." He took in a deep breath and exhaled a deeper sigh. With his nerves settled, he continued. "This thing has been here for centuries, maybe longer. I really don't know how long. All I do know is that if it wants ya, it takes ya. There's no escaping it." The prisoner paused for a moment looking up at the limestone ceiling of his cell. "It's evil, this thing is. It's dark and bloody evil."

Odin's emotions were cooling as he listened to the man describe the thing that had been brought up so often during their conversation. As the man finished, he responded. "Darkness. I remember how dark it was. It wasn't like the color black - it was darker than that. Yeah, and it had this man. It was... eating him or consuming his body, I don't know what it was doing to the poor bastard."

The man began to nod with each word that came out of Odin's mouth, squinting his eyes tight. "Yeah, ya have seen it, no doubt. That same creature was in ya cell yesterday eating Borque and his men, boy.

Survivin' it once is a miracle, how did ya manage to stay alive after seeing it twice?"

Odin couldn't believe what had just been said. He's seen this creature more than once? He could remember pieces of his encounter in the alley but nothing from the day before. He began to run the experience through his mind over and over again. The alley was a clear, coherent memory now. He started to backtrack in his mind all of the events before the alley, straining to remember and piece together the fragments.

How did I get there, and why was I there in the first place? He thought to himself. Instantly something clicked and a name popped into his mind. In a muffled voice he said, "Simon." He looked at the prisoner across the corridor and continued with his newly found memory. "I was with a man - a sailor - and I helped him get home after he had too many drinks. Yeah, I remember, and then I went into the alley."

Upon listening to Odin ramble on, the prisoner on the left's face changed from inquisitive to worried. Something about what the man with the lost memory was saying caused some alarm in his behavior. "Boy, did ya just say the sailor's name was Simon?"

Odin looked at the man with hope. His memory was slowly returning to him, and he remembered a good friend. A friend that he had been through a lot with recently. "Yes sir, Simon is his name. Short little guy with a long beard."

The prisoner dropped his gaze to the floor, deep in thought. Eventually, he looked back up towards Odin with distress wrapping every inch of his face. "Do ya know if ... if Simon is okay?"

The strange change in conversation and behavior was unsettling. Odin observed as the man's eyes frantically scanned the floor of his cell, impatiently waiting for a response to his question. Sensing the nervousness of the man and his inquiries, Odin answered to the best of his ability, given his limited memory of his friend the sailor. "I think so, I left him in his room that night. He must be okay."

The response did little to change the man's demeanor. Odin's disorientation and vague response to Simon's well-being certainly didn't put him at ease. The prisoner said nothing further about the mystery of the streets, the dungeon, or Simon. He simply stood up and slowly walked to the back of his cell, spontaneously ending his part in the conversation and leaving Odin and the prisoner on the right bewildered and confused.

Odin looked to the prisoner on the right, concerned that he had said something disheartening. "Did I say something or do something to offend him?"

The prisoner on the right took a few moments to respond. Staring at the floor, he swallowed heavily and finally answered Odin's inquiries. "Well, ya see... that bloke ya mentioned, Simon. I think he sort of raised Simon like he was his own son. All he's done since he got thrown in here a few weeks back is talk about Simon and his daughter. He's really concerned about both of them and ..."

Odin's eyes widened as he heard the man speak, sharing this valuable information. The more he thought about Simon, the more memories began to flood his brain. Flats in the market, the teal tent, hiding in the wagon were all vividly swirling around his mind once again. But with all of these memories another face began to emerge. A beautiful face, olive colored skin, and plump lips. Light brown eyes and dark, brunette hair braided and hung over her shoulder. Instantly Odin blurted another name, "Lilly!"

With the name echoing through the dungeon, the man on the left came running back to the bars, gripping them as tight as possible. His eyes were different now, anxious and full of despair as he locked eyes with Odin. "Do ya know Lilly, boy? Is she okay, where is she?"

Caught off guard by the demands, Odin stumbled with his words, trying to gather himself. "Umm... yes, I know her. She works at the-"

The man cut him off, not allowing another syllable to be spoken. "I know where she works ya idiot, it's my bar! Where is she?" His voice was hostile, angry for answers.

Odin eyed the man with astonishment. As the memories of Lilly came back, like a sweet dream that he never wanted to be awakened from, he remembered. "She's gone, I remember now, she's..."

"What do ya mean she's gone? What happened to her?" He paused and let out an animalistic roar, raging with anger. He began to shake the bars he was squeezing, demanding answers. "If ya did somethin' to her, I'll kill ya boy! Where's my little girl?" The man's eyes were fuming with hate, ready to strike as he screamed between the corridor at Odin.

Shocked and terrified at the same time, Odin had no choice but to try to clear his name. "I didn't do anything to her! I was trying to help her and they took her. I didn't hurt her, I swear. It was someone else."

The man calmed himself down through a series of heavy breaths. Pacing his cell like a wild beast waiting for his cage to be opened. After a final exhale, he asked Odin a question. One that meant everything to him. "Who took her, boy?"

The question lingered in his mind for a few seconds while he strained his memory, searching high and low for that answer. It was in there somewhere, hiding in the shadows of consciousness and dream. He reached deep and finally came across something. The merchant James told him who has her. With confidence and faith, Odin slowly stood up from the dirty floor of his cell, lightly dusting off his already ragged breeches. He looked the man square in the eye and said, "Randall. Randall has her."

The man didn't respond or say a word. He just glared at Odin, the look of despair and worry taking over his face once again.

Without notice though, the sound of the iron door at the top of the stairs opening and closing diverted everyone's focus and attention, followed by footsteps. Sheer panic ran throughout Odin as he leered at the opening, awaiting to see who had come down into the dinginess of this prison.

The footsteps, rapidly descending at first, slowed towards the bottom of the stairway. Black soldier boots were the first part to be viewed followed by the man's lower half. He continued forward and stepped off of the final stair revealing a thick torso, especially around the midsection, bedazzled by golden ropes. A teal cape hung from his shoulders, adorned with twin Golden Kraken brooches at the shoulders. His hair was thinning and cut very close, grey in color. Each finger housed a precious stone emblazoned with gold and silver.

That's not Randall. Odin thought to himself, paralyzed with fear.

Across the corridor, the prisoner on the left defiantly called out in a mocking fashion towards the dungeon's new guest. "Well, well, well. Nice to see ya again, Jardin. Come back to finish Borque's handy work? Might want to be careful, or ya might disappear too. It looks like ya beast is on the loose."

The bejeweled man ignored the man's taunts. His eyes were locked on a different cell. He stepped forward, not giving the prisoner a second of his attention.

The prisoner began shaking his cell bars violently once again, screaming at Jardin as he walked the corridor. "Look at me ya bastard. Where's my daughter, Jardin? Where's Lilly?"

The man didn't show an ounce of emotion as he turned and glared at the prisoner. His calm demeanor was unsettling, and there was a presence to him that was eerie, almost inhuman. In a soft voice he finally responded to the defiant, agitated prisoner.

"Don't worry barkeep, I'm not here for you. I will deal with you soon enough though, that is a promise. I'm here for that one," He paused and pointed a gold and emerald scepter in the direction of Odin's cell. "Today is his day and he will get his wish. Randall will see you now boy, but let me warn you, he is not in good spirits." Behind Jardin was a group of guards, all heavily clad in plated armor. He glanced back towards them and gave instructions. "Chain him up and take him to the throne room. Randall will be waiting, and he is not very patient these days. Don't make a mistake." Jardin handed one of the guards a golden key and proceeded to walk back towards the stairway. The last thing Odin could hear before the guards stormed his cell was the sound of the man whistling as he ascended the stairs.

33

A BLAZING fiRE ROARED in the hearth in the back of the wide throne room. Easily six feet tall and twice as wide, the arched stone feature demanded anyone's attention the second they walked into the room. An intricate carving, possibly made of mahogany, hung above the archway, displayed for all to see. It was the kraken, with its far-reaching tentacles stretched from one end of the hearth to the other, surrounded by a ring of the beautiful wood. It was an amazing sight, but the real focus of the throne room was of course the immaculate throne. Forged some forty years earlier, Randall's seat was plated in solid gold, on a steel frame. The plush arm rests, padded and layered with the finest silks from Opal, were dyed the familiar teal of the house. The oval shaped headrest, teal as well, adorned with a capital R in brilliant stitching, was encrusted with hundreds of fine rubies and emeralds. The brilliance and luxury of the throne cast little doubt about who was in control here. Thousands of peasants and merchants had kneeled in front of this great symbol of oppression before, and now it would be Odin's turn.

Odin knelt, shackled to the floor by his ankles and wrists. The iron cuffs were tight, chafing and unforgiving. He was currently alone in the lavish room, thinking to himself about how bad this had turned out for all them. The vision of Simon, arrow thrust deep into his shoulder and falling backwards continuously flashed before his closed eyes. Odin prayed that the sailor was dead before hitting the ground on the other side of Randall's wall. He deserved better than that.

There was also the thought of Lilly, and how she was violently hauled off by the puppets being controlled by Randall's strings. He had no idea of her whereabouts or her well-being. This was a nightmare that he wanted to wake up from. This was not the way his new life was supposed to end. As he knelt there, head lowered deep in thought, the agonizing silence became too much for him. With a bellowing scream, he called out for the lord he had tried so hard to come and see. "Randall! Randall!"

The yells continued for several minutes, echoing through the wide throne room. No response ever came. He was there alone, lost in his thoughts, seeking answers to questions that could not be real. Eventually, reality began to set in and he stopped the screams. Tired, angry, and out of breath, he slowly slumped over, giving in to this form of torture. He laid on the paved floor of the throne room, shackled to the ground, not caring about what was going to happen to him.

What did he have to live for? His friend Simon was dead, Lilly probably was too. Her father Mitch, defiant and maniacal, will be murdered before too long. The love of his life had been buried for months. What was left? There was nothing. Then...

A small wooden door to the right of the throne opened.

The door was stained very dark, almost black in color, with matching rivets and handle. The first to come through the opening was the man with the magnificent stomach, known as Jardin. As he entered, carrying himself with a sense of self-worth, teal cape floating behind him with each step, he eyed the broken man lying on the floor without a will to live. As he approached, he asked Odin a question in that soft, confident voice of his. "Are you ready to see your lord, boy?"

Odin's spirit had been broken; he didn't care about the plan any longer. Nothing was going to be accomplished here. He locked eyes with Jardin but didn't respond. He just continued to lay on the paved floor, wishing that this could all be a dream after all.

"It would be wise of you to cooperate, lad. I myself am a generous and forgiving man, but your lordship doesn't exactly possess those qualities. He doesn't quite tolerate insolence or insubordination." Jardin glared at Odin and looked towards the hearth. His eyes averted up towards the magnificent carving of the kraken, proudly displayed above. "Do you know why Lord Randall chose that creature as his sigil?" He paused for a split second but didn't give Odin a chance to respond. "Of course, you don't, so why would I ask? Lord Randall has his tentacles in all aspects of this city: the docks, the brothels, the markets, and even the Manors. He owns this city, boy. He owns Floria."

As the man was speaking, Odin slowly lifted his head off of the cold paved floor, and began to get into a seated position. This was not a sign of respect, he just felt like maybe if he sat up this man would stop talking. He was ready to die, and he knew Randall would be the executioner. The end was near.

"Ahh, yes. That's much more appropriate for your lordship. Thank you. When Randall comes in here, be prepared to answer two questions." The man paused once again, admiring the wooden kraken above the hearth. "The first question is why did you want to see him? From all that Borque discussed with me, that was your only response during your entire stay in our fabulous dungeon. You wanted to see Randall. Why? I want you to think about your answer to this question very carefully. Your response may decide your fate." He paused once again turning his back to Odin, admiring the sights of the hearth, the carving, and the throne itself.

The answer to the question was easy. He recalled everything now. The night in the alley, the attack at the docks, the merchant James and his brutal death, and Lilly. Where was Lilly and was she still alive and well? He now realized that he had two answers to the first question.

At the start of their journey, the three of them wanted to find Randall and seek answers about the mystery in the streets, the so-called Eyes that haunts the city. When you had a problem that you couldn't solve yourself, the right thing to do was to seek out your lordship. This all changed after he and Simon had visited the merchant James and found him lying in a puddle of his own blood, breathing his last breaths.

The second answer was Lilly. He knew that Randall had her, locked up somewhere in this very castle, or worse. The real reason he and Simon came all of this way was for her, to rescue her and if someone got in their way then so be it. The more he sat there, head hung low thinking about her, Lilly, the woman that made him feel like a man once again, the more he needed to find out her fate. Maybe he wasn't quite ready to die after all. If she was still breathing, then there was a reason for Odin to breathe as well. Taking all of this in, he lifted his head and responded.

"Randall has answers."

Jardin turned around, confusion plastered across his smug face. He stared at Odin, sitting on the floor of the throne room, shackled and unable to move like a common criminal. "Of course, he has answers, boy. He is your lord and mine. He has all of the answers." He paused momentarily, shaking his head. "What answers are you searching for? Remember, be careful and cautious about your response."

"I need to know where my friend is. Her name is Lilly. I was told that you took her, after you killed James!" Odin's voice was hostile, aggressive.

The loud outburst didn't impact Jardin at all. He stood there, arms behind his back, glaring holes through his next victim. The man's eyes were terrifying, and his lack of emotion in all situations was incredibly unnerving. He had just been accused of murder, a crime punishable by death, and he didn't even blink an eye. After a few, painfully silent moments, he finally responded.

"Boy, I take many people and do terrible things to them all the time. That is my job. I do the dirty work that Lord Randall doesn't need to be bothered with- and I enjoy it." Jardin stepped closer to Odin, getting within a few feet. He leaned down, so that the two could be at eye level. "Tell me, who is this Lilly that you are searching for?"

The defiance was slowly boiling over in Odin's veins as he listened to the man. Hearing him discuss how he abducts and tortures people without an inch of remorse wasn't the hard part to hear. It was the fact that he didn't know who Lilly was. How could he not know that name? Or was there something deeper occurring here, like a game of cat and mouse.

Either way, Odin's anger was escalating, and he began to fling it at the emotionless man in the teal cape. "You know who she is, the bar-keep's daughter! She went to get help from James and you abducted her! Where is she!"

The man remained unfazed. He kneeled there, face to face with Odin, sneering. Looking at Odin as if he was a cockroach scurrying for the dark to hide. "Ahh ... the barkeep's daughter. She's a pleasant peach that one. I believe you had the pleasure of meeting her father in the dungeon. Mitch, is it?" His facial expression was condescending. "Yes, that's right, Mitch the barkeep and his beautiful daughter. What is she now, say twenty five or so?"

"Why do you care? Where is she dammit! If you hurt her, I'll ..."

Jardin cut him off before he could finish the threat. "You'll do what, boy? You are shackled to the floor, slowly awaiting the execution that is certainly coming your way for whatever you did in the dungeon. You know something and you better start talking."

Odin's rage calmed for a second, not understanding the rapid change in the conversation. This man was not to be trusted, that was a fact. But what was he searching for?

"What are you talking about? What do you think I did in the dungeon?"

Jardin glared at Odin with frustration in his eyes. "Boy, stop playing games! How did you do it?" He paused for a moment to gather himself, sighing deeply. "Lord Randall will be here soon, and he is expecting answers. Now let's get back to our original conversation. There is a second question that you need to answer. I want you to really think about this one, too. Why did the creature come into your cell and kill Borque?"

The question caught Odin by surprise. The first question was easy to answer, he knew why he sought out Randall. How was he supposed to answer a question like this though? There was no answer because there was no explanation.

From all of the lore that he had learned about the creature, it either feeds off those in the streets after dark or it seeks out those that had been marked for death by someone controlling it. He had no answer.

"I ... I don't know. I don't even remember it coming. That bastard Borque was slicing up my hands and then I blacked out. I don't remember it at all, I swear."

With heavy insolence, Jardin replied. "You are holding something back, boy. I can smell it. I've interrogated thousands of people and they all have one thing in common. Do you know what that is?" He didn't allow Odin to respond. "They cooperate and give me what I want. Are you going to give me what I want?"

Odin looked at the man with astonishment and confusion. He didn't know why the creature was in his cell; he didn't even remember it happening. How could he answer the question? With most of his anger and defiance spent once again, Odin dropped his head and answered. "I don't know, I really don't."

"So be it. If you are interested in seeing your friend again, I suggest you start cooperating." Jardin turned and walked back towards the black as night door to the right of the throne and opened it. He looked back one final time in Odin's direction, smugness filling his entire demeanor, before slamming it shut.

34

AFTER AN HOUR OF agonizing silence, the black door once again reopened. Four armed guards entered and lined up near the throne, two to each side. These were Lord Randall's personal guards. Their ten-foot lances were pointed directly at Odin.

A few seconds later, Jardin came out of the door once again and took his place to the right of the throne. The only thing missing from this party was Lord Randall, and being that he was rather impatient these days, Odin wouldn't have to wait much longer to learn of his fate.

Without notice, Jardin, hands clasped behind his back, began to speak. "You've requested to see your lord and he has granted your wishes. Be prepared to answer his questions boy, as I've instructed you to do. Your life and your friend's may depend on it."

Odin couldn't control himself. "Where is Lilly? She's alive, isn't she? Tell me! Please tell me the truth! I'll tell you whatever you want to hear!"

Jardin's face showed a bit of guile. A slow, deceptive smile started to cross his lips as he eyed Odin. This was fun for him, a game, and he was very good at this type of game. "It sounds like you are ready to cooperate after all, boy. Soon enough you will see your friend, I promise you that. Be prepared, your lord is ready."

Without notice, all four guards redirected their lances away from Odin and towards the ceiling of the throne room in unison, eyes still focused and peering at the prisoner shackled in the center of the room. Jardin, standing tall, turned and faced the black door, hands still clasped behind his back. Odin's eyes followed Jardin's to the door, now abruptly opening. Lord Randall had finally made his appearance.

Walking through the door was an older man, grey streaks throughout his thick hair. Equipped with black soldier boots, teal breeches and a golden surcoat, this man had all the qualities of a king. Each finger carried a precious gem and a crown sat atop his head, shining in the light from the hearth. Emeralds and rubies were encrusted within each tooth. Like his trusted advisor, a teal cape was clipped to his shoulders by two golden kraken brooches, swaying behind him with each step that he made towards his throne. A golden sword hung from a leather belt strapped around his waist. The pommel of the sword was adorned with a massive teal stone.

He quickly made his way to the throne and began to sit, signaling the house guards to again change the direction of their lances from the ceiling back towards Odin. Finally comfortable on his ornate throne, he eyed Odin directly in front of him. His expression wasn't angry or menacing, but inquisitive.

"My advisor has informed me that you wish to ask me some questions. Is this true?"

As the lord was speaking, something connected within Odin's mind. He had never seen the lord before but maybe he had heard his voice. The uniqueness of his accent could not be forgotten. It was strange. Now locking eyes with Randall, the man he had been through so much to finally see, he answered with authority of his own. "Yes Lord, I do have questions."

Randall continued his gaze at Odin, searching for any hint of fear or uncertainty and finding none. "Very well, ask away. I have a few questions of my own."

Odin reflected on the conversation he had earlier with Jardin. Why had he come this far to Randall? It was for her - it was for Lilly. "Where's Lilly? The barkeep's daughter," he asked with confidence.

Lord Randall's expression didn't change. He wanted to dig into this even more now. "You are a brave one, I'll give you that. Not many souls would come into my household and ask questions about fugitives." He gestured towards Jardin on his right, and the man left the room, exiting through the black door. "Let me reassure you, since you are so worried about your friend, that she is alive and well. She has been my guest for the last week. A precious gift from my trusted advisor."

Odin didn't know whether to be relieved or terrified. The news that Lilly was alive and well reduced almost all of the despair and heartache that had plagued him since leaving James's tent days ago. But in the back of his mind, the idea of her being a guest, or more likely prisoner, within these walls caused more anxiety. He knew deep down that she was alive - Randall has no motives for deception. But was she well? That was another question that he needed to find the answer for.

"If she is alive, show her to me."

"All in good time young man, all in good time."

Frustrated and worried, Odin blurted out. "If you or your henchman have hurt her, I'll..."

"Silence!" The thunderous outburst practically shook the room. "You dare come into my household making threats. I rule here, with an iron fist if needed." The inquisitive look that had plastered his face thus far was gone. Anger and arrogance began to surface. "Listen here boy, I have answered your question with honesty. As the lord of this keep, that is my duty. You have already answered my first question with your own. I understand that you seek my new guest and I will grant that wish shortly. In the meantime, you will answer my questions. Do you understand?"

Odin looked on defiantly. As the lord's temper came to the surface, his voice seemed even more familiar. "Yes, I understand."

"Very well then, answer this question and I will bring her to you." Randall leaned forward on his throne, smiling from ear to ear.

Odin nodded in agreement.

"How did you get inside The Manor's walls?"

At this point in the journey, there was no reason to be dishonest. "I hid in the back of a cargo wagon and the guards at the gate didn't check the merchandise. Once I was inside, I came looking for you."

Randall's eyes widened at the response. Curiosity once again entering them. "Very interesting. Very resourceful, too. So, I'm sure you had a chance to see all of my supplies in the cargo lot."

When Randall said the words, a memory finally clicked with Odin. That voice, he had heard it before, when he and Simon were in the back of the wagon. It was Randall having a conversation with the waggoneer. It was Randall discussing the celebration for a new beginning.

Odin didn't understand what any of this meant yet, so he merely answered the man's question. "I did. I saw all of it. I also heard the waggoneer state that all of the goods were for a celebration of some sort."

"Ahhh, you are correct about that young man. What is your name by the way?"

Odin kept his eyes locked with Lord Randall. Was this some ploy or was he being genuine? Why did he suddenly care about his name? "My name is Odin."

Lord Randall slightly cocked his head to the side thinking. "You are not from here are you, Odin? As I recall, the name derives from the continent to the south - Milstone, correct?"

Odin gave the lord a slight nod.

"Very well Odin, all of the supplies are for a celebration. A grand celebration that will change this city forever. It will change and cleanse it forever." The words chilled Odin.

He wanted to see Lilly, to know that she was alive. "I've answered your question Lord, now be a man of your word and bring Lilly here." With a shackled hand, he pointed to the paved floor he was kneeling on.

"I am a man of my word. You will see that very soon. My advisor is fetching her as we speak, bringing her here to this fabulous throne room." He paused for a moment to take in his tremendous creation, lusting over every inch of it. "Tell me something else, Odin. When you were vividly helping me understand how you entered our impenetrable gates, you used the pronoun I. Are you sure you were in the wagon alone?"

This was some sort of ploy, and Odin was not going to let him toy around like this. "You know I wasn't alone Randall. You know I had a friend with me and your men killed him. Filled him with arrows and he plunged to his death off of your wall. Don't ask me questions that you already know the answer to."

The hostile, authoritative voice was returning. "You do not have the right to tell me a thing, boy! I am Lord Randall, proprietor of Floria, and ruler of this forsaken city. I swing the axe, noose the rope, and pull the chains. One more comment like that and you will truly see my fury." He held Odin's eyes, disregarding him as if he was a speck of dust. Staring right through his inner soul. Once the heat cooled, Randall continued. "Respect is important Odin, and in order to receive it you must earn it. I'm sure you understand that reasoning coming from Milstone where respect is so highly regarded. I am aware of your friend, the sailor. I wanted to see how honest you are, even in a situation like yours. I appreciate the honesty, I truly do. But there is something that you are not aware of."

The vagueness of the comment left Odin's mind spinning in circles. What was he not aware of? Why was this man still playing games with him? He refrained from another outburst, halting the man's cruel intentions, or giving him a reason to show his wrath. "What am I unaware of Randall? What don't I know?"

A slight chuckle could be heard coming from the lord's mouth followed by a sly grin. Victory was right around the corner and he could taste it. "We will discuss that soon, but first, as a man of honor, I will deliver on my word. You wanted to see the barkeep's daughter, correct?" Odin didn't answer, instead opting for another nod. "Well, let's see her. Jardin," He paused and looked over at the black door, "Bring my guest in."

Odin's attention turned to the black door once again. It opened rapidly and behind it was the figure of a woman. He instantly recognized the curvy features of her body. Lilly was still wearing the tight fitting blue dress, but it was soiled and had several rips in the hem. Her hair wasn't neatly tied back in the long braid she would wear - it was down, hiding her face from his view. Bruises and scrapes covered her bare arms. She wasn't a guest in Randall's house. It looked more like she was a toy, tossed around and forgotten after playtime was over.

Behind Lilly was Jardin, holding a silver chain. The man gave Lilly an aggressive shove in the back, forcing her to stumble out of the door and into the throne room. While doing so, Odin noticed that the chain that Jardin was holding was connected to a black colored choker wrapped around her lean throat. She was a prisoner just like Odin and the many others that had come before them. Jardin entered the room next, violently yanking on the chain and forcing Lilly towards the throne, still occupied by Randall. Both she and Jardin took their places to the right of the throne, fully on display for all to see.

"As you can see Odin, she is alive. I am a man of my word."

Odin's relief became too much to withhold. Seeing her in the flesh and finally knowing that she was alive caused an emotional outbreak. "Lilly, Lilly, it's me Odin! I'm here! You're going to be okay - I promise you!" Sobbing, and tears streaking his cheeks, he turned and faced Randall again. With rage in his voice he asked, "What did you do to her?"

Randall's voice, full of ruse, slowly answered the question. "Like I do with all of the pretty little things that are presented to me as a gift. My advisor here takes care of all of my interests, financial or personal. She is alive. I will give you that."

"What's wrong with her face? Why can't I see her face, Randall?"

Lord Randall looked over at his confidant. "Show him our handy work Jardin, show him what happens to merchants when they try to get involved in my affairs."

Jardin yanked on the chain connected to Lilly's neck, pulling her head back. Her thick, dark hair flung over her head exposing her face. The sight was very concerning. Her bottom lip, split on the right side, still leaked blood that covered her chin. In addition, her right eye, black and blue, was severely damaged, exposing broken blood vessels.

As Odin gazed at Lilly, beaten and bloodied, his anger exploded once again. "I'll kill you! I'll kill you!" Trying to stand and straining against the shackles, he screamed at the lord like a madman, fragile mind snapping in two. "How could you? How could you do that to her?"

During the entire exchange, Lilly remained motionless, eyes glued to the paved floor. Her skittish mannerisms were so alien. She had been broken, in so many ways.

Meanwhile, Odin continued to pull on his chains, fighting with every inch of his being, trying to break loose from the shackles that held him tied to the floor while cursing at the lord. Randall simply shook his head back and forth in disappointment, disregarding the violent attempts as if they were a bothersome gnat flying around one's head.

"You have disappointed me, Odin. I thought that you would learn from your mistakes. Apparently, I was wrong."

"You're a murderer and a liar! Look at what you did to her. Look at her, you monster!"

Randall stood from his throne, aggressively pointing at Odin. "Boy, you have pushed me too far! I am a reasonable man, but I will not succumb to your pathetic insults. Listen here Odin of Milstone, you will die today, here in this very throne room. But before I unleash my vengeance, I have another question for you."

With hate and agony in his eyes, Odin nodded once again, not saying a word to the lord or mentioning the guarantee of his death.

"Tell me how you did it."

"How did I do what? What are you talking about?"

Lord Randall rolled his eyes in frustration as he again took a seat in his lavish throne. "Listen very carefully. How did you summon my beast How did you summon The Eyes?"

Confusion and bewilderment struck Odin like a hammer and an anvil. What was the lord talking about? He hadn't summoned the monster, it just appeared in his cell when Borque was slicing him up. Where was Randall getting this theory from?

With defiance and repulsion, Odin responded. "I don't know what you're talking about. Your monster just appeared out of nowhere. I don't even remember it happening."

Lord Randall's eyes narrowed to a squint as he stared at Odin, shackled and helpless in the center of his throne room. "Well Jardin, I think you were right after all." He turned to his left to eye the trusted advisor standing at guard, hands tightly clasped behind his back. "It does not seem as though Odin from Milstone is going to be very cooperative."

"I agree my lord. How should we do it?" Jardin snarled while twirling a piece of Lilly's hair in his fingers.

A slight laugh came from the lord's mouth. "Ah, that's the easy part. I will summon the beast and that will be his fate. I know he has seen it before but today will be the last time. Unless he changes his mind and answers my question."

Jardin dropped the piece of hair and faced his lord. "I hope he does change his mind my lord but unfortunately, I have my doubts. He is rather defiant, this one. Unless of course he knows the truth."

With much sarcasm, Randall quickly responded. "That's right, Jardin. I almost forgot. Odin from Milstone, if I don't have an answer within the next hour, you will not be the only person to succumb to the beast today." Lord Randall paused and looked over at Lilly, still trembling, hiding behind the long locks of dark hair obscuring her battered face. "Oh, I don't mean her. I enjoy her too much to waste a perfectly ripe peach like that."

Odin listened on, even more confused. There was no way to answer a question he didn't understand, and who was this other person that Randall had mentioned would perish as a result of a wrong answer? "If not Lilly, then who?"

With a deviant smile, Lord Randall held his hands together, finger-tips touching. "Jardin, humor your lord and bring me the girl, then go fetch the sailor."

35

SEVERAL MINUTES PASSED BEFORE Jardin returned, giving Odin adequate time to think about all that transpired in such a short amount of time. He couldn't believe what he heard.

Simon had survived the fall somehow. The thought of his friend, still alive and breathing, brought hope to his heart, despite knowing that they would all be dead soon. He knew deep down Randall had no intentions on sparing Lilly.

His eyes continued to move between the lord, smiling deeply in his direction, and the black door. Lilly sat on Randall's lap like an obedient child while the man's gaze bore through Odin's soul. The agony of waiting was dreadful, but eventually, the black door opened again.

Standing in front of it was Simon, alive but in rough shape. The arrow was still lodged in his right shoulder, broken off mid shaft, and he was very weak. Infection had taken over, based on the color of Simon's skin and lips. Once again, Jardin shoved his victim in the back, causing the sailor to fall face first on the paved floor of the throne room. As he stumbled to his feet, Odin observed a significant limp in his left leg. Possibly a broken leg, based on how he favored it when setting his foot down. Perhaps that long fall did some damage after all.

Odin had no words. He couldn't believe it was going to end like this. All three of them together one last time. In their short time together, they had been through so much. They were already like family to him.

"This was the surprise I was waiting for Odin. I wanted to see your eyes the moment you realized your friend was still alive. This is why I do it Odin. This is my pleasure."

Odin gave a slight shake of his head. He then looked up at the lord, still holding Lilly on his lap. "You are worse than that creature of yours. You know that right? You are the real monster in Floria."

"Ahh Odin, compliments are not going to get you out of this young man. You and your friends are already dead. Make no mistake about that. Before I unleash my fury, I'll give you one last chance to tell me the truth." Randall paused waiting for acknowledgement. Once he received it, he continued. "I am the only one that can summon the creature, yet it appeared in your dungeon cell, and you were not harmed. How did you do it?"

"I've already told you. I don't know what happened. You don't have to do this. You don't have to kill all of us. It's me you want. Let my friends go, please!"

"If it was only that easy. You already know too much to live young Odin from Milstone. Since you are not going to tell me your secret, I have no choice."

Jardin gave another violent shove to Simon's back, causing him to stumble forward towards Randall and his throne. Walking behind the wounded sailor, Jardin approached his prey, reached around and grabbed the end of the arrow shaft. He yanked and twisted the shaft causing a violent scream to pour out of Simon's mouth. Holding the shaft tightly, he forced Simon to the right of Randall and made him kneel on the cold, paved floor facing his friend.

After the violent act subsided, Lord Randall continued. "You see Odin, all of you know too much, and I am becoming rather impatient.

I have a celebration to attend. The great cleansing of Floria. It's a shame you and your friends will not be alive to see any of it."

Odin's rage had escalated to new levels, sitting bound and helpless, while this madman planned his death. There was nothing that he could do, but he still had a voice and an ounce of need. If he was going to die today, he needed to at least get the answers that the three of them sought at the beginning of this tragic journey. With tears in his eyes, he locked onto Randall once again.

"Your Lordship, I have answered your questions to the best of my knowledge, whether you believe me or not. I have one more question for you before this all ends. Give me and my friends that last request."

Lord Randall looked over towards Jardin, still hovering over Simon, with a look of puzzlement. He was used to those being interrogated giving in and telling all. A last request by someone close to death usually involved something about one's family or finances, but it had never been to answer a final question before. Jardin simply shrugged his shoulders, acknowledging that he was also confused by the request.

After a few intense moments, Lord Randall began to nod. "Your proposition intrigues me. I find it humorous that you wish to ask me a final question knowing that the answer will die as you take your last breath. But, as you and your friends already know, I'm an honorable man and I will grant this final request, young Odin of Milstone. Ask away."

"How do you do it? How do you control the creature that everyone in the city calls The Eyes?"

Lord Randall's expression changed from intrigued to disturbed immediately. He had never told a soul his secret before, except his trusted advisor Jardin. The idea of relinquishing the truth behind his power was not a comforting thought, let alone an intelligent one.

If someone else knew the truth, would they be able to control the creature in the streets the same way that he had for over forty years?

His immediate thought was to get this over with already, kill the three of them and continue with his plans for the rest of the city. But the more he thought about the inquiry, the more he liked the idea. Jardin was the only living soul that knew the truth, and he had never been able to boast about his strange, powerful ability openly before. This was a chance to show others why he was the most powerful lord in Floria.

"Odin of Milstone, most would be executed immediately for asking such a bold question, yet, an idea has recently sparked within my mind that may help this poor city and its crude inhabitants. You wish to know my secret," Lord Randall paused and leaned forward on his throne making sure that he was eye level with Odin, "Or more importantly, you wish to know our secret. Is that correct?"

Odin's mind couldn't understand the angle that Randall was trying to play here. He had told him everything that he remembered about the night he was tortured by Borque. Why was this madman still intent on assuming Odin knows more than he is revealing? "I ... I don't understand Randall. I've told you everything, I swear it. Just please ... tell me how you do it. I need to know!"

Lord Randall's eyes tightened, listening for any clue of deception in Odin's voice and hearing none. Maybe the man shackled to his floor was being honest after all, but something happened in that cell and it wasn't Randall's doing. Even if this man discovered the truth, he would be dead soon and never have the ability to use it.

"Very well. You see Odin, I didn't always have this gift, this strength. I acquired it after an event that left me broken, both physically and emotionally. When I was a young man, long before I was Lord Randall, I was just Randall, a lord's fifth son with little claim. I did have a beautiful wife and a child. You've probably noticed that there is no wife or child running through this throne room."

"What happened to them?"

"They perished. They were murdered in the streets by a peasant. He was hungry you see, would do anything for a few coppers, so he killed my wife and daughter for her purse. Slit both of their necks for eight coppers." Randall's voice was stoic, emotionless.

Odin remained silent, breaking eye contact with Randall, thinking about his own past, about Mia.

After a brief pause, Randall stood and started to pace in front of the throne. "You see, as a young man, I was devastated. I had just lost everything and I would do almost anything to get it back. My heart was broken and I had given up the will to live. I wanted my family back and the only way to see them again was to die myself."

Odin averted his eyes from the lord momentarily, thinking about his past. "What happened to the peasant, the one who murdered your family?"

"I witnessed the peasant put to death from the gallows. His head came clean off as the rope snapped, but it wasn't enough to take the pain away." He paused for a moment to let the vision set in. "Later that day, I recalled the stories about the creature. I'm sure you have heard a few of them yourself. The evil that hunts young children in the streets if they are out past sunset."

Randall eyed Odin briefly, looking for acknowledgment that he knew of the stories. Once Odin gave a slight nod, Randall continued.

"Well, I wanted to die and I wanted the creature to take me to see my wife and daughter. One night, around the witching hour, I went looking for it, but it never came to take me. Night after night, I continued to search for my escape, but I always returned to my empty keep, mourning my losses and the fact that I was still here. It wasn't until the sixth night that I finally found it, or more precisely, it found me."

A slight shiver ran throughout Odin as he listened to the story, recalling his own experience in the alley. Based on what he had been told, this thing had interacted with him on at least two other occasions, but why? He had to know the truth. "What happened? Why didn't it give you the peace that you longed for?" As he spoke, his eyes shone with his desperate need.

"Interesting inquiry, young Odin. Unfortunately, I do not know for sure. When I saw it for the first time, I was instantly immobilized, frozen in fear of what my eyes were showing me. My beast slowly approached, pulsating, humming it's rhythmic, beautiful tune, and then I saw them. The Eyes, red as the coals of a scorching fire. Red as the blood coursing through my very veins. But then... the beast stopped. I can't explain why, but it communicated with me somehow. It felt my pain, my agony from within. It...saved me."

Odin started to shake his head, not believing what he just heard. "No, that can't be true. That thing doesn't think. It just feeds. It's a monster, just like you!"

"Believe what you wish Odin. You will see that it is the absolute truth soon enough. From that day on, I found that I could reflect on my pain, my suffering, and aim it at any soul within the city. My creature did the rest. I have become the most powerful lord in Floria because of this gift. I have built my empire behind this secret and have helped many along my way to the top. This ability has not been used only for selfish advancements. Many have come to me asking for help and I have granted that request more times than I can count."

Randall paused and ran his fingers through Lilly's thick, dark hair, exposing her battered face once again. He gripped a large handful, holding it tight, yanking her head back in the process.

"Take this little peach here. Her father came to me many years ago, vengeful and broken. His wife had just been killed as I recall. A mugging gone wrong in the alley behind his tavern. It must have been, what, twenty something years ago? He and I made a deal the next day and the murderer received his justice. I make the same deal with all of them, Odin. Once your first born reaches the age of twenty five, you belong to me. You met Mitch, in the dungeons."

Randall was practically glowing at this point. Pride and arrogance seeping out of his pores, filling the entire room.

"All of the peasants, merchants, and putrid beings scraping by in this forsaken city will soon be at peace. The cleansing is coming." Randall abruptly stood, causing Lilly to fall to the floor, once again hiding her face with her thick hair. "Now Odin, all of your questions have been answered and I am growing impatient. Are you ready for all of this to end? Are you ready to see the beast for the final time?"

As Odin contemplated all that was just said, Lilly, still laying on the floor, looked to her left and found Simon. He was mere feet from her and she scurried towards him and embraced the sailor, holding him tightly around the waist as he knelt. The pain and shock of his injuries couldn't keep Simon from returning the loving touch. He reached over with his right arm and held her around the shoulders. The two sat there together, on the cold paved floor, accepting whatever was going to happen next, and not caring as long as they were together.

Meanwhile Odin was frantic. He began to violently pull on his shackles, blood trickling from his wrists as a result. This was not supposed to be how it ended for him. Floria was supposed to be the start of his new life. He had traveled too far and had been through too much to just wait for all of it to be over. He had seen that creature enough too and wasn't about to see it again.

As he struggled to break free from his bondage, he cursed the lord, adding fuel to the fire. The more he struggled and strained though, the more energy he found. Adrenaline pumped through his very soul and he felt truly alive, as if the shackles bound to his limbs would simply disintegrate at the next tug. He stretched and stretched, tearing his own flesh, screaming in the process until, with a twisted grin on his face, Lord Randall initiated the summoning.

36

THE TORCHES LIGHTING THE throne room began to flicker as if a swift breeze flowed through the area. Even when the flames fully returned, their luminance was different, much weaker. Lord Randall stood in front of his throne, arms outstretched from his sides. He gazed towards the ceiling, his eyes rolling back, exposing only the whites.

The fear of what was coming subsided Odin's attempts to break free. He knelt in front of the lord, blood covering his arms, disbelieving that this was real. The thought of seeing this creature once again flooded his veins with sheer panic. His heart was racing. The adrenaline and anxiety flowing through his body began to take over, causing haziness with his vision.

Simon and Lilly continued to hold each other on the floor. Lilly's expression was emotionless, as if in shock. Simon on the other hand, despite being physically weakened from the infection, exhibited absolute terror. His eyes were as wide as saucers as he gripped Lilly with what little strength he still had. As the three waited for the inevitable, Randall continued.

A strange chant began to pour from his mouth. As the chant's volume increased, the torches in the throne room began to flicker more intensely. They began to extinguish, one by one, leaving only the blazing heart to light the room. Instantly, Lord Randall lifted off of the paved floor and hung in mid-air, tilting his head back while continuing the chant.

Odin followed the events as best he could, his vision was becoming hazier with each passing moment. As he knelt there, watching the lord floating in the air, something changed dramatically. The light flooding out of the hearth seemed to dissipate, as if a shadow penetrated the middle of it. There was a blackness in front of the hearth. Now that his full attention was on this new darkness in the room, he observed how it slowly moved. All around the darkness, curves meandered in and out in a rhythmic motion. The entire shadow was pulsating, and then the humming began.

Simon instantly released his grip on Lilly's shoulders and covered his ears with both hands. The deafening sound echoed throughout the long throne room while Lilly attempted to bury her face in his side. There was no escape from the thunderous noise.

Odin followed the darkness as it left the area in front of the hearth, moving towards the throne and Randall, still hanging in the air. Its motion was effortless. It seemed more liquid than anything. Once it was within feet of the throne, the pulsations running through it amplified along with the hum. Blood was trickling out of Odin's ears as he followed it.

The beast was here.

Both the darkness and Randall hovered in the air for several moments. Immediately, Randall dropped, losing his balance as he fell to the floor. His eyes remained rolled back as he lay motionless. The creature above him slowed its pulsation, and then began to split apart. Not into two pieces but three, equally the same size as the original. One of the pieces began to move once again, pulsation quickening, in the direction of Simon and Lilly.

Simon began to scream as the thing slowly drifted towards him. With all of his strength, he pushed backwards with his hands, sliding across the floor. Shock had taken over and the screams stopped, but his mouth continued to hang open. He looked up to see this darkness, now feet away, but was unable to retreat further. He was frozen, paralyzed.

As the hum and pulse strengthened from the darkness, Simon began to levitate several feet off of the ground. His legs buckled and his shoulders pushed backwards. His head involuntarily leaned back as he drifted in mid-air waiting for the wrath to finally be unleashed. The sailor forced out a final, blood curdling scream before he began to move in the darkness' direction.

Like Simon, Lilly was motionless, immobile. Her gaze was on her brother, but she was helpless, forced to be a spectator in this event. Until, the second piece began to flow in her direction. Her eyes quickly diverted from Simon to this new threat slowly approaching.

Odin's cries and screams couldn't be heard over the deafening hum in the room. Like his counterparts, his efforts fell through as the third piece began to move as well. This third piece approached slower than the previous two and it was crossing the room right for him. With his heart slamming in his chest, darkness began to fill his very soul and consciousness was escaping. It was all over. He would soon have the gift that he had longed for. He would soon be with Mia once again.

Meanwhile, Simon continued his slow progression forward towards the first piece of the monster. The rippling and pulsation emitting from it grew stronger with each inch of movement. He was no longer screaming though; the shock of reality had taken full control by now. He was helpless to resist. It started with his skin. Small strips of flesh began to peel away from his arms and legs, revealing saturated muscle and tendons below. As the small pieces were removed, they accelerated away from his body towards the darkness, disappearing within. Layer upon layer of flesh continued to be stripped away, until bone and tendons only remained in his limbs. These too slowly began to deteriorate and flow towards the monster, leaving Simon's head and torso as the only part of him left to be consumed.

Lilly began to scream as her body rose off of the floor, floating toward the creature in the same manner Simon had.

Odin was laying on the floor now, eyes glossed over as the third piece of the beast approached. Physically, he was moments away from being torn apart, but consciously he was not in Lord Randall's throne room. He was somewhere else.

He was back in his father's bakery on Milstone. The scents of fresh baked bread still lingered in the air as he looked around, astonished by the sights. Smoke rose from the clay oven in the back of the bakery, billowing through the plume of the chimney. As he turned around, he noticed an assortment of wicker baskets lining the front of the bakery, each filled and marked with its specific variety of bread. Everything about this was real. All thoughts of Floria, and the events that led him to Lord Randall were forgotten. Peace surrounded him, he was home.

A giggle was heard to his left, gathering his attention. As he turned, he saw her. It was Mia, smiling at him the way she always did - with love, affection, and care. Her long red hair was down today, not in the customary braid that she wore when helping out in the bakery. She was restocking a table of muffins, fresh from the oven, protecting her hands from the heat with the bottom of the apron tightly secured around her waist. She was perfect and she was here.

This was all he ever wanted.

As he watched her, falling in love all over again, something behind her caught his eye. They were not alone in the bakery. There was a man there too, with soiled and tattered clothes. All of the joy and love that filled Odin's heart in the few moments he saw her quickly vanished as he watched the man.

Something was wrong, the man's actions were nervous, shifty even. Without notice, fear flooded Odin, believing that Mia was in danger. He unsheathed his dirk and began to approach the love of his life, attempting to get between Mia and the peasant, but it was too late. A dagger was already in the peasant's hand, sinking it deep into Mia's abdomen. The thief had already taken the world from him.

Odin ran to her, sliding on the dirt floor of the bakery. He cradled her head in his lap, watching the crimson life flow out of her and collect in a puddle. Those beautiful green eyes, filled with uncertainty and fear, began to blink heavily. She was leaving him, again. Mia's breathing became scarce until she finally stopped. Why was this a part of his vision, why did he have to live through this horror once again?

All the positivity he felt when the vision began came crashing down in an instance. All of his love that he felt was replaced by hate. Agony filled his very soul, supplanting the joy that was once there. And finally, the grace that overwhelmed him quickly took a seat to one dominant thought and feeling: vengeance. He wanted it, needed it, *yearned* for it. With all of this brewing within, Odin snapped back into reality and opened his eyes.

The beast had continued to approach at its steady, slow pace.

Odin's eyes quickly darted towards his friends to the right of the throne, Lilly was hovering in the air, head tilted back, legs buckled, but Simon was gone, nowhere to be seen. The hum in the room was chaotic, almost distorting the entire room, but Odin's focus was new. He felt reborn, alive again, angry. He forced himself off of the floor and stared at the third piece of the darkness.

Something was different though; he wasn't afraid. This beast, with its rippling, liquid-like matter wasn't frightening - it was inviting. He held out his shackled arms, stretching towards this once haunting entity, embracing it. The cuffs that had recently torn at his wrists and ankles dissolved into nothingness, freeing him from the bondage. This is when he saw them, The Eyes.

Swirling mists of crimson floated throughout the two gazing ruby orbs lodged inside the darkness. They were mesmerizing, hypnotizing even. Odin looked on as The Eyes viewed him back, observing every inch of his being. They were inquisitive, alive with wonder, searching for answers as they scanned Odin's body and mind. He was connected to it somehow, he could communicate with it, he could ... control it.

Odin searched deep, gathering all of the melancholic feelings that had ruled his life for so long. Hate, agony, despair, and vengeance all collected, circling his inner being. In the moment, nothing else mattered. All of this negative energy was redirected away from him, towards someone.

Odin aimed his indignation at Lord Randall, who was slowly regaining his own consciousness. Instantly the beast halted, turning towards the throne. Lilly inadvertently dropped from the air, falling down to the floor as the piece directed on her changed its course as well. All three pieces were now flowing in the same direction - Lord Randall.

Getting himself off of the floor, Randall held up his left hand towards one of the pieces, shouting for it to stop, commanding it to finish his bidding. But he had already lost control. Instantly, paralysis took hold of him like all those before him, as the three pieces converted on their next victim. His reign as the master of the beast had ended.

Jardin, already side-stepping towards the black door, looked on with horror in his eyes. His constant threat to those around was his driving force, his reason for living. Without it, what did he have left? That power and strength was gone. His reign of torture and terror was disintegrating before his eyes as he watched his lord slowly begin to levitate off of the ground. His retreat was complete as he exited the black door, slamming it shut, safe for the time being.

Lilly quickly ran over to embrace Odin, burying her face in his side, wrapping her arms around his head. The shock of the situation was still fresh, but in all of this chaos, he was her only safety.

A slight look of grimace crossed Odin's face due to the broken ribs, but he held her affectionately as he watched the finale of the beast's wrath. As he looked on, the defiant commands and threats that were seeping out of Lord Randall's mouth were now replaced with screams of trepidation and panic. Odin's pain turned into a smirk as Lord Randall was slowly torn apart piece by piece. Soon it would be all over.

37

IN AN INSTANCE, THE atmosphere in the throne room changed. The torches lining the walls were reignited, providing adequate lighting. The constant humming emitting from the beast stopped as the three pieces of the darkness dissipated into nothingness within a blink of an eye. Odin and Lilly were alone, left to sort through all of the hell that had just occurred.

Odin couldn't believe what had just happened. How did he do it? Where did that strength come from? Questions continued to cycle through his mind, not entirely comprehending that he was still alive. They had survived. A sob broke his concentration and he acknowledged that he was holding Lilly.

He held her tight, stroking her dark hair. "It's over, it's all over. I'm here."

Her eyes were wide with wonder and despair as she looked up at him, shaking her head. She didn't have the ability to speak, still shaking slightly. Eventually she forced out a single word. "Simon?"

He gripped her tightly, holding her the only way one can when delivering such horrifying news. A slight shake of the head, the question was answered, followed by hysterical wails. Lilly tugged at Odin's shirt, screaming that it wasn't true, not accepting the fact that Simon was gone. Odin held her, taking the blunt of her attacks and listening to her mourn for her brother.

Eventually, the aggressive sobs began to slow, allowing Odin a chance to try and speak with her. "Lilly, I'm here. We're okay. We're going to be fine. It's over now. The beast is gone."

She looked up once again, tears streaking her battered face. With a shaky voice, she asked him a question. "How ... how did ya do that?"

Odin shook his head in confusion. He didn't exactly understand what had happened, but he did remember the story Randall told him about The Eyes. Mia's death was a similar experience and he housed all of the feelings that Randall had. The fact that he had been in this creature's presence several times unscathed began to make sense now. Was it protecting him?

He tried his best to explain his theory but wanted to open up to the woman he risked his life to rescue. He told her of his past, of Mia and their hopes of a future together, and everything else. Lilly was the first soul outside of Milstone that knew the truth and he found comfort in that.

The emotional speech seemed to lessen the blow of her grief some, too. As he was speaking, he thought about what they had said before committing to stow away. *Until the end, whatever that means.* He realized in that moment that he didn't just care about her, he loved her.

Odin gazed into her eyes as he thought about their future together, how happy they would be, even with all that had transpired. This was his future, his life - not the past that had haunted him for so long. He was finally ready to lay Mia to rest. She was the first love of his life, and her kind-hearted soul would want him to be happy.

As the future swirled around in his mind, reality quickly set in and worry once again flooded him. They were still in the recently deceased Lord Randall's castle, and they were still in danger.

"We need to get out of here Lilly. I think we're safe, but Jardin slipped out the door over there." He pointed towards the black door to the right of the throne. "Who knows where he is or how many guards he is returning with?"

Lilly's eyes were frantic, scanning the entire throne room, watching for any bit of movement. Her voice began to tremble once again. "He's coming back? He's gonna kill us, isn't he? Don't let it happen Odin, please don't." She wrapped her arms even tighter around Odin, embracing the safety of this man.

Odin held her eyes, making sure that she knew that she would always be safe with him. He would do anything for her. He would die for her. Deep down he knew that he held the power now, that he could keep her safe no matter what. He could control The Eyes. Odin leaned down and kissed her, deep and long, stroking her thick, dark hair for every second of the embrace. As he finished the kiss, he answered her. "I need you to understand something, Lilly. You never need to be scared again, ever. I'll protect you wherever you go, wherever you are. You don't need to be afraid. I love you Lilly, and I'll do anything for you."

She didn't respond. Her eyes told the whole story. She had been looking for love for so long and now this merchant's son from the bloody continent of Milstone with his checkered past and new abilities was her loving savior. Feeling the safety of his touch, she placed her head upon his chest.

After a moment, Odin broke the quiet. "Let's get your dad and get out of here. He's down in the dungeons."

Lilly quickly lifted her head from his chest, confused and relieved at the same time. "My ... My daddy? He's alive? He's here?"

"Yeah, I met him in the dungeons. Big guy, pretty angry too. Randall took him after your twenty fifth name day. An agreement that they made years ago after your mom passed. Can we go?"

Lilly broke her gaze from her savior. "My daddy's alive. He's here. Yes, let's go. Come on, come on." She stood, pulling on Odin's arms, yanking him off of the floor. "Where are the dungeons, where are they?"

Odin was forced to his feet, feeling the excitement and passion flowing through this woman. In mere minutes, she had learned that her brother had perished fighting to rescue her; the man that had fulfilled the rescue loved her and would protect her until her last final breath; and that her father, who disappeared weeks ago without a trace, was alive.

He didn't have much to say except, "The dungeons are through there." Once again, he pointed to the black door. "Let's go get him and get out of here. I have a feeling there isn't going to be a celebration or a great cleansing, so it should be pretty easy to find a ride home to the Whisky Dip. I know a guy that will help us."

They walked swiftly towards the black door together. Odin reached down and grabbed Lilly's hand, holding it firmly.

ONE YEAR LATER

He approached the cabin with caution, remaining silent with each step. The windows were covered with dark drapery, preventing the rising sun from penetrating the rooms beyond. It had been weeks since his last visit, and he wanted this to be a surprise.

Standing at the oak door, he carefully reached down and turned the handle, opening the door just wide enough to slide his thick frame through. Once inside, he closed the door quickly, still maintaining the silence from before. He didn't want them to know he had come, and he didn't want to startle anyone that may be awake this early in the morning.

The family room he was standing in was warm, blanketed from the heat the hearth had provided during the frigid night. Red coals still glowed below the charred logs within. The stone block walls made for great insulation. The warmth was inviting, comforting after the morning chill.

He approached the room to the left with stealth, making sure not to step on a creaky plank. Once outside of the room, he slowly pushed the door open with his calloused palm, peering inside in hopes of finding them awake. The room was lit by candlelight, but he could see them, sitting in a rocking chair in the corner. He stepped inside carefully, again closing the door behind him.

The light in the room was dim, but he knew his daughter. He could feel her presence, the way only a father can. Mitch quietly approached Lilly sitting in the chair, wrapped in blankets. Her eyes were closed, head leaning back, enjoying the few moments of silence that came sporadically. In a whispered voice, he called out to her. "Lil? Lilly bug, it's daddy. Are ya awake?"

Lilly slowly opened her right eye, blinking heavily from the lack of sleep. A smile crossed her lips as she realized that her father was in the room. "Daddy, where have ya been? I haven't seen ya for weeks now. Ya missed my day, ya know. What time is it anyways?"

"It's early baby. Sun just rose less than an hour ago. I'm sorry I couldn't make it sooner. Where is he?"

"He's here, swaddled up nice and tight." Lilly pulled the blankets down from around her chest, exposing the tiny head of her newborn baby.

"Oh Lil, I have to hold him. I can hold him, right? He's fine, isn't he?"

"Daddy, calm down. He's fine. Everything is fine. He's just sleeping. This little monster was up all night, hungry as a bear." She slowly cradled his hairless head in her palm, whispering to her son.

"Lil, he's beautiful, he's perfect. I need to hold him, though."

"Okay daddy, okay. But if he wakes up, ya gettin' him back down."

Mitch reached down, carefully cradling his grandson in his strong arms as Lilly supported his head during the exchange. With the baby's head resting on his shoulder now, Mitch began to slowly pace the room, cherishing every moment with his new grandson. After a few moments, he whispered to his daughter once again. "Did ya name him what we talked about? Odin was fine with it, right?"

Lilly looked up at her father with joy in her eyes. Once she found out she was expecting, one name continuously came up. "Yeah daddy, Odin loves the name. His name is Simon, just like we talked about."

Mitch gazed at his new grandchild in awe, not believing there could exist such a beautiful thing. In a whisper, he introduced himself. "Little Simon, I'm ya Pappy. Ya gonna grow up to be big and strong like ya uncle, huh buddy." His eyes were tearing up as he spoke, love and sorrow both crossing his mind.

The bedroom door slowly opened again. It was Odin, quietly sneaking back in after getting a few hours of sleep in the other bedroom. He approached carefully, making sure not to make too much noise. "Hey Grandpa, I'm glad you made it. Lilly's been wondering about you for weeks now."

"I know, I'm sorry I missed the birth. That won't happen again, I promise. I'll be here for the next two or three." He paused and cocked his eyebrow, hoping they would agree with the thought.

"One at a time Grandpa, one at a time. What do you think of him?"

"He's perfect, absolutely perfect." Mitch paused for a moment and then continued, but the joy in every word was missing. This new tone was serious, concerned. "Listen Odin, I need to talk to ya, in private if ya have a moment."

"Yeah, yeah, we can do that. Here, let me take the baby and give him back to Lil, and we can go out into the family room and talk."

With little Simon back in the safety of his mother's arms, the two men closed the bedroom door, giving them some privacy. They each sat in wooden stools near the hearth, enjoying the vibrant heat still emitting from the stone structure.

Odin leaned in knowing something was on Mitch's mind. "What's going on Mitch? You seem a little concerned."

"Well, to be honest with ya, I am worried. I don't mean to bring up headaches of the past, but he was spotted near the docks last week." He paused for a moment to make sure Odin knew who he was talking about. "Jardin is here, in Floria. I saw him with my very own eyes, son."

Odin didn't respond immediately; he allowed the news to brew in his mind for a few moments. Jardin had escaped that day in Randall's castle, hiding out for a year now without incident. "Why do you think he's back now?"

Mitch shook his head, not understanding the reason or the timing. "I really don't know, but he was with some of his old goons. They're planning something Odin."

"Well, we better do something first. I didn't think I'd have to do it again after he disappeared, but I'm not taking any risks Mitch. Not with Lilly or my son. I'll do it tonight. He'll never see it coming."

Mitch nodded in agreement. "That's what I hoped ya would say Odin. Finish it, for Simon. Finish it for all of us.

"Consider it already done Grandpa, I'll send it at dusk."

PORT OF FLORIA

ACKNOWLEDGEMENTS

There are so many individuals playing a part in this project.

First and foremost, I have to thank my daughter, Aubrey. Without her inspiration and charisma, I would have never picked up the pen. Her motivation and drive to write and produce a beautiful story of her own will forever resonate in my heart.

I'd also like to thank my loving wife and eldest daughter, Emma, for their unconditional support and love. You guys are my rocks! Without your patience, enduring love, and compassion, this would have never happened.

And thank you to my littlings for keeping me youthful, my imagination clear and fresh, and for digging out my love that can sometimes be buried.

To my secondary family, the Lopez's, for always being supportive, listening to my ideas, reading unfinished, raw pieces, and always showing forever unconditional love.

To all my amazing advocates, Dicy, Lizzy, Terri, and Angie. Thank you for putting your agendas on hold to listen to me babble and monologue about my writing endeavors. Having your ears and hearts cannot be applauded enough. Your feedback and support drive me to be the best.

To my editor, Dani Yeager. Thank you for cleaning up my mess and bringing the story of Floria into the light. Your brilliant ideas and suggestions helped tame this menacing beast. Let's do it again?

To the prolific Chad Miller. Thank you for your honest, unbiased friendship, your advisory, and all of your support during this meandering journey. *To Life and Light.* Rock on, brother.

All of you guys kick ass, love you!

ABOUT THE AUTHOR

From an early age, JB knew he could create mind-blowing, emotionally charged stories filled with enigmatic characters and story arcs. Fond, nostalgic memories still loop in his mind about

the three or four-page thrillers he wrote in middle-school for his friends. Around the same time, he discovered Stephen King and Dean Koontz. Both prolific writers influenced his creativity and helped hone his love for the craft. But the love remained dormant for years.

In the early stages of the Covid pandemic, JB's genuine passion came to fruition. Now happily married and a father, his inspiration bloomed after hearing his second daughter's desire to write a novella. Day after day, the two sat at the kitchen table, exchanging ideas, creating treacherous villains, and building a majestic fantasy world through the use of a pen. He was hooked, and the passion to write came rushing back like an avalanche.

Since then, he has completed two manuscripts: The Streets of Floria and Exit 202. The latter will be released late 2023. You can also find his numerous short stories published through online magazines and websites. His current work in progress (WIP) titled The Chronicles of Barbasos, is an anthology of shorts, due out early 2024.

JB lives in sunny California with his wife and four children; three daughters and a son. Oh, and there's his writing partner; his gray tabby, Max. When he isn't writing, he loves to read, play golf, and listen to 80s rock and 90s metal.

For more information, check out:
www.jbarnold-author.com